Root Beer & Roadblocks

Orchard Hill Romance #4

Susan M. Baganz

Root Beer & Roadblocks
COPYRIGHT 2017 by Susan M. Baganz

Contact Information: titleadmin@pelicanbookgroup.com

Quoted Scripture, unless otherwise indicated is from the English Standard Version of the Holy Bible.

Cover Art by *Nicola Martinez*

Prism is a division of Pelican Ventures, LLC
www.pelicanbookgroup.com PO Box 1738 *Aztec, NM * 87410

The Triangle Prism logo is a trademark of Pelican Ventures, LLC

Publishing History
Prism Edition, 2017
Paperback Edition ISBN 978-1-943104-89-5
Electronic Edition ISBN 978-1-943104-99-4
Published in the United States of America

Dedication

To Mark Steele (1956-2011).
A boss, friend, and fabulous pastor.
You gave the best hugs.
Gone too soon and terribly missed.

Other books by Susan M. Baganz

Orchard Hill Contemporary Romances

Pesto & Potholes

Salsa & Speed Bumps

Feta & Freeways

Root Beer & Roadblocks

Bratwurst & Bridges (coming soon!)

Black Hill Regency Suspense Romances

The Baron's Blunder (novella)

The Virtuous Viscount

Historical Christmas Novella

Fragile Blessings

Also featured in print in *Love's Christmas Past*

Short Stories

Little Bits 'O Love

1

The worst thing that happens to a man
may be the best thing that ever happened to him,
if he doesn't let it get the best of him.
Anonymous

February 2014

Johnny jogged to his car and grabbed his Bible. Fatigue weighed him down as he locked the sedan, the book tucked under his arm. Heading back toward the church, a movement caught his attention. A little boy from his Sunday school classroom escaped his mother's grasp and bolted his way, blind to a car backing out of its spot.

"David, stop!" Johnny bolted and managed to get behind the moving vehicle to shove the child out of the way. The rear bumper struck his own leg and knocked him to the ground.

The car's wheels stopped just short of running him over. *Thank you, Lord, for big tank cars with huge trunks.* The child cried, and a woman picked up the boy. "It's OK, David, you've only scraped your palms. This nice man saved you. How many times must I tell you not to run in parking lots? You are too small for cars to see you." She hugged the little boy tight.

Johnny dragged his legs out from under the car

and struggled to his feet, bracing himself against the trunk to catch his breath. The elderly woman, who had been behind the wheel, toddled around to him. "Are you OK? I'm sorry. I didn't see him. You moved so fast."

Johnny nodded. "No one would have seen him. It was an accident." He patted her on the shoulder before he limped across the parking lot. Pain seared through his hip and leg with every step he took. Reaching the curb, he sank down to the cement, thankful it was clear of snow.

His cousin Niko ran out of the church and knelt by his side. "Johnny, what happened?"

"He rescued my son from getting run over by a car that was backing out. He took the hit." A woman wearing a stocking cap and winter coat came up behind Niko with the weepy boy in her arms rubbing his eyes.

Johnny shrugged. "What she said."

"You OK? Do we need to call an ambulance?" Niko's gaze bore into him. The greater unspoken question loomed.

Teeth gritted in pain, Johnny returned his cousin's stare. "I want to sit through worship. You're on stage in a few minutes. Help me inside. I have an appointment with my doctor tomorrow. It can wait until then." He motioned for Niko to help him rise, and he did. The older woman came up to him and handed him a piece of paper.

"Here is my name, phone, and insurance information. Do you want to call the police and file a report? I wouldn't blame you if you did." Her arthritic, wrinkled hands were clenched tightly together as if in petition for mercy.

"I doubt that's necessary. Thank you, May." He took the paper and shoved it in his shirt pocket. David's mom passed him his Bible, which he'd dropped. The leather was brushed clean.

"Are you sure you're OK? I'm a nurse. I could take a look." Her face instantly turned three shades of red as she realized her inspection would involve him taking off his jeans.

Johnny smiled and leaned forward. "In my younger days, that would have been an offer too good to pass up, but I visit my doctor tomorrow. It'll wait." He turned to Niko. "Help me in?"

Niko frowned but walked along with him to the sanctuary and helped him settle into a cushioned seat. Then, Niko went to lead the worship band.

Johnny sat through the service even when everyone stood to sing. His left hip and leg ached as well as his shoulder, which had also hit the cement. *A nap. I just need a nap.*

After the service, a staff person took down all the information on the accident for an incident report for records at church. Niko approached with his guitar case.

"Ready to go?"

Johnny nodded and swallowed hard. Now would be the moment of truth. How bad was the damage? Ninety minutes sitting in one spot probably made him stiff. He pushed himself up with his good arm and stood. He closed his eyes and took a deep breath to fight against the nausea.

"Johnny?"

He raised his hand. "Give me a moment. I'm just stiff," he lied. It was worse than that. With his Bible tucked under one arm, he stood up completely and squared his shoulders. "Let's go." He grabbed his coat and slowly limped out the door and to the car.

"I'd like to drive you to the emergency room." Niko's voice brooked no argument, but Johnny wasn't to be defeated.

"No. I want to go home and take a nap. I'll put on some sweats first and see how bad it looks. If I change my mind, I'll let you know."

"You're too stubborn for your own good."

"True. I could have had that cute nurse taking a peek at my bruise, and I even passed that up."

"Who was she?"

"I'm assuming she was David's mom. He's a young boy new to our Sunday school classroom who has quickly attached himself to me."

"How old?"

"I'm not sure. Five or six maybe?"

"The woman seemed familiar."

"We've met thousands of women over the years, Niko. They all start to look the same."

"No, I mean like I should be able to identify who she is, but I couldn't place her."

"Yeah, I had a sense of that but was in too much pain to really pay attention."

"Do you think this will impact—"

"my cancer? Go ahead, Niko. It's not like we can never talk about it. Could it escalate the cancer? I haven't got a clue."

"Sorry, dude. Oh, hey, I almost forgot. Tia said she invited someone over for lunch today."

"Probably a single woman. I can't seem to convince her I'm not in the market for a wife. I'm a poor gamble for anyone."

"Don't talk like that."

"Why not? It's true. Marry me, remain childless, and quickly become a widow. Yeah, the scale is all weighted in my favor there."

They pulled into the two-car garage, and Niko came around to help Johnny out. Johnny had come to live with his cousin Niko and his bride, Tia, after he'd received the diagnosis.

"Please, Niko. I have a little dignity left—let me hold on to it as long as I can."

Niko grabbed his guitar instead. "Fine. Just remember who picks you up when you do a face plant on the stairs."

"There's a rail, and I plan to use it." Johnny limped up the steps, half pulling himself up using the rail for each level, and opened the door into the breezeway. Niko followed close behind. Entering the kitchen area, he saw Niko's wife. "Hey, Tia. I'm going to take a rain check on lunch." He walked down the hallway to his room, shut the door firmly behind him, collapsed on the bed, and let the tears fall.

After a few minutes, he dragged himself back up, kicked off his shoes, and slipped off his jeans to inspect the purplish-blue mark along his hip and down his leg. He shrugged on some sweats and left to use the bathroom. Tia confronted him as he emerged.

"Niko told me what happened. How bad is it?" she whispered.

Johnny swallowed hard. "Bad, but I don't think I broke anything."

"You could have a hairline fracture."

"I promise not to run any marathons and risk cracking it further."

Tia shook her head and leaned forward to kiss his cheek. "We love you, Johnny, and just want to help.

I'm sorry if you think I'm smothering you."

"Nah. It's nice to know someone cares."

"We do. Can I get you anything?"

"Something for the pain, perhaps. What was for lunch?"

"Salad and some paninis."

"You made me one?"

Tia nodded. "I'll bring you a plate."

"Great. You're the best."

He hobbled back to his bed and propped himself up against his headboard. Tia arrived with a drink, medicine, and lunch.

"Just set the plate aside, and I'll come and get it later."

"Sorry to spoil your Sunday plans."

"Johnny, you're more important than any plans. As it happened, she cancelled out as well."

"OK. Thanks, Tia."

"Anytime." She left and closed the door with only a tiny click of the latch.

He downed the pain medication with the cold root beer she had brought. Johnny leaned his head back, and the smell of toasted feta cheese and other goodies on his sandwich aroused a grumble from deep within. In spite of the savory flavors Tia had blended, he only managed a few bites. He set aside the plate and slid down in the bed to find the least painful position.

He awoke later in the afternoon and stumbled to the family room. Johnny levered his way into an antique chair with stiff wooden arms. Niko had been sitting nearby reading and making notes.

"Working on your next worship set?" Johnny inquired.

"Yeah. It's hard with Pastor Dan on leave right

now. He'll be back soon, but something happened, and they asked me to fill his shoes even after his return. At least for a while. I've also been thinking about the youth band and how to inspire them to grow as worship leaders. They'll be scheduled in a few weeks."

Johnny nodded. "You'll do great."

Niko set his Bible and notebook aside. "I appreciate the vote of confidence. It's a different preparation than what we did with Specific Gravity performances. How are you feeling?"

"Really sore. In pain. Wishing I drank something harder than root beer." Johnny gave a dry laugh.

"Tia has some news for you."

"As my friend or manager?"

"Manager." Tia walked in and sat across from them on the couch. "Wanna hear?"

"Sure, it'll distract me."

"Got a call from Abbey Road Studios. They have an artist demanding you for playing electric guitar on her album. I have basic downloads I can put on your tablet to listen to if you're up for a plane ride."

"Cool. Wow. Hit by a car. Cancer eating away at me and now one of the highest honors—to play at the most famous recording studio in the world?"

"Was it on your bucket list?" Niko asked.

"I don't have one. And even if I did, I'd never have dreamed so high." He took a deep breath and glanced back to Tia. "When do they want me there?"

"Well, that's where this gets interesting. They'd like you to fly out of O'Hare late Monday night. Do you even have your passport?"

"Yeah. I do, and it's up to date although I'm not sure why. It's been years since we've toured internationally. Guess I always thought I'd get a chance to go on one of those short-term mission trips someday."

"Maybe this is your mission?" Niko suggested.

"Hard to say. So if the doctor clears me tomorrow morning…will it be too late to book a flight at that point?"

"As long as there are seats on the plane, I can arrange it. As things stand, you should be fine."

"Are you sure you're up for this, Johnny? You can barely stand right now." Niko asked.

"I can play my guitar sitting if I need to or even flat on my back. Managing pain would be my main concern."

"Sure you don't want to go to the emergency room and get an x-ray tonight? Could speed things up tomorrow if you have those to take with you."

"And it would ease your mind, right?"

Niko frowned. "Yeah. Sorry, but I worry about you."

"I know, and I appreciate it." Johnny leaned back. "I'll let you drive me in to get it checked out. Better to have that information now, to see if this trip is even possible. I doubt any doctor would allow me to fly if my hip is broken, right?"

Tia nodded. Niko rose and helped Johnny to his feet.

"Let me retrieve my wallet. Gonna need my insurance card."

Tia jumped up. "I'll get it for you, and your shoes. Why don't you sit down to put those on?" She flew out of the room before he had a chance to respond. She returned with some slip-on canvas shoes. "There. Good to go."

A cry came from down the hall. "Apolo is up."

Johnny stepped forward, but Niko steered him toward the garage door. Apolo was Tia and Niko's infant son, and Johnny adored him.

"Tia will handle Apolo. You can visit him later."

"Fine."

~*~

Katie settled David down for his afternoon nap. He kept asking after Johnny and wondering if the man was OK. She told him he probably was and hoped she wasn't lying. Something about the man triggered memories of years ago. An old flame she'd loved dearly but who failed her when she needed him most.

She flipped up her laptop, started to search out his name, and soon had pages of images and videos of Johnny Marshall. The young man who wooed her in high school had grown and achieved his dreams. Dreams her parents claimed were foolish. Back then, Katie had demanded he seek a serious job. She refused to marry, a struggling musician.

While there were photos of him with the band from years ago and a few concert pics, most of those focused on Niko. Johnny wore a cap and glasses. He was fierce as he played and amazingly good. *Was* this the same person who saved her son? David called him Johnny, and she recognized Niko now that she watched the online videos of their band and checked out their website. The Johnny she once knew was never camera shy, but the one here refused to look at the lens. His expression was serious, intense, and sad. Not the exuberant, idealistic guy she'd fallen in love with all those years ago. Her Johnny had hair on his head—this one was bald. She shook her head. If it was him, she wondered what had happened to change him so drastically. Could it be the same man, or was it just one of those weird coincidences?

"Mommy, where is Johnny? I wanna see Johnny." David asked as he bellied up to the table, kneeling on the chair to grab his milk.

"Honey, I realize you like Johnny, but I don't know him, where he lives, or who he really is. I doubt you'll see him again."

The little boy set his glass down and slumped onto his heels. "Never?"

"I don't know, honey."

"But every week, he's in my class. He plays with me, reads me stories, and talks about Jesus. Sometimes he sings."

"Maybe he'll be there next Sunday."

David gave a loud sigh. "OK, Mommy. Sunday is tomorrow?"

"No. Seven more days. One week."

"Too long. I don't wanna wait," he pouted.

"I understand, sweetheart, but wait you will."

"Can I pray for him?" The little boy with the dark brown hair bent his head, held his hands together, and began to mumble under his breath.

"Sure. You can do that." Katie whispered as she placed glasses of water on the table and went to grab the hot dishes. "Mom! Dad! Dinner is ready." She sat down next to David and waited for her parents to make their way to the dining room.

"Where is Mabel?" asked her mother.

"We let Mabel go, Mother."

"What? Did you hear what she said, Herbert?" The older woman slammed her fork down in a childish fit.

"Huh?" The older man reached for the spoon to

put the potatoes on his plate. "Whatever you say, dear."

Katie closed her eyes so her parents wouldn't catch her rolling them. Her father couldn't hear well and suffered with the after-effects of a small stroke. Her mother was in the early stages of Alzheimer's. Katie had moved back to the area to help care for them. Her older brother, Ken, lived two towns away and couldn't sacrifice his family to provide the kind of care their parents needed. Katie dreaded the decisions that were going to have to be made. As a nurse, she hoped she could keep them here, together, for as long as it was safe.

"Eat, Dad." She spoke loudly. Her father smiled, nodded, and grabbed a slice of ham to put on his plate. Seemingly forgetting her mild tantrum, Katie's mother served her own food. Katie tended to her son. Bedtime would be welcome, except she wondered if memories of a certain set of brown eyes reflecting deep pain and longing would haunt her dreams. What had today's Johnny longed for?

~*~

The morning was a rush to get David off to school and make it to the oncology clinic on time. Winter was not much fun, but she was grateful for the neighbor snow-blowing the driveway and sidewalks for her parents. Thankfully, they had a few weeks of a dry spell but insanely cold temperatures. Cold so brutal that it was unusual for February in Wisconsin. Katie would not complain.

She settled in behind the counter to schedule and register clients. She did some of the initial check-in at the rooms too, but this early in the morning and new on the job, she was still getting used to the front office procedures before they threw her into the full-fledged fray of dealing with cancer patients.

The bell at the door rang, and she glanced up as the man from yesterday limped in. His coat was zipped with a knit cap pulled low, covering his ears. Even though the clinic was inside a larger medical center, it wasn't too far from the entrance. Gloved hands reached up to take off his scarf. He tugged off the gloves and made his way to the counter.

"Johnny Marshall. I'm here for my eight fifteen with Dr. Osgood. I brought some x-rays with me." He pulled a folder from under his arm. Handing it over, he stopped. "It's you—from yesterday."

"Yeah."

"How is David? Is he OK?" Johnny asked.

"He's fine. More concerned about you. He prayed for you several times yesterday."

The man gave a smile. "He's a cool little guy. Tell him thanks for me, OK?"

"Sure. Would you have a seat? The doctor will be with you shortly."

"Yeah, thanks, um, Katie." He squinted as he looked forward. He tipped his head and went to sit down, gently lowering himself into an armed chair.

Katie took a deep breath. Her suspicion had been correct. This Johnny was the same one from her high school days. The one who had crushed her heart and given her the best gift ever at the same time. Her son adored him, and now Johnny sat in an oncology clinic, which could only mean one thing.

The man she loved had cancer.

2

Character is a habit long continued.
Greek Proverb

Katie's fingers clicked on the keyboard, and he scrutinized her. She looked up at him, and recognition slammed him in the gut. He blinked rapidly. Deep grooves lined her forehead. She had those same gray eyes that bewitched him years ago, and she wore her dark brown hair cropped shorter in the back and longer on the sides. She parted it to one side, and it shimmered in the fluorescent office lighting. She wore simple silver jewelry and pale lipstick and minimal makeup. A fresh and clean appearance of a woman not in the first blush of youth. And a mother as well. A single mother if his guess was correct. There were no rings on her fingers, and David asked a few questions in class about fathers.

Johnny struggled to breathe. David's mom was Katie? She was back in town? *Chill. Cool it.* He took some deep breaths and glanced over to the desk. She was busy on the phone and looking at the computer. More beautiful than she had been at eighteen. He slid over to a seat out of her line of sight, blinking back the tears, not from the pain in his hip but from a crack in his heart. The woman who abandoned him, turned her back on his love years ago, had returned, and he'd have to see her every time he came in. If he didn't like his doctor so much, he'd switch, but it was the best oncology clinic covered by his insurance. His options were limited.

Grow up, dude. He was a man now. He could handle this. She'd gone on with her life and had a kid. He'd gone on with his and was possibly nearing the end. As depressed as he was before he walked in the door, his spirits sank even lower. *Why, God? Did you do this to slap me in the face? Kick me when I'm already down?* It didn't make sense.

A nurse called his name, and he rose to follow her to an exam room. Blood pressure was high. *Really? Wonder why?* Pulse rapid. *No duh.* He remained quiet, only answering questions he was asked, and awaited the doctor, who arrived within a few minutes.

Doctor Osgood scanned the x-rays and reviewed lab work. He sat down across from Johnny. "You managed to escape with some deep bruises, and I can write a prescription for a pain reliever to get you through this week. I'll clear you for travel. But, Johnny, we do need to put a plan in place for your treatment. Are you sure there isn't anyone who could be a match for a bone marrow transplant? It might mean a cure."

Johnny's shoulders slumped. "I'll think about it. You said you cured me last time, though. Who's to say I'd lick this one? There's no guarantee another won't pop up in the future."

"True. But there's no guarantee you're going to make it home alive this morning. Car accidents, heart attacks, yes, even at your age. Anything could happen to you to end your life at any point. There are no guarantees. Listen, Johnny, I'm a fan of your work. You love the Lord. Don't you think He would want you to do whatever it took to continue your ministry here on earth?"

"Maybe." Johnny shrugged.

"Should I prescribe an antidepressant as well? I can. I suggest you get in some counseling or in a small group at church for support."

"I got Niko and Tia," he protested.

"You need more than them. You dump on those two, and they will take it until it weighs them down so far they can't get back up. Sometimes people can care too much. You have to share yourself with a few others at least. Even let the public know. You've not shared a word on social media about what you're struggling with, yet after your last battle, you guys had no trouble stating why you had pulled off from touring."

"True, but we were on the other side. It's easier to share the victories, isn't it?"

"Yes, but you might have a bigger impact if you're honest about the struggle and let others care for you through it. Just think about it, Johnny. I want you back next week after your trip to see how you're doing."

"OK."

"Have a safe journey to Great Britain, and don't forget to get up frequently to walk about the plane cabin." The doctor rose. "And Johnny...I'm praying for you."

Johnny struggled to his feet and shook Dr. Osgood's hand. "Thanks. I appreciate it."

Johnny came out to schedule his next appointment, and Katie was at the desk. "I'm supposed to come back sometime next week. Do you have any openings on Wednesday or Thursday?"

"I can get you in at eight thirty on Wednesday. Will that work?"

He blinked rapidly. "Can you write that down?" He barely got the words out.

His Katie was back. His? *Ha!* She'd left him high and dry. He lost count of the number of letters he sent with no response. The disconnected phone number. The roadblocks her parents threw up when he tried to contact them. She thrust a piece of paper at him. He slowly took it. "Thank you, Katherine Bailey." He held her gaze for a moment, placed the appointment card to his forehead, and tipped as if he wore a top hat. He turned and shoved it in his back pocket, pulled out his gloves, and limped out the door.

~*~

Katie watched him leave. Even sick, his jeans fit him well. A pang of loss stabbed her deep in her gut.

"Katie, can you type up these notes for me?" Dr. Osgood handed her the chart. "Oh, and call in this prescription for Mr. Marshall. He's going to need it."

"Yes, doctor." She took the chart, looked up the information, and logged the prescription in through the computer system. Sent. She hoped it helped with his pain. She started to type up the doctor notes. She now had a good idea exactly what plagued the man she had once thought to marry. Her heart grew heavier at the secret she carried. It could possibly be the very thing that, if revealed, would give him a reason to fight.

The bigger question was—did she have the courage to confess the truth to Johnny? And did she risk her greatest love to help the one who had hurt her so deeply?

That should be David's choice, shouldn't it?

But he's just a kid, Lord. How can he know what is best?

You've raised him well, Katie. Trust Me.

Katie sighed. God had spoken, but how did she obey without letting Johnny know she had read up on him in his chart?

Definitely beyond normal nursing duties.

She picked up David from school and hugged him tighter than ever until he complained. "Mom, you're hurting me."

"Sorry, sweetheart." She set her son down, and they walked into the house. David went to play, and Katie rifled through her purse to find the phone number Tia had given her. She was married to Niko, so she probably knew how to get in touch with Johnny. She grabbed her phone, took a deep breath, and dialed.

"Hello? This is Tia."

"Tia? It's Katie. We met on Sunday?"

"Yes, Katie. I'm sorry it didn't work out for lunch. Things fell apart here too, so it was just as well. I hope we can do it again soon."

"I would like that. Listen, I'm calling for a favor."

"I'll help if I'm able."

"I need contact information for Johnny Marshall."

"Johnny? How do you know Johnny?"

"We went to high school together."

"Oooo-K. I'm his manager as well as his friend, so I can't give out that information. I can take down yours. When I am in touch with him, I can let him know you called and wanted to connect."

"That would be all right. How soon before you'll be in contact?"

"He's out of town right now, but he'll be back in a few days. I don't expect him to contact me until he returns."

"I guess that'll be fine."

"Any special message to send?"

"Um, yeah. Tell him…" Katie glanced over to her son playing with his toys in the other room. "…I have something of his he might be interested in." She closed her eyes. Why did she do that? She couldn't ever really tell him, could she?

"Great, I've written it down, and I'll give him the message. He'll be working, and with the time change, I doubt we'll hear from him unless it's an emergency."

"Thank you, Tia. Maybe I'll see you Sunday."

"I hope so. Niko gets to worship with me on Sunday, and I'd love to introduce you. Have a great week."

"Thanks, Tia. You too."

~*~

Johnny read over chord and lyric sheets while listening to rough mixes on his tablet. He wanted to be prepared to hit the ground running when he landed in London. Time was a premium in the studio, and he had never worked with this band or producer. He needed to come in ready to perform at the top of his game. Pain might make that more difficult. He rose and walked around the cabin periodically. Limped would be more like it. The medication at least took the edge off, but it made him drowsy, and with the time change, he needed to rest. He finally dozed a few hours as the plane soared across the pond.

His dreams filled with memories of the summer after graduation. The fun. The fears. The mistakes and the final heartbreak when Katie left for college, asking for a separation, as she was doubtful about any future with a daydreaming musician.

He wondered what brought her back to town. Her little boy was adorable, and Johnny's heart ached that he would never have that kind of blessing in his life. It was the reason he volunteered in the children's ministry now that Specific Gravity was back in town and not touring all the time. He loved kids. He had always longed to be a dad. Bedtime stories and sticky kisses had been stolen from him with his first round of cancer and the defection of his wife. The wound had cut deep, and the tourniquet of divorce severed any chance for a family. In his rebound from Katie, he had not made the wisest choice in marrying Donna.

Donna. The girl who didn't want kids right away...now had two in three years and another on the way by her second husband, whom she had an affair with while Johnny toured the world singing about God. He really couldn't blame cancer for his destroyed dreams. The marriage was over long before his diagnosis. The results shut a door he had always thought would be open to him. To be a dad, like Niko was to Apolo.

Well, for seventy-five minutes a week, he had a table surrounded with shiny eyes, mischievous smiles, high-octane energy, and lots of questions. Maybe God had denied him being a father, but he could pour love on those kids. Thankfully, Niko and Tia allowed him to be a doting uncle to his second cousin, Apolo. What a blessing to be able to be a part of his life. At least for now.

His eyes flickered open. He peeked through the shade at his window to witness the sun rising over the horizon. In just a few more hours, he'd be at Heathrow and letting his fingers leave another legacy that would outlive him. Music. His balm. His comfort. His career that, so far, had been fairly good to him. Phil Keaggy and John Mayer might be more famous, but he had made his own dent in the music industry and kept busy. The down side of this trip was that he would miss church on Sunday. It couldn't be helped, and he prayed his "kids" would be OK.

He pondered what the doctor said. The possibility that a bone marrow transplant could cure him. But at what risk to the donor? What if it didn't work? To ask that of Niko or any other relative seemed selfish. It's not like he hadn't lived his dream already in his career. He had. Dreams of marriage and family flushed down the toilet years ago. There was no redemption for him there. So, what else did he have to look forward to here on earth? Was the specter of death going to follow him forever even if he made it through this time? Wouldn't heaven be preferable?

Johnny had no fears about eternity. He'd repented his youthful follies and clung to Jesus. He knew how desperate he was for a Savior when life had fallen apart. Niko and Tia had been there as was his family and church, but still…only God understood the depth of his physical and emotional pain. With the new diagnosis, those scabs ripped wide open again, and inside, grief hemorrhaged unchecked. He would allow that to feed his performance this week.

Johnny limped his way through customs, located his baggage, and hailed a cab to his hotel. He checked in, dropped his bags, and caught a quick shower and shave. He picked up the phone and called in.

"Hey, Peter. I'm here. Can I come over and check out the studio so we're ready to roll early tomorrow?

Maybe I can record some possible tracks."

"Sure, I'll send a car for you. Fifteen minutes?"

"I'll be ready."

Johnny donned his jacket and stuck his knit cap on his head. London was more temperate than Wisconsin in February, but there was still a chill in the air. He grabbed his music and guitar and headed out to catch his ride.

Arriving at the studio, Peter greeted him. "Nice to meet you, Johnny. I've listened to some of your work and have been impressed. I want to see what you can add to this album. It's been going well, but both Pamela and the band have felt it was missing a spark. She was the one who asked me to call you."

"I hope I can fulfill everyone's hopes. I have some ideas. Do we have time this afternoon to play around on a track and see what I might be able to do? It's all in my head."

"Go ahead, Johnny. We'll do some practice sessions and record you, and maybe we'll strike gold."

"That would be nice, wouldn't it?" Johnny grinned as he took out his guitar, tuned, and hooked them up into the system. After a quick sound check, he spoke to the engineer. "Can we try that first track?"

Johnny jammed and recorded several takes on a few of the album's rough tracks. He yawned. The hours had flown by. "I think it's time to call it a night. Jet lag is going to catch up with me, and I need to get a bite to eat before I crash."

"There's a pub around the corner with great fish and chips. My treat." Peter was all smiles as they walked a few doors down to the spot, got a seat, and placed an order.

"Can I get some ice in my water, please?" Johnny

handed back his menu.

"From the Colonies?" The cheeky waitress asked and turned to leave before he could respond.

"Tell her to have a good evening when you're done, and you'll make her day," Peter suggested.

"And mark myself as a tried and true American, huh?" Johnny chuckled.

"Absolutely. But that's what you are."

Johnny nodded and managed to eat half of his meal. Between his ongoing pain and the encroaching fatigue, he was beyond done for the day. "Sorry, bloke, but I have an important appointment with my pillow. Thank you for dinner."

~*~

Johnny had drifted off into a pain-reliever-dulled sleep when the telephone by his bed rang.

"'ello?" he scratched out.

"Johnny Marshall? This is Pamela. I listened to some of your tracks and...wow! You were just what we needed for this project. I'd love to come by and visit or treat you to a few drinks at the hotel bar."

"Thanks, but no. Horrible jet lag. Need rest. See ya tomorrow." He hung up the phone.

A short time later, there was a knock on his hotel room door. Johnny rolled to his back and slung an arm over his eyes as he groaned. "Who is it?"

"Johnny? It's Pamela. Open up."

Johnny stumbled to his feet, went to the door, and looked out the peephole. A stunning woman, with a low-cut knit top that clung to every curve and who knows what else, stood on the other side of the door. The bright red lipstick made him think of a hooker and brought to mind verses from Proverbs.

"Come on, Johnny. Let me in. I just wanna hook up with you."

Those words were like a cup of cold water splashed in his face. He whispered to himself. "For the lips of a forbidden woman drip honey, and her speech is smoother than oil, but in the end she is bitter as wormwood, sharp as a two-edged sword. Her feet go down to death; her steps follow the path to Sheol; she does not ponder the path of life; her ways wander, and she does not know it. Proverbs 5:3-6." His head dropped against the door.

"What? I couldn't hear what you said. Come on, Johnny. Let me in." Her voice pleaded.

"Leave or I'll ask the hotel to call security or the police or whatever."

"You can't mean that? I'm Pamela. I'm a star in this town. Open the door."

"No. Leave me alone."

"No one rejects Pamela."

"I'll call my agent and catch the next flight home."

"No! You can't do that! I need you for this album."

"Let me sleep. I'll see you in the studio and not before."

She huffed.

Johnny didn't wait to see if she left or not. He checked the deadbolt and stumbled back to bed. He glanced at the time. He picked up his phone and called Tia.

"Hello, Tia Acton."

"Hey, Tia."

"Johnny, it has to be late there. Are you OK?"

"Tired. Listen. Does my contract hold a morality clause?"

"Morality clause? I don't recall anything like that at all, except for your behavior needing to be professional."

"That part isn't a problem, but this singer is coming on to me, and if she's not listening and leaving me alone, can I bail on this?"

"Let me check with Roberto. Tell me specifically what happened."

"Nothing much. Yet. But she's determined. She called and wanted to buy me drinks. Later, she came to my door wanting to hook up."

"Oh, my."

"Yes. Apparently, my playing today has seduced her. We've not even met or been introduced. I fear she's going to come on to me tomorrow and make this more difficult. I want to know if I legally have an out if I need it."

"I'll call Robbie and email you. You can check that in the morning after you have some rest. Don't worry, though, Johnny. Morality clause or not, we'll make a way for you to leave if you want."

"Thanks, Tia."

"Sleep well, Johnny. We're praying for you."

~*~

The next morning, Johnny shaved and dressed. He was afraid to leave his room lest Pamela waited for him. Instead, he ordered room service. He sipped his coffee and ate what the menu referred to as a classic British breakfast of smoked bacon, Cumberland sausage, black pudding, grilled tomato, Portobello mushroom, baked beans, and two free-range eggs, fried. It was more than he normally ate at home, but he enjoyed every bite.

Finally, he grabbed his guitar and headed to the lobby. He called a cab, afraid Pamela might come with the studio car. Everything in him urged caution. He was tired, in a foreign country, and physically in pain. Regardless of his marital status, or lack thereof, he was not interested in any kind of relationship with this particular singer.

He arrived at the studio and grabbed another cup of coffee. He set up, tuned, and started to practice for the next song. He had gotten a brief hello from the sound tech, and soon the manager arrived. When Pamela came in, he ignored her and kept his focus. She pushed herself forward when he rose to use the loo.

"Johnny, finally, we meet. I'm Pamela."

"Hi, Pamela. Thanks for inviting me to be part of your project." He tried to step past her to leave the room, but she wrapped her arm around him and pressed herself against him. Her bright red lips angled up with a sly smile. Her overly made-up face reminded him again of a prostitute. This was a studio recording—who dressed up for that?

"Excuse me?" Johnny peeled her arms off, and she pouted. He strode out of the room to the bathroom, but when he turned around, she was there with her arms crossed and a scowl on her face.

He washed his hands, dried them, and moved past her. She grabbed his arm. "You are not running from me."

Johnny stopped and glared at her. "I'll run across the ocean if you don't stop touching me. I'm here to do a job. A job you are paying me for. I don't need the money or the ego strokes to be on your album. I have no trouble packing up and flying home today." He wrenched his arm free and winced at the pain radiating through to his bruised shoulder. He stalked out and grabbed some coffee.

"Good morning, Johnny," Peter cheerfully greeted him.

"Peter?"

"Yeah?"

"Keep Pamela away from me. No phone calls, or showing up at my hotel, or stalking me in the men's room. One more time and I'm packing up and gone. Contract or not, this is not conducive to my process as an artist. I deserve respect. I will quit if this continues."

"You've got to understand Pamela, she's a—"

"Diva?"

Peter frowned and nodded. "She's used to everyone fawning all over her and getting any man she wants."

"Not interested. I came here for work. That's it. I'm warning you." Johnny sipped his coffee and turned back into the studio to pick up his guitar. Pamela awaited him.

She wore a short skirt and black work boots with some silly socks sticking up. Her long, lean legs didn't appeal to him. Her low-cut top stretched tightly across her ample chest and came short of her navel, leaving an expanse of skin. Her purple and red hair was a messy style. Clunky bracelets, big earrings, along with a red-lipped pout rounded out her fashion statement.

"Johnny, I just want to get acquainted with you. To be friends."

Johnny raised one eyebrow and snorted. He picked up his guitar and sat down. "Please leave. I have work to do."

She folded her arms and shook her head. Johnny

shrugged. He put on the headphones and nodded to the engineer on the other side of the glass. The music began, and he started to play, closing his eyes to ignore the woman as she tried to distract him by sitting in an indecent position on the stool in the corner. Eventually, she got up to leave but stalked him whenever he left the room.

The day drained him. Pamela fawned over him, complimented him, and tried to engage him in conversation. When he packed up to leave for the evening, she came up from behind and thrust her hand into his front jeans pocket. He pulled it out and turned, holding her wrist firm.

"That was your last shot." Johnny grabbed his guitar and walked out of the room. He strode over to Peter, who bit his lower lip. He must have witnessed the incident.

"Peter. This isn't your fault. Thank you for having me." He put the guitar case down and offered his hand. Peter shook it.

"Is there any way…?"

"No. I cannot and will not work like this." He picked up the case he'd set down. "I hope that you have some tracks you can use. I've fulfilled the terms of my contract. She violated it. I'm done."

Pamela barred the door for his exit. "You can't leave."

Johnny frowned. "You're holding me prisoner? I think that's against the Geneva Convention."

She scrunched her eyebrows. OK, so she might be a gifted musician, but she was dumb as a box of rocks. "I just want to explore what else those talented fingers can do."

Johnny's face grew warm at her words. "They can

call the police, my lawyer, and my manager."

"Not man enough to fight your own battles?"

"Man enough to recognize which battles are worth fighting. You, Pamela, are an annoying fly buzzing around. All I want right now is for you to go away and leave me alone."

Her eyes grew hard, and before he knew it, her hand let loose to connect with his cheek in a resounding crack. He bit back tears at the pain. He looked at Peter. "Either you control her or I'll be filing assault charges."

He never anticipated the kick that followed, causing him to drop his guitar, thankfully well-protected in its travel case. He stumbled against the wall, pulled out his phone, and called information to get the police.

Unfortunately, when the police arrived, they were also accompanied by the paparazzi.

3

When you've got nothing, you've got nothing to lose.
Bob Dylan

Johnny limped outside Abbey Road Studio amidst the flashes of cameras and the shouts from reporters. He ignored them all and flagged a taxi to his hotel. The police had arrested Pamela, but he was certain that within an hour, she would be on the streets hunting him down. His shoulders tensed, and a headache formed at the back of his neck. Arriving at his hotel, he packed up his bags, checked out, and took another cab to a hotel not far away. He signed in using Niko's name and account per Tia's instructions. She had already taken care of the payment for him. He would get a few hours of sleep and leave on a plane the next morning.

He ordered soup through room service. Along with a certain pain, his stomach roiled as he remembered Pamela's provocative attempts. He wasn't so naïve or inexperienced, but having played primarily in the Christian market, overt attacks had not been as prevalent. When they toured as a group of men, there was safety in numbers. He chuckled. Niko used to get the most heat from the women, until Tia stole his heart. Of course, Tia almost dying to save Niko from a delusional man had shocked his cousin into recognizing he loved her. For all the love Johnny had for his cousin, the leader of the band had been slow to recognize love even when it was right in front of him.

If Johnny was honest, he was jealous of Niko's happiness. He didn't begrudge him that by any means. Niko had done things mostly right. Johnny, however, had messed up his own life. While he understood cancer was not God's punishment for past sins, in many ways, he thought he deserved it because of how he had screwed up in his younger years. Especially with Katie.

Was that why she never responded to his letters and changed her number? They had both crashed at the bottom of that slippery slope of intimacy one time. He had repented, and she was adamant that he get a "real" job. A few days later, she was gone, leaving a gaping wound in his soul. It saddened him that someone else had been able to give her what he couldn't, and he hoped the loser supported David. The little boy was obviously desperate for a father figure in his life. Why else would he cling to someone like Johnny, who resorted to helping out in children's ministry to fill the empty void in his own heart? Did David know how much that meant to him? Probably not. He was just a kid responding to love and attention.

With the help of the pain medication, Johnny slept well with no interruptions and took a cab to the airport.

He waited in the concourse for his international flight when his cell phone rang.

"Hello?"

"Hey, Johnny, it's Peter. Listen, I'm really sorry about Pamela, and we'll make sure you are compensated for your work."

"Good. My lawyer has already been informed of what happened."

"Don't think too badly of us. Pamela's a diva, and she's not used to hearing a 'no' from anyone, much less a man."

"Glad to have contributed to her growing up." Johnny couldn't hide the sarcasm. "This is a rough industry, and she can't expect to stay on top and always have crowds fawning all over her forever. Reality is going to cash a hard check someday."

"Reality might have already done so. The media are raking her over the coals for last night's arrest. I wanted to warn you that the paparazzi snapped pics of you both coming out of the studio, and you might find yourself in the news. You should be aware there might be some brutal lies spreading through the entertainment industry."

Johnny groaned. "I knew the cameras were there, but I wasn't worried because I hadn't done anything wrong. Thanks for the heads-up. I'll let my lawyer know to watch for any slanderous articles. I won't take abuse from her, the press, or social media."

"It might get nasty, but I'll do all I can on my end to refute the lies. As a witness, I can testify to your integrity. By the way, the police arrested her a second time when she went to your hotel and banged on the door of a young couple in the room you had occupied. Smart move."

"I appreciate you informing me. Consequence is a hard teacher. I hope she learns from it."

"She's angry and willing to smear you however she can, in the press or social media."

"Thanks for the heads-up."

"Have a safe flight home."

"Thank you, Peter. This trip to London has definitely not been what I expected."

After he hung up, he caught his flight and said farewell to jolly ol' England. He wished he'd had more energy and stamina to explore the historic city of London and beyond while he was there, but right now, home was all he longed for. Given Pamela's perseverance in pursuing him, it was better that he disappear from the island. The up side was that he would make it to church and hang out with his kids in Sunday school. The thought of seeing little David again made him smile.

~*~

Johnny limped through customs in Chicago with nothing to claim but an undeserved national reputation as a playboy. Photographers snapped pics of him as he limped his way to baggage claim. His sunglasses and knit cap didn't hide his identity well enough. The guitar case was probably a giveaway. Niko met him and helped him collect his luggage. They shouldered their way through the paparazzi to the car. Johnny slammed the door and buckled up as flashes made him blink hard. Niko got in and, with a grim set to his lips, took off and into Chicago's rush hour traffic. They stopped at an oasis for coffee and a bite to eat and managed to get in and out without any media attention.

"Sorry, Niko. Maybe you should have sent someone else. Now they'll smear you in the media too and paint Specific Gravity with this brush."

"We've been there before. Remember Tia's father? That wasn't even a year ago. The scandal blew over.

God will make this work out too."

"I regret taking the job."

"Did you pray about it?"

"No. My first mistake. I wanted to run away from my pain, my diagnosis, and even myself."

"Didn't work, did it?"

Johnny snorted. "Blew up in my face."

"I've got more bad news for you." Niko's voice was hesitant as his hands gripped the steering wheel, leaving his knuckles white. Traffic wasn't heavy as they headed north.

"Is this the needle on the camel's back?" Johnny asked.

"Maybe. Sarah at church called. They have requested you not serve right now in children's ministry until they can verify you aren't guilty of what the media is accusing you of."

Johnny closed his eyes as it hit him that the one good thing in his life had been stolen by Pamela. He removed his glasses and wiped away the tears. "How did they find out so fast? This only happened a day ago."

"I'm sorry, Johnny. Once things hit social media— Twitter, Facebook, and the online entertainment news channels, it goes viral. I tried to defend you, and Tia has been talking to Pastor Andrew."

"It's not your fault. I don't understand why God would strip away everything good in my life. What's the point anymore of fighting?"

"Fighting the rumors or the cancer?"

"Both, I guess. Although it'd be nice to die with my reputation restored."

"Your integrity is still there, Johnny, and you will be vindicated in time. Psalms talks often about that.

David was pummeled with false accusations and hunted. Psalm 7:8 says, 'Vindicate me, O LORD, according to my righteousness and my integrity that is in me.' It's hard, but if you wait, you will see the restoration of your reputation. All is not lost. This is a temporary setback, not a permanent mark on your character."

"Thanks. I'll have to go back and read that chapter in its entirety. My doctor suggested an antidepressant. I might take him up on that."

"If it'll help, do it."

"It might be weeks for the benefits to be seen, and right now, I don't care. You take away my kids and what's left?"

"Tia, Apolo, and me? Your family and friends?"

"You'll all be fine without me."

"Think so? Who helped me with Tia? Who was brave enough to slap me in the face to wake me up to my own sin and help me be a better husband and father? You. Do you think your work here is done?"

"What if God is saying it's OK to quit?"

"What are you suggesting, Johnny?"

"I'm tired of fighting."

"Do you have an option that could help you win your battle with cancer you've not told us about?"

"There's no promise or guarantee with any options before me."

"If it's a choice that has potential, would you seriously consider disregarding it?"

Johnny slipped his sunglasses on and stared out the window but said nothing.

"Johnny?" Niko's voice had a harder edge to it.

"We always have choices, Niko, and God can be glorified in any of them. What I choose is between Him and me."

"Even if you disobey Him?"

"Yes."

~*~

Katie hadn't heard from Johnny. His name was mentioned in a report on an entertainment news show, which disturbed her. Johnny wouldn't be cavorting with some pop star in London, would he? She dressed with care as she prepared for church, in hopes of being able to speak with him. Maybe when she picked up David. All David could talk about was getting to church to see his friend Johnny.

She peeked in the room when she dropped David off but didn't find Johnny anywhere. David scanned the room and hesitated to step in farther. She knew he could be clingy, so she scooted away and rushed to get a place in the sanctuary before the worship service started. She walked toward the front and spied her new acquaintance, Tia. She was sitting with her husband, Niko.

"Tia," Katie whispered. "Got room for one more?"

"Sure." Tia and Niko scooted over a seat and made a spot for her. Just as they stood for the first song, movement at the opposite end of the aisle caught her eye. Johnny slid past a couple to come and stand next to Niko.

When it came time to greet, Tia gave her a hug, and Niko offered a strong handshake. Johnny gave her a nod and half a smile, not attempting to reach around his friends. Katie sat down, her mind consumed. Questions warred with a longing to connect once again with the man who had stolen so much from her. Pieces of her heart remained buried in the wreckage of their past.

When the service concluded and they had finally stepped into the aisle, she stood aside to wait for Johnny. He glanced at her as she walked alongside him to leave the sanctuary.

"Johnny?"

"Yeah?"

"Why aren't you in with the kids this morning?"

"Long story. This isn't the time or place for it." They entered a large café area and stepped off to the side so others could move past them. He avoided eye contact, staring instead at his shoes.

"I need to talk with you and wondered if there would be a good time for that."

This time, his eyes bore into hers. "What about?"

"It's kind of personal…"

"My schedule is fairly open this week. Even this afternoon would be fine." He frowned, and she noticed the dark shadows under his eyes.

"That'd be great. Can we meet somewhere? Say, the coffee shop off Appleton Avenue?"

"What time?" His tone was clipped, and he scanned the crowd almost like a cornered animal.

"Two?"

Johnny nodded. "Great. See ya, Katie. Give my love to David. Tell him I missed him." He moved away, but she grabbed his arm and noticed him wince. She released him.

"Why don't you come with me to get him?"

"I wouldn't know how to explain things to a kid his age. Tell him I really wanted to be there, but something happened I had no control over, and I'm not sure when I'll be back."

"Oh, that's clear as mud for a six-year-old."

"Sin is like mud. Filthy and sucks you in. It's a hard truth in our world." The edge to his voice was tinged with weariness.

"Your sin or someone else's?"

"Does it matter?" Johnny turned and limped away with his head down and his hands in his pockets. She watched as a few people spoke with him briefly, and he hurried past them. Almost as if he couldn't escape the place fast enough.

She picked up David.

"Mommy, Johnny wasn't here. I'm not going back if Johnny's not here."

"I'm sorry, honey. If you really want to sit in the service with me next week, that's fine, but you have to be quiet unless it's time to sing."

"OK, Mommy."

"Let's go home."

~*~

At two o'clock, Katie sat with her cinnamon dolce latte waiting in a comfortable set of chairs for Johnny to arrive. She had been there for only a few minutes, trying to calm her heart. David was home taking a nap, and her parents were capable of watching him if he awoke before she got back. She reflected that this would likely not be an option for much longer. But at what point did someone make that decision? She prayed God would show her how and when and that her brother would be supportive. It was ultimately his call as to when their parents moved to supervised care.

Johnny strode in, noticed her, and gave her a tip of his head as he went to order a beverage. Too soon and not soon enough, he sat adjacent to her with something hot to drink.

The place was light on company, and the murmur of the baristas mixed in with the alternative folk music playing in the background. Johnny's knee bounced to the rhythm of the song.

"Thanks for coming," she started.

"So, what did you need to talk about?" Johnny's voice was soft and void of emotion. He wore his sunglasses, and she couldn't see his eyes.

"I, um, have a confession to make."

One eyebrow shot up from behind the dark frames.

"Well, really, two of them. And I need to beg your forgiveness."

"Do I listen to the confession first or do I need to give you the promise of forgiveness in advance?"

"Well..."

"Cut the crap, Katie. Seven years ago we had something special, and I wanted to marry you. Apparently, I wasn't good enough, so you left me high and dry. You refused to answer any of my letters and refused my calls. I didn't dare try to visit you after the way you ditched me for being a—how did you phrase it? 'A flighty musician.'"

The bitterness in his voice shocked her. "I never got any letters or phone calls from you. No voice mails or even a missed call number showing up on my phone. I felt terrible for the way I left things and kept hoping you would call, but I'm partly glad you didn't. I had a weakness for you that was my undoing. My parents never forgave me for dating you."

"Ah, yes. Your estimable parents, who had their noses stuck in the air and couldn't countenance you seeing some pagan Greek who had delusions of making it by playing guitar. I should have known it would come back to them." His apparent fatigue took some of the sting out of his words.

"Listen, Johnny. I can't undo the past, and I'm glad you wrote even if I never got the letters. But what I wanted to tell you was—I was only intimate with one man my entire life."

The brow furrowed above those glasses. "Are you saying you and I—?"

"—was my first and only. Yes. That's what I'm saying."

"But David? Who's his father?"

"You didn't do the math?"

His hand came up and pointed to his chest as his mouth dropped open. "Me? David's *my* son?" A tear escaped and made a run for his chin as he bit his lip and bowed his head.

Katie nodded. "I'm so sorry."

Johnny's head rose to face her. "Sorry? What for? I couldn't be more thrilled. He's the best kid. You've done a fabulous job raising him. Why didn't you contact me? I've lost so much. You can't know how much I always longed to be a father."

"I wanted to let you know, but my parents convinced me not to. You got married, and I didn't want to interfere as you moved on with your life. I didn't follow your career. I only found out about your marriage when my parents called to tell me. They said it was good I hadn't married you or you'd have probably left me for her."

"Never. Listen. I may have been an arrogant, pompous jerk back then, but I would not have left you to struggle on your own. Didn't you name me on the birth certificate? The State would have come after me for support, and I would have gladly provided it even if you had never wanted to see me again."

"I can change the birth certificate to make you his legal father."

"Does David know?"

Katie shook her head.

"I'm a dad." The glasses came off, and he wiped tears away. "You can't begin to understand what an answer to prayer this is. I always wanted kids. A family. Donna didn't, and the door slammed on that with my last bout with cancer. You've just given me my dream. A son. A wonderful son." He choked up, closed his eyes, and pinched the bridge of his nose before taking a few deep breaths. He put the sunglasses back over his swollen lids. "Is this what you wanted forgiveness for?"

"For not telling you. Yes."

"Done. You're forgiven. I admit to some anger at losing all those years...I want an opportunity to get to know my son, though."

"We'll work something out."

"You mentioned two things?"

"Yeah." She let out a sigh and tapped her cup with her finger. "I had to type up the doctor's notes last week after your appointment."

"Privacy laws?"

"Sorry. I've not said anything to anyone. And I won't. But have you asked anyone for possible donation?"

His body stiffened. Johnny shook his head. "No."

"Why?"

"I've been out of the country for one, and secondly, well, it's none of your business."

"You're a father, Johnny. David needs you in his life. Don't break his heart by killing yourself."

"It's not suicide."

"It's passive suicide. Yes. And it's wrong."

"That's between me, God, and my doctor." Johnny flipped her a business card with his cell phone number on it. "Here's my number. Call me when I can visit David. I have a great lawyer who will help us come up with some kind of compensation plan, and once we get the birth certificate changed, I'm sure someone in the government is going to want me to fork over a piece of my paltry musician's wages. I'd like to avoid their involvement and will gladly come to terms with what I owe and what is reasonable for the past few years." He rose to his feet. "It's been nice seeing you, Katie." He sighed. "If it's any consolation, my heart never recovered from your rejection. I've only ever loved you." He set down his cup and zipped up his jacket. Grabbing his coffee, he strode out the door without another word.

Katie leaned back in her chair and let the tears fall. "I've only ever loved you too, Johnny," she whispered to the empty space where he had sat.

4

A loving heart is the truest wisdom.
Charles Dickens

Johnny came back home and went downstairs to the studio and picked up his guitar and started to play. He let the tears flow freely as his fingers moved with emotion and precision over the guitar strings. When he finished with that particular song, he glanced up to find Niko there.

"Hey, need a friend?"

"When don't I?" Johnny answered.

"What's up?" Niko picked up his guitar and started a light strum.

"Found out some earthshattering news."

Niko stopped playing. "Good for a change, I hope?"

"I have a son. David is my kid."

"The little boy you rescued?"

"One and the same."

"Katie?"

"Yeah. One time and it split us up."

"You never told me. You were so devastated and close-lipped about it I didn't ask back then."

"I felt so guilty about what happened I asked her to marry me as soon as possible. I loved her and figured we'd have married eventually, but I wanted to do what was right, and not just because I could have gotten her pregnant. But Katie wanted me to find a real job, in a factory or something, and give up my dreams of playing guitar. I refused. Within days, she moved away and cut me off. Never heard from her again until last week."

"Whoa. How do you feel about instant fatherhood?"

"I forgave her for not telling me, but that doesn't mean I'm not cheated out of six years with him. I always wanted to be a dad. David is a great kid. I'm thrilled and terrified."

"What scares you?" Niko asked.

"I'll want to pay back child support. I think I can manage it. But I have cancer. Will I even be around to watch him grow up?"

"Maybe this gives you more incentive to fight?"

"I could do everything and still lose the battle." Johnny groaned.

"What?" Niko asked.

"Now all I need is for the media to come out with my 'mystery love child' as further proof of my wicked ways."

"Let him who has no sin…"

"Right, that's why I wasn't allowed in Sunday school today." His shoulders slumped.

"They didn't stone you, but they want and need to be careful of parents' perceptions."

"I understand. I get that. I had equal parts of people greeting me and some who turned away and wouldn't acknowledge me. Then there are those who just don't recognize me, which is fine.

"Grow your hair. Let your beard out or cut it in a goatee. No one will recognize you then." Niko grinned.

"Thanks. Might just consider that. The goatee would come faster than the hair on my head, though."

"You could always purchase a wig. Dolly Parton swears by them and wears them all the time."

Johnny chuckled. "Do you want me to get one like hers or a toupee?" He let his fingers start to move on the strings, and Niko strummed to keep up with him in the improv jam session. A half an hour passed before Tia made an appearance.

"Hey, guys, sorry to interrupt, but Apolo's awake and asking for Unka Johnny."

Johnny grinned at Niko. "How much you wanna bet there's a stinky diaper Tia's trying to weasel out of?" The men laughed as they trudged up the stairs. "Hey, will you tell Tia about this for me?"

"Why not tell her yourself?" Niko pushed him from behind as they reached the top. "I'll do diaper duty, and you let my lovely wife in on your news. She adores you, Johnny. She's not going to judge you."

Niko grabbed the little boy and headed to the nursery, leaving Johnny alone with Tia.

Johnny swallowed. "Um, can we talk?"

An eyebrow rose. "Personal or business?"

"Personal."

"Come to the kitchen. Want a cup of coffee?"

"Nah, this calls for a root beer." He went to the fridge and drew out two of the beer-style brown bottles of the beverage and handed one to her as they sat down at the kitchen table.

"What's up? This must be pretty serious."

"It's a combination of confession and good news."

"I already figured out you read my journals when you gave them to Niko."

He sat back, stunned. "What? I...OK, I did glance

at them."

"Thought so."

"You weren't sure?"

"You just implicated yourself. I know that was a long time ago now, but payback might be sweet. What are friends for anyway?"

"Come on, Tia. Overall, it worked out pretty well for you."

"It did. So, thank you."

"I'm forgiven?"

"I suppose."

He gave a sigh of relief. "But that's not what I wanted to talk to you about." He took a long drink of the soda and let out a belch. Tia just shook her head and sipped her own.

"Well? I'm waiting."

"Today I learned that I am a father to a six-year-old boy named David."

"I thought you said…"

"I can't. Not since my cancer treatment. This was one slip-up right after high school. Katie, his mother, and I were dating. I wanted to marry her. One night we went too far, and within days, she disappeared, and I couldn't get in touch with her. Gone. Broke my heart."

"So now she wants your money?"

"No. She just wanted me to know. Of course I'll do the right thing by her and our son. I'm thrilled I can be a father after all. Just sad I lost six years of his life."

"Congratulations, Johnny. David is a blessed little boy to have you for a father."

"You really think so?"

"Yeah. And Katie was a fool to walk away from you."

"Not so sure about that."

"You never did get over her, did you?"

Johnny shook his head and lifted his bottle to his lips and swallowed deep.

"I'm sorry, Johnny."

"Yeah. So am I."

~*~

Once Katie was home, she went to her room. She pulled a box out of the top of the closet and opened it. Maybe if she waded through a little bit of a lifetime of memories and junk in this house, she would have it pared down by the time her parents needed an assisted living facility. She managed to toss the contents of the box before David came in. She had taken down another one, so he sat with her tablet and played while she sorted. She began a pile for Goodwill but hid it in her closet so her mother wouldn't come and undo her work.

A third box came down, and she opened it up. On the top was a shoebox. Opening it, she found the proof of what Johnny had said earlier. He *had* written to her—over and over. Her parents had refused to give him her new address and had withheld the letters. She shoved them under her pillow to read later.

She hauled stuff to the garage to dump in the garbage. It was time to get dinner started, so she took David with her to the kitchen to take care of that task.

When they sat down to their meal, something Johnny mentioned haunted her.

"Mom. Dad. Remember that boy I dated in high school?"

"The second-class bum?" Her father asked.

"Oh, he was a musician, wasn't he? With some go-nowhere dreams? I'm glad you left him behind when you did." Her mother forked more spaghetti into her mouth.

"I ran into him recently. He mentioned he had mailed me several letters I never received."

"Did he? Well, I never believed half of what he said. He's probably just trying to, well, you know. You are older but are even prettier than you were back then, Katherine. You really should find a nice, upstanding man to date. Someone who can provide for you and David. We won't be around forever for you to sponge off of." Mom continued to eat and began to hum, which was usually a sign she wasn't in the real world with them anymore. How like her to stay in reality just long enough to insult her.

Katie ditched the idea of getting to the truth, but she suspected her parents of withholding the mail even though they would likely never confess. She had the proof under her pillow.

After the dishes had been washed, put away, and lunches packed for tomorrow, she settled next to David on his bed to read before bedtime.

"Mommy?" David snuggled up beside her, his dark, straight hair soft as silk.

"What is it, honey?"

"Why wasn't Johnny there today? I missed him. He's really sad and needs me."

"You might be right. We should pray for him, don'tcha think?"

"Yeah. I really like him, Mommy. He makes himself my size to talk with me and reads me books. He can sing too."

"Do you want to pray for him right now?" Katie

asked.

The little boy folded his hands and bowed his head. "Jesus, I missed Johnny today. Please let him come back to my class. And let him know that I love him. Amen."

Katie swallowed hard and quickly wiped away a tear. She had already suspected her son had Johnny's tender heart.

"Time for bed, sweetheart."

"Do you think God heard my prayer? Was it good enough?"

Katie smiled as she tucked him in. "Sweetheart, it was perfect. I'm sure He heard." She kissed his forehead and left the room, closing the door behind her. She went to check the doors and make sure they were locked. She set the alarm, not so much to alert them to a break in, but more in case her mother decided to wander. Her parents had already turned in.

She made a cup of tea, headed to her bedroom, and shut the door. She grabbed the letters from under her pillow and settled on her bed to read.

He'd mailed the first one the day after she'd left.

Dearest Katie,

I can't believe you are gone. I didn't mean what I said about regretting our last night together. I regret that we weren't married when it happened. I never intended to dishonor you this way. Please reconsider marrying me? Choose me. I can't give up the dream I feel God is calling me to, and I would never ask you to give up your dream of being a nurse. Somehow, we could work it out and be happy.

Your parents won't give me your number or address but promised to forward your letters. I know they don't like me, and I'm sorry for that. I can't change who I am for them, or for you.

I love you, Katie. I always have. I'm sorry for the way things ended and am praying you'll change your mind and be mine.

Yours forever,
Johnny

She folded the letter up and opened the next one, sent only a week later. Perhaps he had waited for her to respond?

Dearest Katie,

I've been praying and praying and hoping you might call. Niko has managed to line up a string of concert events for the fall, so I'll be traveling some with the band. I'm excited to see what God will do and thrilled He would let me play music for Him, much like King David did. I know it's not the same as leading in church or playing on the worship team, but I really believe we make a difference by bringing God's truth to people who might never set foot in a church building. Maybe ease their suffering with skilled musicianship much like David did for Saul.

I miss you terribly. Your smile. The way your eyes light up after we kiss. The feel of your arms around me when you hold me tight. I'm only half a person without you here, and I'm not sure how to go on without you. How could you set me aside so easily? Could you really walk away from what we had? Did I matter so little to you? These thoughts torment me night and day. I pray and ask God to bring you back to me. But He won't make you do something you don't want. At least write and let me know one way or another. My heart cannot grasp that it's over between us, and I keep hoping it was a horrible mistake.

Forever yours,

Johnny

She read a few more letters in the stack recounting their adventures on tour but always faithful in his love for her.

Dearest Katie,

It's been several months now with no word from you. My heart rebels at the thought of moving on. I met a woman. She's sweet and believes in my music, and we plan to marry soon. It sounds foolish, and Niko even says he thinks it's a rebound romance. Maybe it is.

Just know that I love you and I always will. I don't blame you for not wanting to marry a struggling musician. Even though we are doing well and will be recording our first album, it's a fickle industry and there are no guarantees. I'm picking up studio work, often traveling to Nashville in-between gigs. Those pay well.

So, I am moving on. As if I can ever recover from loving you. I will continue to pray for God's best for you, even though I wanted to be His answer to that prayer. I love you, Katie.

Forever yours in my heart,
Johnny

Katie folded the letter up. David was born a few months later. Johnny's marriage took place shortly after that. Her parents had helped her out financially so she could finish school and care for her son. It was hard. So hard. She had avoided friendships and dating to escape the questions of David's parentage. Her parents refused to let her acknowledge whose child he was. They didn't want that kind of association. She suspected that back home, they informed friends that she had adopted. Right. Like a single nineteen-year-old still in college could do that. She wondered what other lies had been spread.

Katie obviously spread a few lies herself in stating she didn't know who the father was on the birth certificate. And the lie of omission in never telling Johnny. Until today.

She had been shocked at the joy radiating from his face at the news that David was his son. Shock and awe. Hadn't that been a battle cry in the Gulf War? It was what she had seen, though in a more positive way, in Johnny. She wanted David to know his father. She wanted David to learn music from a master. She wanted David to learn faith from a man of God. Funny how David had been in Johnny's classroom and connected so instantly with him. God must have planned that when she selected Orchard Hill as a church home.

And Johnny saved David's life just last Sunday… and still suffered the pain, if his limping was any indication.

But Johnny had cancer. A potentially curable form of leukemia. She sensed defeat in him. She'd not worked in oncology long, but she suspected that this was unusual. Most cancer patients were tired, yes, but eager for the fight and determined to win. Even until their last breaths, they rarely seemed to let the cancer defeat them. So why Johnny? He had always been an upbeat guy. Where had his zest for life gone? His passion?

She bent her head as she bundled the letters together. Now it was her turn to pray.

~*~

Johnny wasn't sure what to tackle on Monday morning. Talk to Roberto about the contract and the slander in the media. Oh, and about the child support and arranging a visitation schedule and what that might entail. Call Pastor Andrew regarding the accusations. It used to be he would go for a jog to clear his mind, but he lacked the energy and still hurt from his fall. He got on the phone to schedule and reschedule some appointments. He'd see his doctor Tuesday morning. He was due to fly to Nashville Wednesday afternoon for studio work. It was a short trip, for which he was grateful. He'd be back home by Saturday.

He managed to see Roberto early in the day, and Tia joined him after dropping off Apolo at her in-laws. They settled in across from the lawyer's mahogany desk.

"Johnny, it sounds like we have a few issues to resolve. Let's start with the contract. They did violate it, and I have been in contact with the studio. They are promising to pay. You should have a check by the end of the week. Thankfully, your guitar wasn't damaged."

Tia nodded. "I'm glad we don't have to fight them."

Roberto smiled. "Me too. International contracts can have a different challenge to them. The fact that Pamela's slander over a supposed affair as well as the fight between you two and her subsequent arrest hit the media and snowballed into something big is astounding. No offense, Johnny, but you've never been in the crosshairs of the paparazzi, and with this tarnishing your reputation as a believer, you have just cause to fight. We can demand retractions and threaten lawsuits, but there's already a long list of media outlets as well, but those retractions can be buried and won't garner the attention the initial scandal caused. We can do all that, but if we do much more, it's going to look like you really are guilty. So, I wouldn't recommend a media campaign at this stage of the game. But if you have a friend in the media who would be willing to do a fair interview, that could help."

Johnny shook his head. "What's the point? It doesn't interfere with my studio work, and if I need to distance myself from Specific Gravity to preserve their integrity, they can always find another guitar player to take my place. I have cancer, so I may not be around long enough to care anyway."

"Don't talk that way, Johnny. You're not going to die," Tia asserted.

"I do think you filing harassment and assault charges against Pamela helps. If we can get a copy of the police report…"

"Niko suggested I file for slander but let the rest fizzle away. Go ahead and do the retractions. I normally fly under the radar of any paparazzi, and if nothing else emerges to titillate them, everyone will soon move on."

Roberto scribbled some notes. "I'll get the letters sent out on your behalf." He shoved a piece of paper in a file and opened up another folder. "Now, let's talk about the fact that you have recently become the parent of a six-year-old boy named David."

The next half an hour involved financial statements and suggestions for visitation to run past Katie. Changing the birth certificate would be central, as well as David's social security card.

The fact that he needed to see Katie twisted his

gut. She had stomped on his heart once, and he was very much afraid she'd do it again.

5

Love is an irresistible desire to be irresistibly desired.
Robert Frost

He spied Katie the minute he entered the clinic.

"Hi, Johnny. I'll let the nurse know you're here," she said.

"Thanks." He gave her a nod as he went to sit down. He jumped back up and came to the counter. "Um. Is there a time we could meet to talk, you know, about David?"

Katie smiled. "Sure. Call me after five, and we'll set something up." She wrote her number on a piece of paper and handed it to him. Johnny turned to sit down again. "By the way, I haven't told him yet. I want you to be there when I do. He's been praying for you."

"Why does he think I need prayer?" Johnny asked.

"Because you weren't in class, and he said you seemed sad."

"Huh. Go figure." His son was too perceptive by half.

"Are you?"

"Am I what?"

"Sad?"

Johnny frowned but was spared answering when the phone rang and another patient entered the clinic. He leaned his head against the wall behind the row of

Susan M. Baganz

chairs and closed his eyes. He hadn't given an answer in words, but he suspected Katie guessed the truth.

Katie escorted him to his room. "Don't worry. I've made it clear that I cannot handle your records. Cicely will be in to get your vitals."

"Oh. OK." He walked in and sat down as she closed the door behind him. It opened only a moment later, and a round, bubbly woman sashayed in.

"Well, Mr. Marshall, I'm Cicely, and I need to ask you a few questions before the doctor comes in."

He shrugged. "Go ahead."

"How are your bruises?"

"Colorful." His face grew warm. Did she want to see? He really didn't want to drop his pants for her.

"Have you talked to anyone about being a bone marrow donor?"

"What even qualifies them? How do you determine a match? I would hate to ask and it not be a good match. I know this was all explained when I got the diagnosis. I think I was too much in shock to take it all in."

"There is a protein called human leukocyte antigen, or HLA, and it needs to be a close match. The closer the match, the more successful the outcome. Parents would be the most likely."

"Cousins?"

"Unlikely, but don't rule it out unless you have them tested. If a close family member doesn't match, there is a bone marrow registry we can go to. They prefer you rule out family members first."

"My parents are older. I doubt they would physically be up to donating."

"You are making their decisions for them, aren't you? You should give them the option to be tested.

Whether they can donate after that…well, the chance is still slim. Seventy percent of recipients cannot find a match in their family. If you can, it makes things so much easier and quicker. I'm gathering you haven't asked anyone yet."

Johnny shook his head. "So even if I ask, they may not qualify, and I'm left without much hope."

"Where there is life, there is hope. There is the registry. Don't dig your grave so quickly."

She rose and left the room.

A dark cloud settled on him. Hope? What was that? *My hope is supposed to be in the Lord, and I'm trusting You for my salvation, but am I obeying and trusting You with this trial?*

And what about David? The son he had always longed for. Didn't he deserve to have a father in his life for a long time? Wasn't that enough motivation to ask for the help he needed?

There was a knock on the door followed by the doctor entering.

~*~

By the time Johnny left, he had a prescription for an antidepressant and information to give to family members who might consider donating. These would be hard conversations, because Niko and Tia had been the only people he had told about his cancer other than his pastors. Katie knew as well. He gave Katie a wave as he walked out the door. She had been on the phone, and he wasn't in a mood to talk.

He got a text from Katie later in the afternoon suggesting he meet David and her at Culvers for dinner at six thirty. She said David was a fan of their root beer. That made Johnny smile. Obviously, the kid hadn't tried the locally brewed brand yet. Now *that* was some awesome root beer.

He called his parents.

"Mom?"

"Yes, Johnny? How are you? I'm still confused why you moved in with Niko. If you are having financial troubles, you are more than welcome back here."

"I know, Mom, but living with Niko gives me free access to a studio to record and practice."

"What do you need?"

"Why do I have to need something to talk to my mom?"

"Because it's about the only time you call anymore. Gallivanting around to Nashville and London. How are you going to find a nice girl to marry and have children with?"

"Yeah, well, I'm off to Nashville again this week but was wondering if Sunday afternoon, I could come over and talk to you guys and invite my brothers and sisters to come as well."

"Sounds serious. Are you OK?"

"I don't want you to worry, Mom. I'll explain everything Sunday afternoon. Would two o'clock work for you?"

"I'll make some fresh baklava for you. I know it's your favorite."

"Thanks, Mom. I might bring Niko too."

"Oh, I would love to see Niko again."

"Great. I love you, and I'll see you Sunday."

"Love you too, Johnny. Have a safe trip, but don't come back speaking Southern now."

Johnny laughed. "I won't."

He hung up and sighed. There. He was committed. He needed to tell them about David too... At some point, David would need to meet his grandparents. His mom and dad would be thrilled to know he had a son. At least one burden of failure he could shake off his shoulders while adding the title of single father to his list of crimes.

~*~

"Mommy! French fries and root beer please," little David said, pogoing around her as she waited her turn.

"That's not a nutritious dinner."

"Butter burger?"

"I'll get you a butter burger meal, and you can also have custard for dessert."

"Yay! Why are we here without Grandma and Grandpa?"

"We're here to meet a friend."

David frowned. "A big-person friend?"

"Yup."

"Boring." His little shoulders drooped as he pouted.

Katie laughed. "I don't think you'll find him boring at all. See?"

Johnny came in the side entrance and stomped the snow off his boots. His gray knit cap contrasted with his bright red scarf. He looked up, and his brown eyes locked with hers. A switch flipped inside, taking her back seven years. He gave her a half-smile as he sauntered toward them.

"Johnny!" David squealed and leapt into Johnny's arms, enveloping him in a hug.

"Hey, buddy, if you choke me to death, I won't be

able to eat dinner, and I hear they have some great French fries and root beer here." Johnny released David. The little boy grabbed his hand and held firm.

Katie thought maybe a tear had formed in Johnny's eye, but he moved away, and when he turned back and smiled at her, it was gone.

They ordered their food. Johnny insisted on paying for their meals. They found a booth, and David sat as close to Johnny as he could.

"I pray over my meals," Johnny said.

"We do when we aren't with Grandma and Grandpa."

Johnny nodded and bowed his head. "Thank You, Lord, for this food and for this time spent with David and his mom. May You be honored by our conversation this evening. Amen."

"Amen," rang David's little voice, an echo of his father's.

Katie watched as the two picked up their butter burgers and took a bite, closed their eyes, and chewed. An "mmm" resonated from both, and Johnny's eyes snapped open and gazed down at his son. There was such love there it took Katie's breath away. Her little boy was no longer just hers anymore.

"Why weren't you in church Sunday? I missed you, Johnny."

"I missed you too. I hadn't planned to come, because I was supposed to be out of the country. Unfortunately, something happened while in London, and I had to return home early. In the meantime, the person who did a bad thing told everyone a lie about me. Because the church didn't know the truth, they decided I couldn't work with kids until they checked it out."

"Did you hurt a kid?"

"No. I would never harm any child. I love children."

David frowned. "Well, they should know you better than doing whatever it is they said you did. That was just mean."

Johnny chuckled. "Thanks for your vote of confidence. It was nasty, and my attorney is working on it. The lies hurt, but it hurt more that I didn't get to spend time with you learning about Jesus."

"I know a lot about Jesus. I can teach you, Johnny. What do you want to learn?"

"I hope I never stop learning about how wonderful our God is. Thank you for being willing to help me."

"Anytime, Johnny. Anytime." David chomped on a French fry and followed that with a sip of his root beer. He let out a belch.

"David!" Katie scolded.

Johnny took a sip of his root beer and released a louder and longer belch.

David stared up at him with wide eyes. "Can you teach me how to do that?"

Katie caught the wink Johnny gave the little boy. "What's a great root beer for but providing loud belches?"

Katie involuntarily burped, and the boys laughed. "You guys are terrible."

Johnny and David smirked at each other and resumed eating.

"Why don't you have any kids if you love them so much?" David asked.

A flash of sorrow passed over Johnny's features. A second later, it was gone. Had it been her imagination?

"I was married, but my wife wanted to wait to have kids. I got cancer, and she left me. As a result of the treatment, my body is not capable of helping a woman make a baby." Johnny's face grew pink.

David nodded. "That's a bummer. You could pretend that I'm your son, if that will make you feel better. I don't have a daddy, so he won't mind."

"What do you know about your father, David?" Johnny glanced over to Katie, and she tensed.

"Momma told me he was a really great guy but doesn't know about me. She won't tell me why, but she always looks sad when I ask, so I try not to bother her about it."

"I think any man would be proud to call you his son, David." Johnny responded, putting his arm around the little boy for a side hug.

"David, Johnny and I have something important we wanted to tell you." Katie's voice cracked as she finally spoke.

The little boy's eyes lit up, and his smile grew big as he swallowed. "You're getting married?"

Katie almost choked. She took a sip of her soda. "No. We're not. But that wonderful man I told you about—your father? Well, he is Johnny."

"And I didn't know about you being my son until a few days ago. I'm really sorry. I missed so much of your life. Could you ever forgive me for that, David?"

The little boy sat back, and a tear flowed down his cheek. "You're my dad?"

"Yes."

"But you said you couldn't have kids."

"Well, that was after the cancer. You were created several years before that."

"Mom? He's really my dad?"

Katie nodded, and her sinuses stuffed up as she fought back the tears. She reached for a brown napkin to blow her nose.

"But you're not married to my mom."

"No, David. Sometimes adults do stupid things, and one of the dumbest I ever did was lose your mother's love."

"Johnny. You can't take the blame there. Sweetheart. David. It's a story that will be better told when you are older. But you were created in love. Fear, misunderstanding, and pride tore me from your father's arms. He would have married me, but I never told him about you. I was selfish and wanted you to myself. I was wrong to have deprived you of such a wonderful man to grow up with, follow, and love."

David slid off the bench, went to her, and wrapped his arms tight around her neck. "I forgive you, Mommy. I love you, and you are the bestest mommy ever." He kissed her cheek, and she held him close for a few seconds before releasing him.

"He's right, Katie. You are the best mommy ever. You've done a wonderful job taking care of our son." A large brown envelope sat on the edge of the table. He now slid over to her. "You can look at these later, and we can make any changes you want. It's my attempt to set things right."

"You did nothing wrong."

Johnny nodded. "I did, but thankfully the most beautiful result came of that. A son. You gave me a son. I am sorry for my sin but am grateful for the wonderful outcome anyway. I regret the suffering you endured."

"If I remember, there were two participants, and I was as eager as you were, if not more so." Katie grew suddenly warm as her eyes connected with Johnny's intense gaze. Passion sizzled there that seemed even more exciting than it had seven years ago. She blinked and watched her son, who bounced on the seat as he ate.

"So, Johnny. Are you going to move to Grandma and Grandpa's house with us?"

"Oh, no, David. He can't live with us. We're not married."

"But mommies and daddies live together."

"Sorry, son. But we won't unless we are married. We've not known each other for seven years. We can't pick up a relationship from then and act like that time never passed."

"Why not?"

"It's complicated." Katie said at the same time as Johnny. They both chuckled.

David belched again, and Katie tried to give him a stern look.

"David, I think it's a God thing that you came into my life when you did, and doing so brought out the truth that I'm your father. I want to be your dad. Regardless of what happens between me and your mom, I'm your dad and we'll get to spend time together, and I look forward to it very much."

"What do you do, Dad?"

"For work?"

"Yeah. Mommy's a nurse, and she helps sick people."

"I'm a musician."

The little boy's eyebrows scrunched. "What's that?"

"I play music. Remember how we talked about young King David a few weeks ago and how he played the harp for Saul?"

"You play a harp?"

Johnny laughed. "No, but it would be cool to try sometime. I play guitar. Mostly electric and acoustic but sometimes bass. I can play a little piano and drums but not as well as guitar."

"Do you play for a king?"

"In a way, I do. I play music for Jesus, but I also play for people. Sometimes I record music in a studio with a band. In the past, I've toured with my cousin Niko and some buddies. We've recorded music that honors God and hopefully encourages people to follow Him."

"You travel a lot?"

Johnny shrugged. "I often travel where the jobs take me, but I can go weeks without touring. Come spring, the band might start playing at festivals again. We're waiting before committing to more."

"Waiting for what?" Katie asked.

"Cancer," Johnny mouthed. Aloud, he answered, "I got sick once before, and the band stopped touring so I could heal."

"Are you sick, Johnny?" David asked.

Johnny nodded. "Pray for me, OK? Your mom tells me you already have been."

"OK. Mommy, can I go get my ice cream now?" David waved his slip of paper, a coupon for a free scoop of custard.

"Sure, honey. Can you handle it on your own?"

"You betcha." The little boy slid off the bench and skipped to the front counter where Katie could see him.

"Is it safe for him to do that alone?" Johnny asked.

"Yeah. I keep an eye on him. I want him to learn to

be more independent." Katie refocused her gaze to the man sitting across from her. "I'm glad David has you for a father."

"Yeah? Why?"

"Because he deserves a man like you to help him grow. He loves music. I've never had the time or money to give him lessons."

"I could teach him."

Katie smiled. "I think he would like that."

"I'm sorry I was rude to you the other day about the transplant stuff. I'm meeting with my family Sunday afternoon to ask them."

"Good. I'm glad. I'd really hate for David to gain a father only to lose him again."

"You haven't dated? There's been no one else?"

"I've had a few dates but none that captured my fancy."

"That's been my life since Donna."

"Did you love her?"

Johnny stared out the window for a few moments. "If love is an action—a verb—then yes, I loved her the best I knew how. It was a chore at times. A duty. A struggle. But I tried. Traveling was a blessing and a curse. The reality is, if I hadn't traveled, the end would likely have come sooner. As for a heart connection? Not so much. I was devastated when she left me, but more because she did it, and then I was divorced. It was like stamping failure on my forehead or wearing a big D on my chest. I missed being married, but I didn't miss her."

"I'm sorry you had to go through that."

Johnny gazed at her, and she forced herself to maintain the eye contact until David slid back onto the bench with his scoop of chocolate custard with blue sprinkles.

~*~

When they finally ended the evening and Katie took David home and put him to bed, she pulled out the letters and opened up one she hadn't taken the chance to read yet. She figured she'd space them out and treasure them. This one was probably written before he met his wife.

Dear Katie,

How is a man supposed to go on with half a heart? If I were Niko, I would have the lyrics to a dozen songs of heartbreak right now. But he's the master poet, and I can only pour out my heart in music without words. Why couldn't we have made it work? Was it because your parents would never have agreed? I realize they are important, and I can't help but be jealous of your devotion to them at the expense of us.

I'm getting more work and making decent money, saving for a house with a nice basement for the band to practice in. Looks like we'll be recording an album soon and possibly touring. We got an agent who's pushy. His assistant is sweet, though, but she has eyes for Niko. He doesn't realize it yet.

There have been some girls. I know I'm free to date, but when I do, I feel guilty. Like I'm cheating on you. How am I to get past what we had? I don't really want to. I want you back in my arms and by my side. I miss you, Katie.

Forever yours,
Johnny

What was that look Johnny had given her when he

talked about not missing his wife? It was almost as if he meant, "Not like I missed you."

She still loved him. She had never stopped. It wasn't just desire, although he was a far more compelling man now than he had been at eighteen. He'd grown in depth, matured through suffering and loss—some caused by her. She was different as well. The idea of a relationship with Johnny thrilled and terrified her.

He'd never said he wanted her back or that there was even a possibility of a future together. He'd made provisions and a reasonable and respectful plea for time with his son. No acrimony toward her at all. Maybe he understood her better than she understood herself. She looked down at the letter. He had resigned himself to being unacceptable to her parents. Katie was guilty of trying to please them to the detriment of her own happiness.

Now her father was impaired with the aftereffects of a stroke, and her mother was losing her mind and identity. Soon they would be in an assisted living facility and no longer in a position to question her choice of a life-mate. All their wealth and savings would go to pay for their upkeep. This house would be gone. It had always been far grander than necessary, anyway.

The question now was whether Johnny would consider her after how she had hurt him. And how did she let him know she was even interested in being more than his son's mother?

6

At the touch of love, everyone becomes a poet.
Plato

Johnny walked into church early Wednesday morning to meet with Pastor Andrew about the media smear and his ability to serve. His body ached, and anxiety over the meeting with his family ate at his insides, twisting his intestines into knots. On top of that, he had music to learn for his studio gig this week. It was a quick in and out session if all went well.

He waited in the lobby for his appointment as worship music wafted through the speakers. He was glad it wasn't too loud. Silently he prayed. *Lord, You've tossed so much at me lately. The cancer diagnosis, selling the house, moving in with Niko, reuniting with Katie, discovering I'm a dad, and the need to ask for help in hopes of a cure...oh, and the fictional scandal with Pamela. Was that how Joseph felt running from Potiphar's wife? Condemned without trial because of one person's lies?*

"Hey, Johnny." Pastor Andrew had come out, and Johnny hadn't even noticed. He rose, followed the man to his office, and sank into a comfy chair across from him. "What brings you here?" Andrew's slight southern drawl contained a level of comfort.

"Life's gotten crazy, Andrew." He recounted what he had just prayed about. "I really want to be able to serve, and I'm working to clear my name...but I don't want to cause problems with the church, either."

Andrew nodded. "There was a knee-jerk reaction to the news, which initially happened without me knowing. I have reassured the Children's Ministry Director of your integrity. You were supposed to have been away Sunday so they anticipated we could get this figured out without denying you the opportunity to serve. I'm sorry about how that worked out. We can put you back in your classroom. You're not a pedophile or accused of abuse of any kind. You've a track record of faithfulness. You're never alone and have been a good role model for the kids who are, at this point, too young to read the kind of magazines those stories are printed in. I believe you even made the *National Inquirer* but only a byline...and they didn't use your name there but probably did on page thirteen. I didn't bother reading it." Andrew winked as he grinned at Johnny.

"There is more to consider, though, and it was not something I had even been aware of. When I was in high school, I dated a lovely girl, Katie, whom I longed to marry. We...well, we went too far. We split after that because of pressure from her parents to find a husband who could provide a more secure future for her. I found out a few days ago that her son is mine."

"Whoa. Is she making demands of you?"

"No. Katie isn't like that. She started attending here recently, so you probably haven't met her yet. We told David last night, and he is thrilled. He is in my class, and we bonded instantly. Now I understand why. He's also the little boy I saved from being hit by a car in the parking lot. I'm doing everything I can to make up for the years of support I financially should have provided. We're working out visitation."

"So, what's your concern?"

"I'm not so famous that this should be an issue, but I would never have imagined the scenario in London, either. I'm no ladies' man. But it happened and what if—"

"—your love-child is exposed publically?"

"Yeah."

"Let him who has never sinned cast the first stone. If none of us had been free of sin, Jesus's sacrifice for us on the cross would be moot. I think you carry too much guilt for the past that Jesus already paid for and wiped out. Yes, there is a consequence in a little boy who needs you now as his father, financially and relationally, but that doesn't mean you need to wear a cloak of shame over that."

"Why not? Doesn't Katie have to wear that as a single mom? Why do I get a free pass while she faces it?"

"At this stage, my guess is she doesn't face it quite as often anymore. We have so many single moms in our church, and while it's regretful that those children don't have fathers involved in their lives, it sounds like you're doing your best, now that you're aware, to take care of your responsibilities."

Johnny sighed. "Yeah. It's just been so much lately. On top of everything else, I need to approach my family about the possibility of testing to be a bone marrow donor for me."

"I'm sorry you have to deal with all this. As you seek to do what's right, to live your life according to Biblical principles, the more your enemy will throw up roadblocks for you. His plan is to derail and destroy you and your message. This is just a reality in the life of a Christian we often forget. You're at war, and unfortunately, you are facing attacks from several sides. This makes it even more crucial for you to enlist others in the battle to help fight alongside and on your behalf. First with prayer. But also with more practical aspects. When you meet with your family to discuss the cancer and transplant options, will you also inform them of David?"

He nodded. "Yeah. Guess I'll take care of it all at once. Seems like that would be for the best."

"Johnny, you're doing everything right. Hang in there. I realize it's difficult. Stand firm but not alone. Let's pray."

Johnny walked away with mixed emotions. A battle. A war. Roadblocks. Yup, the enemy certainly had been attacking him—his health, his emotions, his reputation…Pastor Andrew had been right though. He had been fighting alone, and he knew Niko and others would gladly step in to help him. So, when had he decided he had to do this by himself?

When Donna left me.

Sure, Tia, Niko, and his family had surrounded him during that time, but he walled a large part of himself away. Avoiding the pain. Refusing to deal with the abandonment of Katie and then Donna. Both women had left when he needed them the most. He had needed Katie to believe in him. He had needed Donna to love him in spite of his illness. Both had walked away.

Katie was back.

Interesting that her departure drove him to deeper faith and dependence on God, while Donna's had driven a wedge. Donna lacked Katie's stronger faith, but he didn't realize that at first. That whole unequally-yoked thing had been a trial from the start, even when passion was good between them. Passion? Lust. Pure and simple. They met a physical need, and when his faith grew stronger, attacks came, and the physical could no longer sustain them. It was over.

Katie had been swayed by her parents. Maybe they were right. He wasn't worthy of her. She needed a nice house and a husband with a six-figure income able to provide her with all the bells and whistles they had provided. Johnny possessed little to nothing at the time she left. But without her parents' support, neither did she. He had thought it would be a level playing field.

He'd been wrong.

It still wasn't level. But when had he ever even been tempted to think that life was fair? He'd always been a realist, hadn't he? Or was there some deep-seated dreamer buried underneath, railing against the injustices of life and broken hearts?

He let out a grunt. If he kept up this kind of thinking, the next thing he knew, he'd be writing songs like Niko. No. Better to bury these musings and concentrate on music. Only once had he written a poem, and it had never helped except to leave him scraped raw and needy. He wasn't going there again.

He had work to do, and he needed the money now more than ever—not just for the medical bills but to support his son and make up for the six lost years he should have been doing that all along. He wished he could make up for that in other ways too, but as a human, he was limited. No *Doctor Who* was going to sweep in and take him back in time to be there for the birth of his son, his first words, first steps…Life wasn't a sci-fi fairy tale where everything ended up happily ever after…

That afternoon, Niko dropped Johnny off at General Mitchell Field Airport south of Milwaukee for his flight.

"Are you sure you don't want me to come with you, Johnny? I could be your bouncer and help keep the ladies at bay."

"Sure, only to find yourself in the news and your marriage on the rocks because of someone's lies? No, but thank you. I'll see you Saturday afternoon?"

"Yeah, unless you need to come home sooner."

"Nah, Sam is putting me up, and hopefully he can help hide me away from any inopportune advances."

"Maybe you'll find your soul mate on this trip."

"I had a soul mate once. She left me."

"You and Katie were both too young."

"Old enough to produce a kid."

"And you'll do right by him. You didn't know or you would have taken care of things then if you'd had the opportunity."

Johnny could only nod as he grabbed his guitar case and looped the traveling strap angled across his chest. "Enough. I need to go."

"I'm praying for you. You're not walking this road without me, Mister Lone Ranger."

"I bet I'd look good in the mask." Johnny winked at Niko and strode away with his carry-on.

He settled into his seat on the plane. He had his earbuds in and his tablet open as he read the chord sheets and listened to the music he would accompany in the studio. Mentally, he composed ideas.

"Hey. Are you Johnny Marshall?" A teenage boy slid in next to him, removing his own ear buds attached to an mp3 player in his shirt pocket.

Johnny halted his audio and pulled out his buds.

"Yeah."

A hand thrust his way, and Johnny returned the handshake.

"Wow. I can't believe I get to sit next to you on a plane. Can I take a pic?"

Johnny shrugged. With a knit cap and his sunglasses on, he was surprised anyone recognized him. The boy leaned next to him holding his cell phone out and snapped a photo. Johnny gave a half-grin in the pic.

"I love your music. I wish I could play like you, but your fingers are too quick and I can't find any fingering sheets of your work."

"I don't make them."

"You don't have anything written down?"

Johnny shook his head. "It's all in my head. Once I get a riff down, it's there, and the more I play it the less I have to think about it. My fingers just play."

"Cool. But how did you learn to do that?" The young man's pimpled face and wide eyes reminded Johnny of his own adolescence.

"I think part of it is a gift, but a larger part is practice, practice, practice."

"When you were my age, how often did you practice?"

"Several hours a day."

"Ouch. My fingers would bleed."

Johnny laughed. "Yeah. Start out slow and build up those callouses, and it won't matter. It became more an issue of my fingers cramping."

"Do you still have to play that many hours a day?"

"No, but I do play every day when I can and for as long as I can."

"Because you need to do that to be fresh?"

"No. I do it to be sane. Music is my passion, therapy, comfort, and peace. When I play, the world fades away, and I find escape and joy."

The young man frowned. "Did you want to be famous?"

Johnny grinned. "Who doesn't? I had great dreams of grandeur that hard work, long hours, and bad reviews quickly cured."

"But you're famous now."

"How did you recognize me?"

"Your picture has been all over the news and magazine rags."

"Do you think that's what I really wanted to be famous for? Because some woman decided to assault me and throw out lies about me?"

"But you got called to play at Abbey Road Studios in London."

"True. That was cool. But it doesn't make me famous. It just means I'm a good guitar player. The fact that you recognized me from those media stories doesn't give me the kind of fame I want."

"There are different kinds of fame?"

"Sure. You have your photo all over the media is one kind of fame, but that has nothing to do with my talent or level of skill. Our band sold bestseller albums and videos...and that's another kind of fame. The best kind, though, will be one day standing before Jesus and hearing 'Well done, good and faithful servant.'"

"I hadn't thought of that. But you make money at what you do?"

"Now I do. In the early days, it was hard. Lived with my parents or roomed with bandmates and slept in a van when we travelled, washing up at truck stops. It was a rough life."

"So where are you headed now?"

"Nashville."

"Cool. I'm going to visit my dad in Atlanta."

"Atlanta's a beautiful city."

"Yeah, but it's too short a visit. I have to fly back Sunday so I can be back in school."

"Parents divorced?"

"Yeah. Three years now. It was hard when Dad got a great job offer and decided to move."

"You miss him?"

"Yeah. He's the best. I love my mom too, but sometimes wish I lived with my dad. I wish they had never divorced."

"Sometimes adults make mistakes."

"Have you?"

Johnny frowned. "More than I'd like to admit."

"Bet you'd never leave your son."

If a knife had stabbed his heart, it wouldn't have hurt worse than those words. The plane was making its way down the runway as the stewardesses gave last-minute instructions. Johnny turned off his tablet for the taxi and lift-off and focused his gaze outside the window at the snow-covered city of Milwaukee. The young man next to him settled in his seat, and the conversation seemed over. At least he hoped it was. Once in the air, the tablet went back on and the earbuds in. He tried to focus on the music he needed to learn, but all he could do was see the eager, shining face of his little boy and miss those sweet arms around his neck when he was last hugged by him. He swallowed his tears. *Focus, Johnny. You have work to do.*

~*~

Susan M. Baganz

Landing in Atlanta, Johnny grabbed his guitar and bags and said farewell to the young man. He headed to his connecting flight and settled in.

Bet you'd never leave your son.

Not on purpose. Johnny closed his eyes to pray. *Come on, God. I didn't even know I had a son. Your Word says there is no condemnation for those who are in Christ Jesus. So where is this attack coming from? Please rescue me. You know I adore David and long to be a full-time father to him. But I can't go back seven years and undo what happened. Now that David is in my life, I wouldn't even want to. You made him wonderfully perfect. A surprise gift when my heart longed for a child, and I had thought the dream dead. But do you give gifts with a side helping of guilt? Please free me from that and guide me to do what's best for my son. And help me on this trip too...so that my integrity can be seen. Protect me from aggressive women.*

He sighed an "Amen" and leaned back to rest. Images of David ran through his mind, combined with dreams for the future of things they could enjoy together. He realized he didn't even know David's birthday. He'd have to get that information soon. He didn't want to miss it when the time came.

~*~

Katie dragged herself home Wednesday night. Her phone beeped, and she reached for it as she stirred the soup for dinner. It was a text from Johnny.

Arrived safe in Nashville. When is David's birthday?

She grinned. She typed a note back.

Good flight? May 6th.

Yeah. It was fine. If you need anything text me. OK?

OK. Have a good few days and play well.

Thanks.

She turned back to the soup and grinned. She could almost imagine getting that kind of text from a husband who traveled. Except the messages might be filled with "I miss you" and "love you" and "give David a kiss for me." She shook her head to clear her fantastical thinking. She had run away from Johnny once. She doubted he'd be chasing her again. He deserved a woman who believed in him and would risk everything for love.

While she might think she was that kind of girl now, she wasn't so sure that vain, parental-dependent girl didn't still exist in the shadows. She might love Johnny—had she ever really stopped? But he deserved better than a woman who ran away and was too afraid to defy her parents' narrow-minded thinking even when she was an adult. Nope. Johnny needed a woman who was more sure of who she was and wouldn't fail him. He'd had enough of that with her and his ex-wife.

Grief sank like a stone in her gut at the thought of what she had lost by her choices. She sat in a chair to catch her breath. She made her bed and walked away from it. She gave up the right to ask for a ring when she refused him, ran away, and kept his son from him. Her sins were many in any tally he might keep.

Johnny never blamed her. He hadn't condemned her. Instead, he thanked her for her care of their son. He accepted her need to honor her parents' wishes even though he didn't like it.

He never thought he was worthy of me. At that realization, she gasped as tears sprang forth. The truth was she hadn't ever deserved a guy as great as Johnny. He had it so wrong.

"Mommy? Are you hurt?" David came to her and put his little hand to her face. Those deep brown eyes teared up in response to her pain.

"I'm OK, baby. Just had some sad thoughts."

He frowned. "I miss Daddy."

She pulled him up into her lap and held him close. "Yeah, baby, I do too. I do too."

She finally set him down, and together they prepared the table and settled down to eat with her parents.

The meal was quiet with only the sounds of silverware as they ate tomato soup and grilled cheese sandwiches. Katie realized how cold her upbringing had been. A maid to cook and serve. Only civilized conversation. Now her dad struggled to talk at all, and her mother didn't always recognize Katie, much less David. She, in essence, lived with strangers. But as their daughter, she had a duty to honor them and provide care. David needed to know them while there was still time. She had been born late in her parents' life...and now with them both retired and in ill health, how much longer would they be around? Her brother was a good seventeen years older than her. She had been all of eight when he had married. He was older now too...and successful. Too busy to be bothered.

She sighed as she cleaned up the kitchen and put away folded laundry. She settled into bed and pulled out another letter she hadn't yet opened. Why did she torture herself this way? Dragging them out little by little? Maybe because that girl from seven years ago still longed to hear the pleas of her lover's heart, and reading them slowly, a little at a time, gave her something to savor.

Dear Katie,
My heart longs for only you
There is not much else for me to do
I weep and pray
Yet you remain far away
Beyond my grasp,
an empty chasm between us
I cannot get there…by train or bus
So my sorry rhyme is my poor attempt
To tell you of love that's left
For you and only you
My heart awaits in vain
And so I write, again and again,
Hopeless, unworthy of affectionate returns
Yet I put myself forward only to be burned
How do I move on after loving you?
Forever yours,
Johnny

She folded it up with a smile. A poem. He always swore that Niko was the songwriter and poet and he could only convey himself through his guitar. She disagreed. His kisses were pretty potent too. This poem was like a kiss, filled with longing and desire and questions and fear. The flesh part of her longed to go to him and kiss away the agony from long ago. But it wasn't her place to do that now. She needed to put those urges and desires on the altar. If Johnny would ever be hers again, it would be through an act of God. She couldn't trust her own heart in the matter.

Johnny, I still love you…don't move on without me.

7

The only greatness is unselfish love.
Anonymous

Johnny worked and made it in and out of the studio each day without incident. Saturday morning, he relaxed at the small dinette with Sam, who used to play with Specific Gravity for years before moving to Nashville to do exclusive studio work as a bass player.

"Good week?" Sam asked.

"If having no one assault me is good, then yes, it was an excellent week." Johnny winked.

"I can't believe that happened to you in London. I mean, sure it's nice to get your name out there, but at what cost? Anyone who knows you at all recognizes the lies exactly for what they are." Sam brought a pitcher of coffee to the table and poured for them both.

"I'm not perfect, Sam. You've traveled with me long enough to know the truth of that. I'm not above temptation." Johnny blew at his cup before taking a sip.

"Sure you are. Prove it." Sam was shaking his head.

"I recently discovered that my high school sweetheart gave birth to our son six years ago."

"Whoa. You're a dad?"

Johnny grinned. "Yup. Dream come true for me." He took out his phone and pulled up a photo of David he had taken the night they had told him. Katie had snapped the picture of David with his arms around Johnny's neck and a smile a mile wide.

"Wow. He's a cutie. Got a pic of the girl?"

Johnny nodded and swiped the screen to a picture of Katie as she had sat across from him at Culvers.

Sam whistled. "No wonder Pamela wasn't a temptation to you when you've got a hottie like that in your past."

"In the past is right. There is nothing between us now except a desire to parent David well." He put his phone away.

"You feel nothing when you look at her?"

"I *feel* a lot of things. I can't act on them."

"You still love her."

"Never stopped. But that doesn't mean she's an option for me."

"Why?"

"Lots of reasons...but, Sam, I've got cancer."

Sam's cup clattered on the table. "Dude, not again. Man, I'm sorry. Anything I can do?"

"A bone marrow transplant might cure me. I'm going to talk to Niko and my family about it tomorrow afternoon. But the match could come from outside my family too."

"Where do I go to get tested?"

"Sam, I wasn't asking..."

"I'm offering. You're like my brother. We've done life together over the years, and if there's any way I could help you get through this, I would do it."

Johnny wrote down the number to call about getting on the national registry. "Call them."

"I will."

"And if you can't help me...maybe you'll be able

to help someone else."

"Yeah. So, you think your cancer means you can't have a relationship?"

"Wouldn't be fair to start dating a woman while I'm fighting this."

"Shouldn't that be her choice?"

"Maybe."

"Come on, Johnny, you need to live and be there for your son. The best thing for him, though, is a mom and a dad who love each other. We both had that growing up. Parents that drove us crazy and even fought, but we knew they loved each other."

"Yeah."

"Doesn't your son deserve the same?"

"I can't force her to marry me."

"Would you have married her back then?"

"In a heartbeat. I even had a ring custom made for her."

"Do you still have it?"

Johnny nodded. "Yeah."

"It was so special you never gave it to Donna, huh?"

"Nope. She got something from the store that she picked out. Apparently, she tried to sell it and didn't get nearly as much money for it on the flip side."

"Some justice in that, huh?"

"Guess so."

"Wanna catch a shower before I take you to the airport?"

"Yeah, probably be good. I should look my best in case the paparazzi decide to stalk me."

Sam laughed. "Only you, Johnny. That is only something that could happen to you."

The flight home was uneventful. Upon his return,

Johnny played with Apolo—in essence, babysitting so Tia and Niko could have a date night. Once the little man was in bed, Johnny headed to his room and crashed into his own mattress. He lay back listening to the dark and the noises of the house and the wind hitting the siding with sharp pellets of snow. He reached into the bedside table and took out the small jeweler's box he had saved. He flipped open the lid to look at the ring he had designed for Katie.

The three braided bands were made of different metals: Black Hills gold, gold, and white gold. Interspersed at the top were three diamonds. They weren't huge, but they were perfect. The center one was largest and white, and the other two were smaller but pink, Katie's favorite color. It was unique. One of a kind because he had an artist friend make it for him.

A cord of three strands is not easily broken. That was the promise he had woven into the ring. Three diamonds because he believed they couldn't survive without God being the center of their marriage. Unique because Katie deserved something special that no one else would have. He snapped the lid shut and placed it back in the drawer and grabbed a matching box of the ring he had bought for himself. It had a similar design minus the stones. Just three tightly bound strands. He pulled the ring out and slipped it on his finger. It still fit. He had never worn rings, and it was strange seeing it there on his hand. Even when he had married Donna, she didn't care if he wore a ring and refused to spend the money on one if it meant cutting out some of the flash she longed for at the wedding. So he had gone without and had always felt cheated by that. Not that it mattered. A few years later, the marriage was over.

He took the ring off and settled it back in the box.

Then he placed the box in the drawer and shut it. He rolled over and felt the bruises on his hip and shoulder. He embraced the ache as it echoed the bruising within his heart.

~*~

Sunday morning was wild in the classroom. David made a beeline for Johnny and leapt into his arms shouting "Daddy!" As much as the little boy had shadowed him before, he was now possessive and even appeared jealous of attention Johnny gave to other kids as he helped them with an art project. When Katie finally came for him, David refused to go with her. The team leader for the room gave Johnny permission to depart, so he did, with David holding his hand and Katie's. They arrived in the café, which was crowded with adults and kids from the first service and people coming in for the second.

"How about I walk you to your car?" Johnny asked Katie. She nodded.

Johnny grabbed his jacket and hat and walked them out to the parking lot, holding tight to the little boy. When they got to the car, Johnny helped him in and buckled him into his booster seat.

"You coming with us?"

"No. I can't right now. I want to attend the worship service."

David started to cry.

"I'm sorry, David." Johnny stood.

Katie frowned at him over the roof of her car. "Maybe you could come by after your meeting this afternoon? Do you remember where my parents live?"

Johnny bent back down to the little boy. "David,

would it be OK if I stopped by to see you later?"

David sniffled but nodded his head.

Johnny planted a kiss on his son's cheek. "I love you, David."

"Lub you too, Daddy."

Johnny backed up and shut the door. He nodded to Katie and mouthed the word "sorry" before walking back inside the church.

~*~

He sat alone during worship, as Niko and Tia had attended first service together. Leaving after it was over, Johnny was even more aware of how alone he was. He missed the fellowship of other men, digging into God's word. He needed to seek out a group.

He saw Pastor Dan Wink and walked up to him.

"Hey, Johnny. How are you today?"

Johnny shrugged. "Nice job with worship this morning, Dan. Glad to have you back. Was your sabbatical refreshing?"

Dan's eyes lit up. "More like eye-opening." He cleared his throat. "When are we going to get you on a team?"

"I really feel called to be in the children's ministry. I love the kids."

"And you ooze music. Hmm. Anything else I can help you with?"

"When we were on tour, Niko led a group of us daily in the Word and accountability. He was a great shepherd, and I'm just realizing I miss that kind of connection with other men. Wondering if there might be a group I could join?"

"For study or accountability?"

"Both. I'm in the Word and could join a study, but with my travel…I don't know, I think accountability would be good."

"Let me see what I can find for you, and I'll give you a call."

"Thanks."

"And pray about the worship teams."

"Yeah, Niko's asked too…I'll pray about it, OK?"

"That's the best I can ask for. Let God lead you, and I'll have no problem with whatever answer you get."

"Even if it's a negative one?"

"Of course."

"Interesting."

"Why? If God tells you to stay in children's ministry every Sunday, He obviously needs you there, and I'm not going to argue with that. But if He tells you that you can play every once in a while, I'm good with that too."

"I had a problem today with my son. He was clingy and jealous."

"I didn't realize you had a son."

"I found out a few days ago. It appears David Bailey is mine."

"Wow. That's a bit of a shocker."

"Yeah, we had bonded pretty well in the classroom, but now that he knows I'm his dad, he doesn't want to be away from me."

"You'll be able to visit?"

"Yeah, we're setting up times. I'll stop by to see him tonight. He cried when I put him in the car and he realized I wasn't coming with them."

"Welcome to parenthood, huh?"

"Crash course. I just feel bad for Katie. It must

make things harder for her."

"I haven't met Ms. Bailey yet. They've only been attending for a little over two months, I think."

"You keep up with all those newcomer cards?"

"I try. I got behind during my leave of absence."

Johnny nodded. "I should get going. I have a busy day ahead."

"Can I pray for you before you head out?"

"How can anyone turn down an offer like that?"

Pastor Dan put his hand on Johnny's shoulder, and they both bent their heads, right there at the welcome center. "Heavenly Father, I ask that You give Johnny wisdom with being a dad and helping out David's mom. And give him guidance too with children's ministry and music. Lord, You know he loves both, and we really do want him to find joy in serving here at Orchard Hill in the way You call him. Bless him today and remind him of how deeply loved he is."

"Amen," they spoke together.

"Thanks, Dan."

"I'll call you when I find a group."

"Great. Have a good Sunday."

"You too, Johnny."

~*~

Johnny skipped going home, headed to the coffee shop, and sat in a corner with a notebook and a cup of coffee. His mom would shovel food down his throat when he arrived at her house. He doodled a bit and flipped the page of his oft-neglected journal. And wrote.

Lost. Alone. Without you
No one to call my own.
God's grace, ever perfect,
But not I, for I lost my best friend and soul mate
My past haunts me with mistakes made
All my longings buried in the aftermath
Because you weren't there
Abandoned by you but not by God
Thankful but lonely
My heart lingers and longs for things I can never have
A family of my own to see me through the pain
The struggle of life
I wander alone, without you
Could you ever see a way to a past love?
To overlooking my mistakes?
To see the man who adores you?
To give me what you once withheld?
Your heart could heal mine
Restore me to life and give me hope
And reason to go on.

Johnny read his scribbles. He once wrote a horrible poem to Katie. Maybe he should be grateful she never read those letters. He was older and wiser and certainly would never have poured out such drivel now as he did then. He shook his head as he glanced at the page in front of him. Nope. He hadn't grown that much, had he? He had it bad for a girl who never wanted him.

Slamming the book shut, he finished his coffee and rose to go to his parents' home so he could humble himself and ask for their help.

Arriving at two o'clock, he walked in and his mother instantly embraced him.

"Johnny-boy, oh, you need to eat." She dragged him to the kitchen and forced him to sit, and soon a steaming plate of some of his favorite foods was placed in front of him. As he dug in, the table filled up with his brothers and sisters and Niko. Johnny's parents sat near one end, holding hands.

Johnny chewed and looked up as he realized two things. One, he was hungrier than he realized, and two, everyone was staring at him.

"Well?" his father spoke.

"Well, what?" Johnny asked with his mouth full. He swallowed and drank some water.

"You called us here," his sister Leandra said. "Spill."

Johnny took a deep breath and glanced at Niko, who nodded his head.

"My cancer is back."

Everyone started speaking at once, but Johnny let out a shrill whistle. They stopped.

His eyes closed. "This type of cancer is potentially curable with a bone marrow transplant, and the greatest likelihood of a suitable match is from family. So, I'm here to ask if any of you would consider getting tested to see if we would be a match." Johnny fought unexpected tears.

Curtis spoke first. "Where do we go for this?"

Johnny handed him a card with the information, and soon everyone had one.

"I have something else to share. Remember when I dated Katherine Bailey in high school?"

"Yeah, we always thought you'd marry her," Stephen said.

"Me too. Well, she's back in town, and it seems an indiscretion on our part resulted in me becoming a father to a little boy, David, who is six years old. So, Mom, Dad, you're grandparents just like you always wanted to be."

Silence reigned for a moment.

"Oh, Johnny!" His mother rose and went to him, wrapping her arms around him and planting kisses on his cheek and shaved head.

Niko cleared his throat. "Johnny, you had me worried when you called this meeting. I thought you were going to tell me you only had weeks to live."

"Without the transplant, I might have a year, maybe more. Hard to know just how fast the cancer will progress. We caught it early."

"Thanks for the honor of giving us a chance to help. If none of us matches, what then?" his dad asked.

"There's a national registry we can search for a match, but family is my best bet."

"We'll all get tested. Johnny, you can count on us."

"Thanks, guys."

"When will we meet David? What's he like?"

Johnny smiled. "He's lively and adorable."

Sophie spoke up. "You gonna marry Katie now?"

Johnny shook his head. "She's been open to me being a dad and providing support, but I've no indication she would welcome any more from me. She's living back with her parents, and they never liked me."

The family dove into food and conversation, and jokes flew around the table. Johnny grinned at the teasing as they mentioned him being in the news, knowing he'd never do what was reported. They had his back.

He glanced at the clock and realized how much time had passed. "Sorry, Mom, Dad, everyone. I need to go see my son. I promised to stop by."

He got his hugs and let himself out. He hopped in his car and drove to the Bailey mansion—at least, that was how he'd always referred to it as in his mind.

He pulled up behind another vehicle that had just arrived in the slippery driveway. Katie jumped out of the car, screaming as she ran into the house.

Flames licked out the kitchen window and smoke billowed from the front door where Katie had just entered the burning house. He jumped out of his car and called 911. Then he ran inside as well.

He coughed as he walked in, disoriented. "Katie! Where are you?"

She emerged from the smoke, coughing too. "I can't find David downstairs. I think he's upstairs in the first bedroom to the right. Could you get him? My parents are probably somewhere down here."

"I'll go." Johnny sprinted up the stairs as the smoke thickened. The blaring smoke alarm added an eerie soundtrack to the thunder of his steps. He burst into the bedroom. David was there…asleep. "David. It's me. Come quick." Johnny grabbed a blanket and tossed it over the sleepy little boy as he hefted him into his arms and exited into the hallway.

Flames licked their way up the carpeted stairs. *Think, Johnny. There has to be another way out.* He lumbered down the hallway to what had always been Katie's room. He opened her door, entered, and then slammed it behind him. He rushed to the sliding glass door to a balcony.

This side of the house was built into the ground, so the drop from the balcony wasn't as far into the rock-hard snow. He closed the glass door behind him and shivered in the cold.

"Daddy?"

"Hey, buddy. Came to visit you, but this wasn't quite what I had in mind."

"Why are we here?" David rubbed his eyes as the sirens wailed in the distance.

Johnny took a deep breath to calm his racing heart. He didn't want his son to panic, but terror clutched at his own gut. "The house is on fire, and I couldn't take you back downstairs. We're waiting for the firemen to come and help us get down."

"Oh, OK. Are we having an adventure?"

"Like Dora the Explorer?" Johnny coughed.

"No. She's a girl. Like Diego."

"Well, of course. An adventure it is." The snow on the balcony behind him began to melt.

Johnny pulled out his phone and dialed 911 to let them know they were on the balcony.

Soon, two firefighters with a ladder arrived. Johnny glanced behind him. The room inside the sliding glass doors was engulfed in flames.

He turned to his son. "You are going to be brave and let the fireman help you down."

"You come too?"

"I'll be right after you."

"OK."

Johnny lifted David to the top of the rung, and with the fireman's helpful words of encouragement, the little boy slowly worked his way backward down the rungs of the ladder.

Warmth roasted Johnny's back. He perched on the porch rail and was about to step onto the ladder when the sliding door exploded with a shotgun of glass and flames. Heat washed over his back as if he'd been thrust into a fiery furnace. He held on to the rail to keep from being blown off the balcony. Ducking his head, he swung around and struggled to find a perch on the hot rungs of the ladder, feet dangling for a moment as the flames raced toward him. All the while, he prayed his son was well. Once he made contact with the rung, he quickly made his way down the rungs as smoke and flames appeared to chase him.

Once again he swallowed his fear. He needed to be brave for his son.

He finally hit the snow and followed the firefighters to a safe place in the yard. A firefighter carried David, wrapped in a blanket, toward the ambulances. Johnny made his way in that direction. Once the firefighter put David down, father and son sat next to each other.

"Thank you," the sweet little voice next to him said to the fireman.

"Yeah, thanks guys. I really didn't relish diving into that rock-hard snowbank from that height." The men rushed away to help put out the fire while paramedics checked them out.

"Katie? Her parents?"

"Everyone's out and doing fine."

"David! Johnny!" Katie came ran across the snowy yard to them. "You're OK?"

"We're fine, Mommy. Daddy and the firemen saved me."

Katie planted a kiss on her son's head and hauled him into her arms to hold tight. "Mom, you're squeezing me."

"I'm sorry." She sat him down and wrapped the blanket around him. She looked at Johnny as tears welled up in her eyes. She took steps to him and wrapped him in her arms. "Thank you, Johnny. I don't know what I'd..." She leaned her head back and looked in his eyes. Then her gaze flickered down.

Before Johnny could react, her lips pressed against his, and he willingly returned the kiss. His skin warmed, and he wrapped his arms around her, pulling her close between his legs as he sat on the back of the vehicle. Heaven smelled like...smoke.

She pulled back with a dazed expression on her face.

Johnny swallowed, fearful she would apologize or reject him once again.

"Ma'am. We need to give him oxygen. He inhaled a lot of smoke." A mask went over his face, but his eyes didn't leave hers. Wide eyed, mouth agape, she backed away.

"Your parents?"

She nodded. "Yeah, seems like while I went to the grocery store, my mom tried to microwave something with metal. At least, that's the best guess we have right now about how the fire started. She went to the living room to watch *Jeopardy* and fell asleep. Dad was napping too."

"Where will you all go now?"

Katie shook her head. "My parents will go to the hospital for observation and from there to an assisted living facility. I've been putting it off for as long as possible, but I never would have guessed... I wouldn't have left him with them..."

He placed a hand on her arm. "Katie. No one is blaming you, and David is fine. I could call my parents and see if you could stay with them while you figure things out. They can't wait to meet David."

"I'll need to see my parents cared for first."

"David can come with me. Looks like we'll have to

stop at the store and get some clothes, though." The mask drove him crazy. He thought he sounded like Darth Vader talking through that thing.

Katie nodded. "David, stay with your father for now." She faced Johnny. "Don't leave without seeing me about a booster seat for him." She turned toward the house. "I doubt either one of us could get our cars out of the driveway right now anyway."

The house resembled a smoldering skeleton. Flames still fought against the water and falling snow. Icicles already formed in some areas due to the frigid cold.

The mansion was a total loss.

Johnny shook his head. All that stuff they thought was important had gone up in smoke. Katie and David were now homeless. He wished he still had his own house to let them stay in. With all he was coming up with to pay for his past neglect, his own profit from the sale of his house was already going to Katie. He wouldn't be surprised if the Baileys had insurance that would pay out too.

"Your blood pressure is dropping." The paramedic said. "Are you feeling dizzy?"

Johnny's world tipped and went black.

~*~

He woke lying down on a stretcher inside the ambulance, covered with a warming blanket. David held his hand. "Daddy?"

"Yeah, David. What happened?"

"You blacked out. Possibly shock," the paramedic said.

"I'm fine." He started to rise, and black spots

floated around.

"No. You need to rest for a little bit."

"OK." Johnny figured sleep sounded good right now.

8

We do not exist for ourselves.
Thomas Merton

Katie trembled. She had kissed Johnny. He had returned it. The only explanation was the shock of the fire. And gratitude for saving their son. And she was happy he had survived, because a world without him in it was too terrible to think about.

Her mother argued with the paramedics, and her father was on oxygen and lying down. They were not ruling out the possibility of another stroke, as he had been unable to communicate or walk on his own. Not that his gait had been very steady anyway. She dialed her brother's phone.

"Ken here."

"Hey, it's Katie."

"I'm kind of busy. This had better be important."

"Well, the house burnt down, Dad might have had another stroke, and Mom's giving the paramedics what-for. David is safe."

"What? There was a fire? How bad?"

"Total loss?"

"Whoa. You're OK?"

"I smell like smoke and my heart is racing, but other than that, I'm fine."

"You and David can come sleep here tonight if

you wish."

"It's an hour away, and we have no clothes. We'll find someplace to stay after I take us shopping and get Mom and Dad squared away at the hospital."

"Do you need anything?"

"I'm good for now, but I think you're going to have to act as Power of Attorney and deal with this."

"You can make the medical decisions."

"You are primary Power of Attorney. Not me. The ball is in your court."

Ken growled. "Fine. They're going to Community Memorial?"

"Yeah."

"I'll call ahead and give my permissions."

"Good, because I really need to take care of my son and the man who rescued him."

"Who?"

"David's father. Remember Johnny Marshall?"

"Vaguely."

"He came by for a visit and ran in to rescue David while I searched for our parents. He also called the fire department."

"OK. Thank him and move on. You owe him nothing."

"Ken?"

"Yeah?"

"Get off your high-horse and start acting human. Johnny's as good as they come."

"Well don't go off and marry the bum. You remember what Mom and Dad thought about him."

"Yeah, well Mom and Dad weren't God and didn't know everything. I'm tired of living according to their script. I'm cutting the cord. They are your responsibility, and I'm done doing your dirty work."

"I'm not supporting you financially."

"Good. I didn't ask you to, and I never asked them, either."

"You certainly didn't refuse it."

"You have no idea what I have or haven't done."

"I'll be checking over the finances, and I'll figure it out."

"Does it really matter, Ken?"

His sigh came through the phone. "No. Sorry, sis. You've had a rough night, and I'm acting like a spoiled brat who doesn't want to do his homework. You've saved a ton of money by staying there and helping them. I'm glad no one was hurt."

"Let me know how things go with Mom and Dad."

"I will. And, Katie?"

"Yeah?"

"Let me know where you're staying."

"I will…when I figure it out."

"All you had was in that house too, right?"

"Yup. We had stored my furniture and all my belongings in the basement. All gone."

"What about the car?"

"They managed to spare the garage. That's the only part still standing. The breezeway and firewall helped, I'm sure."

"Good. I'll come and pick it up later."

"Why do you get it?"

"I don't. I'll need to sell it to help pay for their care."

"Sorry for being so suspicious."

"Nope. You had every right to question me. I'll call you tomorrow."

"OK. Bye, Ken."

"Bye, sis."

She hung up and surveyed the ashes of her family's history. *The letters.* She sank to her knees. What did it mean that the things she grieved the most were the seven-year-old letters from Johnny? Some she had never had a chance to read. Poof. Gone. Up in smoke like everything else.

"Miss? Are you OK?"

"Hmm?" She gazed up at the fireman standing by her side helping her to her feet. "I'm fine. It's just hitting me…some of what we lost in the fire."

The man nodded. The shield on his helmet was up and his face wreathed in black from the fire. "The most important things were saved. Human lives. The rest you can replace."

She shook her head. "Some things can never be replaced or restored."

He followed her gaze to the remains of the house. Firefighters walked through the ruins shining their flashlights. "I'm sorry for your loss."

"Thank you. And thank you for all you did to try to save the house. None of your men were hurt?"

"No, thank goodness for that. The person most at risk was the man in the ambulance. He was smart to hold out on that balcony, but even that was a narrow escape. He took great care of that little boy, though. Never saw a kid so calm coming down a ladder with such terror going on around him. May need to ask him how he did that. He's your hero, miss."

"He most definitely is."

"Only one engine will stay behind. You'll be able to leave with your cars in a few minutes."

"Good night. I hope the rest of your evening is uneventful."

"Me too." He tipped his fireman's hat to her and strode away, directing the men as they wound hoses and cleaned up the area.

The ambulance carrying her parents had left. She wandered to where Johnny and David were. She was surprised to see Johnny reclining and covered with a blanket, his eyes closed.

"What's going on?" she asked the paramedic outside.

"He passed out. Shock. Happens to the best of 'em. He'll be fine in a few minutes, and then you'll be able to drive him home.

"He can't drive himself?"

"Wouldn't advise it. He's refusing to go to the hospital to be checked out further."

"Oh. OK."

"Mommy!" David waved to her with a broad smile. "Daddy and I had an adventure today, but we didn't get to rappel from the balcony like Diego would."

"Hmm, I'm guessing that's OK. Kind of cold to rappel in socks, don't you think?"

"Yeah, I suppose."

"Shall we take Daddy home?"

"Home?"

"We can drive him to where he lives, and then we'll find a place for us."

"Daddy said we could stay at my new Grandma and Grandpa's house."

"That might work for tonight. I think we need to buy some new clothes, though, don't you?"

"Yeah. I don't even have a coat or boots or pajamas."

"I know, sweetheart. We'll get you taken care of."

Exhaustion sapped her strength as her adrenaline crashed. She slumped to the edge of the ambulance, soaking in the warmth from inside.

~*~

"Come on, Johnny, we're home." She had already retrieved David from the back seat and was now unbuckling the man in the front. His eyes blinked.

"Home? I sold my house. Too empty."

"Come on. Niko and Tia are waiting for you."

Surprisingly, he managed to pull himself out of the car. He shivered from head to toe and moved forward to the front door. He inserted the key, but the door swung open and he almost fell in.

"Johnny?" Niko asked as he grabbed his friend and glanced over to her. "Hi. Katie, I assume? We've only met once. And this must be David." He took a sniff. "Where have you been?"

"Remember how we used to play firefighters? Well, it paid off today."

"Come in. Why does this little boy have no coat and shoes?"

Johnny shook his head. "Fire. No time. I grabbed him and ran."

Niko led them to the kitchen and shoved Johnny down into chair.

"From the beginning, please."

Tia walked in with a little boy on her hip. "What's going on? Oh. Hi, Katie. This must be David."

"Hi. I wish we were here under more pleasant circumstances. Johnny came by to visit David tonight and drove up just as I arrived home from the grocery store. David was napping in his bedroom upstairs, and the house was on fire. Johnny rescued David while I located my parents to get them out of the house. Johnny's had a bit of smoke inhalation, and his blood pressure's low, making him dizzy. Is that normal?"

"No. It's not." Niko said, concern written in the wrinkles on his forehead. "I think you need a shower and fresh clothes. You stink." Niko dragged Johnny up and hauled him to the bathroom.

"Can I bring my groceries in from the car? I have no use for them now." Katie asked.

"That'd be fine. David, do you need a bath? We can take care of that in the master bathroom. Katie, you can use the shower after Johnny is done."

"If you don't mind, I'm going to make a quick run to the store. We lost everything. David and I both need some clothing. Will you watch him while I do that? He doesn't even have a coat or shoes right now."

Tia smiled. "Niko can help with the groceries before you leave, and we'll get David cleaned up. He can wear one of his father's T-shirts until you get back. It'll be fun. Is that OK with you, David?"

"I'll stay with Daddy?" The little boy's dark eyes implored.

"Yes, sweetheart, you'll remain with Daddy until I get back. Is that OK with you?"

David smiled and nodded. "He saved me."

Tears crept into her eyes as she hugged her son. "Yes, he did. And I am grateful for that." She glanced at Tia. "Thank you. I'll be back soon."

"The front door will be unlocked. Just come in."

Niko followed her out to get the groceries.

~*~

Johnny almost fell over in the bathtub.

"Strip and throw your clothes out here, and I'll be back." Niko ordered.

"I'm old enough to take a shower by myself." Johnny pouted.

"Right now, I'm not sure you can even stand up without help. Please don't hurt yourself before I return."

Johnny did as he was told and relaxed as the hot water hit him, washing away the smoke that clung to him. He suspected it was in his lungs too. How did one wash that away?

Being caught in a fire was his biggest fear as a kid. He had almost panicked when he had David in his arms and the flames were licking up the carpeted stairwell. He was amazed David stayed so calm, but the kid was half-asleep and not aware of the danger they were in. Now it all crashed back in on him.

The flames burning up the door to Katie's room and engulfing everything within. The heat from the glass. The force of hot air like a blowtorch hitting him as he climbed over the balcony while glass sprayed everywhere, almost propelling him into the snow bank below.

He could feel the heat on his back as if it were happening all over again. He suspected he'd have nightmares now for a while. He'd had them every time they'd had fire safety week in grade school.

God had been with them today. There was no way he could have saved his son on his own. Fear would have paralyzed him. But they survived. They had made it out, and the little guy had been such a trooper about the whole thing.

He lathered his face, head, and hands with soap

twice to try to get the smell out but realized it was probably in his sinuses, and the smell of waterfall or ocean breeze or whatever "flavor" Tia had purchased wasn't quite covering it. He heard the door open and close. Niko had returned.

"You still alive in there?"

"Yeah."

"Good. I brought you some clothes." Niko set down the clothes and left.

Johnny finished rinsing, turned off the water, and grabbed a towel. He dressed and went to the living room, where Niko waited, and sat down.

"Tia's giving David a bath in our suite," Niko said.

"The kid was amazing."

"Care to tell me the story?"

"Not right now."

"You were always terrified of fire." Niko leaned forward, elbows on knees.

"Still am...probably even more so now."

"I'm glad you saved him and are OK."

"Me too."

David appeared in one of Johnny's T-shirts, which hung to his ankles.

"Daddy." He ran and almost tripped.

Johnny picked him up and settled him on his lap. "What you got on under there?"

The little boy giggled. "Mommy went to buy me underwear."

"Good."

"Are you hungry?" Tia asked. "I could make a quick pizza for you since you missed dinner. Niko said you guys had a veritable feast at your parents' home."

"Pizza and root beer!" David exclaimed with a fist pump.

"That's right. I wanted to introduce you to a local brand. Do we have any, Tia?"

She grinned. "But of course, and chillin' in the fridge as we speak. Like father like son, huh?"

David giggled, and Johnny hugged him close. "Yeah."

They ate the pizza, and Johnny and Niko held a burping contest much to the entertainment of David and little Apolo, who wasn't too sure about his Uncle Johnny bestowing affection on another boy.

Katie had not returned.

Niko asked the question on Johnny's mind. "Will David and Katie spend the night here?"

"I thought maybe I'd take them to my parents' home. But if it's OK, they could take my room, and I can crash on the sofa in the basement."

"That bothers your back."

"Yeah, but it's more comfortable than the floor, and it's freezing out there. I'd hate for them to have to go out again tonight."

"I'm OK with that arrangement," Tia said as she glanced at Niko, who nodded his head. "It's the least we can do for tonight. It's not a good solution for them beyond that."

"I know. Wishing I still had my house... I could have moved them there."

"It's not your problem, Johnny. It's Katie's. Why are you acting like the burden falls on you?" Niko asked.

Johnny shook his head. "Because David's my son."

"And Katie's been a great mom to him so far," Tia added.

The little boy yawned. "I'm tired."

"Didn't you just have a nap..." Johnny looked at

the clock. "...four hours ago?" Johnny yawned too.

"Why don't you take him to your bedroom and rest? I'll have Katie come and wake you so you can go to the basement."

"You sure?"

"Yeah, I'll bring a pillow down there and some blankets for you." Tia gave him a wink and picked up Apolo. "Time to get this boy ready for bed too."

"But, Daddy," David whispered a little loudly, "I don't have any underwear."

"You'll be fine. Your mom will bring you some you can put on later."

"OK."

Johnny took David to his room, leaving the door open a crack. He tucked David into the queen-size bed and lay on top of the blankets snuggling his son. He threw a light fleece blanket over himself to keep warm although his sweatpants and Packer sweatshirt were comfortable. He figured he'd need them downstairs in the cooler basement area.

"Will you pray for me tonight, Daddy?"

"I'd love to." He held his little boy close. "Dear Jesus, thank You for sparing David's life and that of his grandparents. Thank You for getting us out safely. Keep Mommy safe as she shops and bring her home soon so she can rest too. Help us find a good place for them to live. We love You and are grateful for Your many blessings."

"Amen." Soon, David's breathing was soft and even.

When he was sure David was asleep, Johnny sneaked out to wait for Katie. Niko sat in the living room by the fireplace.

"David's asleep?" Niko asked.

"Yeah. He's a sweet kid."

"Definitely." He paused. "I'm glad you came out here. I wanted to show you something." Niko held up Johnny's leather jacket.

"My jacket. So?"

Niko turned it around. The leather was burnt away, exposing the lining, and most of it was charred.

Johnny frowned. Niko held up Johnny's jeans, and they too were singed a toasted brown as if he had been roasting a marshmallow.

Johnny gulped.

"I think God must have intervened for you or David to have no burns at all."

"David was covered by a blanket. I never did see how it fared."

"This was your only jacket, right?"

"Yeah."

"I guess you'll be doing some shopping tomorrow too, then. You can borrow one of mine. I know it'll be big on you, but it'll keep you warm."

"Thanks."

"I looked it up on the news, and they said it was a three-alarm fire."

"I wasn't counting trucks."

"I'm sure you weren't. Johnny, I'm really proud of you. You were great with your family, and it took courage to ask for help. Tia and I will take the test too. To follow it up with a rescue of this magnitude knowing your fear of fires...well, it just reminds me that God's not through with you yet by a long shot."

"Maybe. You wanna know something silly? I got so introspective that I even wrote a poem today."

Tia overheard as she walked in. "You did? Can we see it?"

Johnny shook his head. "I only once ever wrote a poem. I sent it to Katie. She never got it. Probably for the better, though. Besides, it's in my car, which is parked near a burnt-down house."

"Aww, even awful poetry can speak to a girl's heart. I don't doubt your artist's soul produced something great," Tia said.

"I'll think about it."

The front door opened, and a cold draft accompanied Katie and several bags from the store. Both men jumped up to help her bring them in. "Is that all?" Niko asked.

"Yeah, I prefer the 'all in one trip' method of shopping." Katie laughed and set the bags down. Johnny helped her get her coat off.

"Where's David?"

"Down for the count."

"I really don't want to have to wake him to go somewhere else."

"You don't have to, Katie. You'll stay here for tonight."

9

Fear brings more pain than does the pain it fears.
Anonymous

Katie wasn't sure how to take Johnny's offer.

Niko stepped forward to hang up Katie's coat. "Johnny's agreed to sleep in the basement on the sofa. You'll stay with David in Johnny's room. There's a queen-size bed in there, plenty big for you and your son."

Johnny rifled through the bags and pulled out some little boy briefs. "He was worried about going to bed without this. Do you mind if I put a pair on him?"

"What's he wearing?"

"One of my T-shirts." He flipped his phone out and showed her a photo he had taken. She couldn't help but smile.

"Yeah, OK. This is awkward."

"You can figure out tomorrow after you get rest tonight," Johnny offered. "Why don't you get ready? There're towels laid out in the bathroom if you want a shower. We have some left-over pizza if you're hungry."

"Yeah, just a slice would be nice."

Niko left to heat up food. Tia came out from the baby's room.

"Katie, wow. Did you find many sales? I love it when I can snag great deals."

Katie grinned. "I didn't do too shabby but couldn't

find anything acceptable for work tomorrow. I'll call in and take the day off to get this all figured out." She knelt down and riffled through a bag. She pulled out some clothes for sleeping and set them aside. "What a day."

Tia embraced her in a bear hug. "It's going to be OK. I'm just so happy everyone came out safe."

Niko placed a plate on the table and motioned them into the dining room. "Yeah, take a look at Johnny's jacket to see how close he came."

"Niko…" Johnny warned.

Tia went to the living room where the jacket lay and picked it up. She brought it back it to the table and flipped it around to the back. Her eyes grew wide. "Johnny. That was too close a call."

"You should see his toasted jeans," Niko commented as he brought a glass of root beer for Katie and grabbed a chair. Johnny and Tia sat as well.

Katie's stomach growled. She closed her eyes to silently thank God and inhaled the cheese, sausage, and spices on the slice. She took a bite and sighed. Before she knew it, the food was gone.

"More?" Tia offered.

"No, thanks. I usually try not to eat this close to bedtime." She sipped the soda. "I'm sorry that my rain check from the other week got cashed this way."

Tia grinned. "Not a problem."

"Wait. This was the woman you had invited to lunch that Sunday?" Johnny asked.

Tia nodded. "I didn't realize you knew each other. Or that you would save her little boy's life that day."

"You rescued David twice now." Katie choked up. She looked across the table to Johnny. "Thank you."

"Maybe it makes it a third time. That lump sum

check should clear the bank tomorrow and give you what you need to get a new apartment at least, if not put a down payment on a little house."

"I hadn't even opened the envelope. It's still in my car."

"You didn't cash the check?"

She shook her head. "It could be worse, though. I could have left it in my room."

"I'd have gladly written you another one." He had dark shadows under his eyes, and he blinked as if trying to keep from falling asleep.

"Johnny, you're tired. Why don't you go to your room and sleep next to David? I can take the sofa."

"Nope. If David wakes during the night in a strange place, he's going to want his mom." Johnny stood and held up the underwear. "I missed diaper duty with him, so I'll take care of this and then I'm heading to the basement. 'Night everyone."

"'Night, Johnny," they chorused.

Katie watched him limp out of the room. "He's still in pain from his fall in the parking lot."

"Yeah, the bruising was pretty bad. Probably worse because of the cancer. Just gonna take a long time to heal."

"Did he talk to his family today?"

"You know about that?"

"Yeah, but couldn't say anything. I work for his doctor."

Niko studied her, and a slow smile spread over his face. "God sure works in interesting ways at times."

"More than you realize," Katie murmured. She rose and took her empty plate and glass to the kitchen.

"Leave them by the sink. I'll deal with it in the morning," Tia said.

"Thanks. Do you have an extra universal charger I could use for my phone?"

"Sure." Niko rose to leave.

"Let me show you where your room is. Johnny's already gone downstairs."

Katie grabbed her clothes and took a peek at her sleeping son. The room was wreathed in shadows but was neat and tidy, which surprised her. Niko came to give her a charger and suggested she plug it in on the vanity in the bathroom if she didn't need the alarm.

"That'll be fine. I'll get ready, then. Good night."

Kate closed the bathroom door, showered off the smell of fire, and got dressed. She made her way to the bedroom and crawled under the covers next to her little boy. The pillow smelled like Johnny in the best possible way and brought back strong memories from years ago, snuggling with him in the car, hiking in the woods…kissing. *Stop! Sleep. I need to sleep. Lord, help me.*

~*~

She was awakened with a scream from somewhere in the house. David slept peacefully. She grabbed her new robe, wrapped it around her, and slipped out into the hallway. Another cry followed, and she saw a door open off the kitchen with a light on. She crept through the dark and followed the frantic cries for help. She took the stairs at top speed.

She arrived at the bottom landing, which opened into a large room where a drum set, guitars, and a keyboard were set up with some amplifiers. Monitors and a soundboard were also in evidence. A practice studio. Off to one side was a small seating area with a few chairs and a sofa, a small sink, and full fridge. She made her way to the screaming and writhing man on the sofa. *Johnny.*

Niko was there talking softly. Johnny was tearing off his sweatshirt.

"I'm burning. Help me. I'm burning!" He screamed.

Niko grabbed for him. "I've got you, Johnny. It's Niko. You got out of the fire. You're fine. It's going to be fine."

Johnny slumped in his friend's arms, sobbing. "I'm burnt. It hurts, Niko."

Katie came to sit on the sofa on the opposite side of Johnny. His back was red. She leaned over to a lamp and turned it on. She checked again. Red.

"Niko?"

"Yeah?" His desperate eyes peered over his sobbing friend.

"He really was burned. His back. It must hurt terribly." She started to pull the sweatshirt over Johnny's head.

Niko stretched his neck around to see Johnny's back and let out a low whistle. "Johnny, listen, I think we need to take you to the hospital."

"Help me. Help me..." Johnny pleaded.

"I will, buddy. You know I will." He glanced over to Katie. "Can you find a T-shirt—or something light for him to wear?"

"Maybe a blanket wrapped loosely would be easier for him to bear?"

"There is a lightweight one on his bed. A Wisconsin Badgers one. Can you grab that for me?"

"Sure."

Katie rushed up the stairs and heard Niko coaxing Johnny up after him. She grabbed the blanket and met them in the breezeway to the garage. "Are you sure you don't want me to take him? I'm a nurse..."

"Thanks, Katie...but I think it's safer for me to do this."

Safer?

She moved to wrap the fleece around Johnny, and his wild eyes forced her to let go. There was something untamed in that gaze and yes...dangerous.

As they left, she sat in the living room, hugged her knees to her chest, and prayed.

~*~

Johnny couldn't stop the tears or the images that threatened him. Had he crossed the line into madness? Niko spoke soothing words to him, but Johnny couldn't even make out what he said.

"Katie..." he whispered.

"Yeah, she brought you the blanket."

"She saw me like this?"

"Sorry, I was too busy rushing to help you and didn't think to lock the basement door."

"No. No locking that door."

"There's an easement window down there—two actually. In a real fire, you could have escaped."

Johnny shivered from the cold and the pain. "It wasn't all a dream?"

"Nope. You really do have a burn. Katie suggested it might be a chemical burn from the fabric baking at so high a temperature. Your skin always seems to delay in reacting even to a sunburn, so I'm not surprised you didn't notice earlier."

"It stung in the shower."

"That should have been our first clue. Why didn't

you say anything?"

"Didn't think it was anything much."

"Enough to wake you up in terror, but I suppose the fire itself accomplished that."

"I expected nightmares."

"Nightmares? More like night terrors."

Once they were at the emergency room, Johnny reclined face-down on a stretcher in a room while a nurse took his vitals and waited for the doctor. He could see his cousin waiting in the corner. "Thanks for being here with me, Niko."

"Katie wanted to come."

Johnny groaned.

"Was that because you're in pain or the thought of Katie being here?"

"The thought that she even saw me like this."

"She's the one who discovered the burns. I probably wouldn't have noticed. I would've thought it was all part of your nasty dream."

"So tired…"

"Rest while you can."

~*~

The sting of a needle woke him, along with the words "second degree burn" and "admitting for observation."

"What?" he asked groggily.

Niko crouched down so Johnny could see him. "They've hooked you up to an IV for fluids, and they'll give you an antibiotic as well as something for the pain. You're dehydrated, and the size of the burn was probably what put you into shock at the scene. The paramedics missed that. I'll stay with you till you get settled, and then I'm heading home to catch some sleep. I'll return in the morning. Just try to rest, Johnny. It's what your body needs."

"Antibiotics…good. Cancer lowers my immune system functioning or something like that."

"Right. They know about the cancer. I told them. Your last tetanus shot was two years ago, so you're good there and don't need that."

"I'll be fine, Niko. Go home and sleep. Make sure Katie and David find a place. I think I'll want my bed back…"

Niko chuckled. "We'll take care of them. Don't worry about that. I'll pick you up a new jacket later too. Your other one was getting kind of worn."

"It was broken in…comfortable." Johnny managed a grin. "Thanks, coz."

"Anytime. See ya later."

Johnny closed his eyes as the stretcher started to move with the transfer to another floor. He was already dizzy enough from the pain and wasn't in the mood for a carnival ride. He only hoped they'd give him something to help him sleep so he wouldn't dream. His nightmares were far too vivid.

~*~

Katie got the news from Niko and finally crawled into bed. She couldn't sleep but didn't feel comfortable wandering around the house. She hugged his pillow tight and inhaled the scent of Johnny, letting her mind trail back to days gone by, when they were both young and filled with dreams.

Listening to Johnny practicing with Niko's band. Times spent hiking in the woods and stealing kisses as they rested at the scenic overlooks at the Kettle Moraine. The changing colors of Horicon Marsh in the fall, listening to the geese and holding hands. Summerfest. ComedySportz. He was always so creative with his dates and providing an experience for her. He had told her he never wanted her to be bored with him.

How could she be? He was creative and had a perceptive heart. If anyone experienced things deeply, it was Johnny. He had been so passionate about God and serving Him. Maybe a bit grandiose in how that would happen, but he succeeded in surpassing his dreams. She couldn't help but be proud of him, while at the same time ashamed that her younger self had been too practical.

It wasn't just her, though. It was her mom and dad. Her parents who now were homeless and had almost cost her the life of her son with their negligence. How do you blame a person with Alzheimer's, though? And her father? In reality, it had been her own fault leaving them alone. But she had been leaving them alone during the day to go to work while David was in school. Nothing had ever happened before.

Well, she had no choices now. No matter how her mother argued when in her right mind, there was no way they could live alone.

The letters. Johnny's letters had also burned. His words of devotion in the few she had read were seared in her heart. She grieved their loss as much as she was angry that her parents had kept them from her. Stealing mail was a federal offense, wasn't it? Did it matter? That was over seven years ago. She had lost so much more than they had in the fire. Her parents had meant well, but what would life have been like if she had made a different choice?

She still might have finished nursing school. Johnny would have helped, and David would have had a father. They wouldn't have been rich, but she would've been able to watch him fulfill his dreams and rejoice with him. Maybe they'd have had more kids. He wasn't able to now, but it was obvious even back then how much he adored little ones.

She would have lost the esteem of her parents, but living life on their terms hadn't made her happier.

Katie was free now. The cords binding her to her home and parents burned away through fire and illness. She was an adult and needed to start acting like one.

She must have drifted off at some point, and David awakened her. He had found the bag of clothes she had dropped by the edge of the bed and was excited about getting new stuff. She'd bought clothes a little big for him, hoping the clothes might last longer. She no longer had the luxury of her mom taking him shopping and showering him with a name-brand wardrobe.

She helped David dress and ran to the bathroom to get prepared for the day. How long had it been since she had bought anything for herself? It felt good to look nice in new clothes. Almost like the first day of school as a kid. She brushed her teeth, supervised David brushing his, and then went back to Johnny's bedroom to pack up their stuff. She made the bed, sat on it, and looked around the room.

She had never thought of Johnny as a neatnik. She'd suspected a musician lived like a slob. How wrong she was. On the dresser was a photo of the two of them from their last summer. Smiling. Johnny had hair in those days, and hers had been long. In the photo, she smiled as she gazed adoringly at him. They really had been in love. An object rested on the surface of the dresser in front of the picture. It was the necklace she gave him for his eighteenth birthday. The silver Celtic Trinity knot was something she had picked up for him at Irish Fest. Even though Johnny's heritage was Greek, there was some Irish in her, and it had fascinated her. He'd worn it all the time. She wondered how long it had been before he had taken it off and why he kept it out. The dresser and the frame were dusted.

Perhaps she still held a little part of his heart. Maybe all those years and her foolish choices hadn't severed hope of something between them. After all, they shared a son.

But cancer could shut that door.

It didn't have to. She might need to be persistent, though. She had much to atone for when it came to Johnny.

David followed her to the kitchen, where Tia already sat feeding Apolo.

"There's cereal on top of the refrigerator, milk, bread for toast, and a cinnamon-sugar combo mixed up because it's Johnny's favorite. There's some fresh fruit too. Help yourself. The coffee will be done in a few minutes."

"Cimmamon toast, Mommy. Please?"

"Cinnamon, honey."

"Cimmamon. That's what I said."

Katie proceeded to make the toast for her son and sat at the table with the freshly brewed coffee.

"You can eat too, Katie," Tia offered.

"I'm not really hungry right now, but thank you.

This coffee will get me through for a while." She glanced at David. "I'd forgotten that cinnamon toast was Johnny's favorite. Funny that it's David's, too."

"Our kids sometimes take after us in surprising ways." Tia wiped cereal off the baby's chubby cheeks. "How can we help you today, Katie?"

Niko walked in with a wave and headed straight for the coffee. Fatigue marred his handsome features, but she had her own dark circles as evidence of her lack of sleep.

"I'm not sure yet. I'll take David to school and visit Johnny. I'll have to call my brother about the insurance to see if there's help to get us a place to stay, but since my parents were the primary residents, I don't hold out much hope."

"Cash Johnny's check. That'll help." Niko said as he sat down at the table and ruffled the curls on Apolo's head, earning him a smile.

"Doesn't he need that money?" Katie asked.

"Don't worry about Johnny. He wanted to provide for you both."

"But…"

Tia spoke up. "Johnny is determined to do what is right. If you had named him at birth, the State would have come after him for support and garnished wages or frozen accounts or even put a lien on his house when he had one. They wouldn't have cared a bit about whether he had enough to live on. Take it."

"I didn't come back to town to cash in on our son. I never expected to run into Johnny."

"We know that, and Johnny understands. He just wants to do what's right, so let him." Niko stated.

"Fine, I'll run by the bank this morning too. If I can't find an apartment today, I'll stay in a hotel tonight."

"No need for that. We have an air mattress we can blow up, and you and David can sleep in the living room. Johnny's going to need his own bed tonight." Niko closed his eyes and sighed.

"Niko?" Tia reached across to put a hand on his arm. "He's going to be fine. Don't think about the worst-case scenario. He's Johnny, and he's going to come through this."

Niko nodded. "I'll bring Johnny home when we get the call for discharge. I'm heading out to get him a new jacket. Can you believe he told me he liked his old worn-out one because it was broken in?"

"You realize he's not going anywhere, jacket or no, until he gets that back healed up enough to wear clothes." Tia reminded him.

"Right. He's going to be strutting around here shirtless. Hmm...do I need to do that too so I make sure your eyes don't wander to his chest?"

Tia giggled. "If you want, but let's wait for that until after Katie and David find a place to live. I really don't want to share your beautiful chest with Katie, even if she is practically family." Tia winked at Katie.

Niko blushed.

Katie's stomach yawned, not with hunger but with a longing for that kind of love. A love she used to have...and had cast aside. *Lord, is it even possible anymore?*

10

The things that we love tell us what we are.
Thomas Aquinas

David went happily into school with the assurance he could visit his father later. Katie went to the bank, and since it was the same bank the check had been drawn on, the funds were instantly available. She found an apartment-for-rent sign a few blocks from the Acton household, where Johnny lived. It was on her way to the hospital, so she drove there. She found a small two-bedroom apartment that was freshly painted and available immediately. She wrote out the checks for the first month's rent and security deposit. Now she had to furnish an entire home, since all her belongings, stored in her parents' basement, burned in the fire or suffered water damage. She made the call to switch the utilities to her name. She'd go shopping after she visited Johnny.

~*~

Johnny's back was bright red and appeared wet. She knew burn wounds wept, and he'd probably have some kind of bandage on it before he went home, but it was such a large expanse of skin. His muscular shoulders and arms caught her attention. Surely, he hadn't looked like that years ago. Even his back under the red showed evidence of a man who worked out.

"Who's there? Please come around where I can see you? My neck grew sore facing the other way, and it hurts to move." Johnny's voice was scratchy, probably from the smoke.

"It's me." Katie walked around and pulled a chair up close to the bed so Johnny could see her.

"Hey. David here too?" Johnny glanced to the side.

"No. He's in school. He slept well and was excited about his new clothes."

"Batman underwear would do it for me too." Johnny grinned.

"Are you on pain meds?"

"Yeah."

"So you're feeling good?"

"No way. It hurts like the dickens, but I just don't care."

Katie smiled. "I'm so sorry. It seems like since we've come to town, David and I have flipped your world upside down. An extra stress you don't need with what you're already dealing with."

"You mean cancer? You can say it. I hate the word, but it's a reality I need to make peace with somehow. As for you guys flipping my world? My ex-wife nearly destroyed me by asking for a divorce when I shared my first cancer diagnosis. It was a double punch. David is a delight, and I've always loved you, Katie. I wouldn't ever regret having an opportunity to see you."

"But the parking lot incident and the fire…"

"Both evidence that I was exactly where God wanted me to be at the time."

"You had a bad dream last night."

Johnny frowned. "Probably the one thing I never shared with you when we dated. I'm terrified of fires. I'm fine with a fireplace, but my biggest fear is being trapped in a fire and being burned alive. Every year in grade school, they did fire safety week. I couldn't sleep for a week without vivid nightmares. Yesterday triggered those."

"Niko was aware?"

"Yeah, it's why I chose the basement instead of the living room. That sofa upstairs is far more comfortable, trust me. I just hoped I'd make it through the night without waking up the house."

"It's a good thing you woke me up. If I hadn't discovered that burn you could have gotten really sick."

"Lucky me." He winked at her.

"I cashed your check."

"I'm glad."

"I also found a two-bedroom apartment and can move in today."

"Where?"

She shared the address.

"Niko used to have a one bedroom apartment in that complex. It's not the nicest place, but it was safe enough. The rent was reasonable. But even if you buy beds today, you'll not get same-day delivery."

"I can purchase an air mattress for David and me. For a few nights, that will work fine."

"I hate that you have to go through this. I wish I could do something to help. As it is, I won't be lifting boxes or anything for almost two weeks."

"Johnny, you've given me more than you realize. You saved our son. I could be planning a funeral today if it hadn't been for you. Instead, I watched our son rejoice over Batman underwear and a new Packer sweatshirt."

"Life doesn't get much better at that age."

"Oh, but it does. He ate his favorite breakfast of cimmamon toast."

Johnny's eyes grew wide as he chuckled. "Really?"

"Really."

"Wow. So, Tia let him use my special gourmet stash of cinnamon and sugar?"

"Yes, and he was in heaven."

"Good. Katie, don't ever apologize for coming back into my life. I'm happy you did. The past is the past, and we can't live in the land of regrets. They only become roadblocks to enjoying the present and moving on into our future."

"Our future?"

"We are both parenting David, so yes. From now on, my decisions and planning will always include you both."

"I found your letters."

"Did you read them?"

"A few, but not all and not in order."

"Did you find my poem?"

She nodded and grinned.

"*Argh*. It was terrible."

"They burned in the fire."

"Small mercies from God." He winked.

"I wanted to read them. They were beautiful. Perhaps, if I had received those letters, the past seven years would have looked much different."

"Let it go. I can write you more if you want and include horrible poetry if that'll make you feel better."

"Would the content be the same?"

Johnny looked at her, and his eyes filled with tears. A nurse bustled in. "Time for more pain medication, Mr. Marshall. How's your pain level right now?"

He held up two hands with some digits extended.

"Six. OK, this will only take a few minutes and you'll be feeling better."

"Thanks, Greta."

"How did you remember me when you can't even see me right now?"

Johnny winked at Katie. "I always try to memorize the voices of pretty nurses."

"Oh, go on with you now." The nurse chuckled as she walked away after adding the medication. Katie watched the overweight, middle-aged woman leave with flushed cheeks and a bounce in her step.

"I think you made her morning."

"And you made mine. Thanks for coming to visit."

"Well, any chance to gaze at a half-naked man is always worth taking."

"You like what you see?"

"You are incorrigible. I see some things you never outgrew."

"What? I've got a pretty woman visiting me and admiring the view. Can't help it if that makes me want to flirt." He yawned. "The medication has a side effect of making me drowsy."

"I'll let you rest and bring David by after school. Either here or at home."

"Good. I sure do love that little boy."

Katie tipped her head, wanting to hide any possibility of him reading the longings in her eyes. She rose to plant a kiss on his cheek. Then she walked to the door but paused at his words.

"I love his mother too."

~*~

Katie wandered to the floor where her mother's room was.

"Hi, Mom."

"Who are you?"

"I'm Katie. I just wanted to visit with you."

"I'm not sure why I'm here. I keep telling them I need to get home. Someone has to watch my baby, and that nanny I hired is probably stealing from me."

"I'm sure your baby is fine, Mom. I brought you a baby to take care of while you're here." Katie handed her mother a lifelike doll wrapped in a receiving blanket.

"Oh, he's beautiful. Oh, sweet baby boy. I always wanted a boy."

"You didn't want a daughter?"

"Nah. Just a baby boy. *Shh*, sweet baby." She rocked back and forth in her bed and hummed a lullaby. Katie waited to see if her mother would acknowledge her again, but her mom was enraptured with the doll in her arms, treating it as if it were real.

Katie rose, sneaked out of the room, and went to talk to the nurses to make sure they understood that removing the doll would potentially bring about violence.

She stopped to visit her father. He lay flat on his bed with his eyes closed and his skin a pasty gray. She looked at his vitals. They were poor. His heart rate was low as was his blood pressure. His last stroke combined with the stress of the fire took the fight out of him.

"Hi, Daddy." She stood by his bedside. His eyes followed her, and he tried to talk, but only disconnected sounds came out. A tear trickled down to his ear. She bent over to kiss his cheek and wiped away the tear. "I'm glad you can hear me. Mom is fine. She thinks she's a young mother again and is worried about her baby. She didn't recognize me. Ken is trying to find a place where you can both stay and be safe."

His eyes seemed to plead with her, but for what? "Dad? Are you scared?"

He blinked rapidly. Was that a yes? "Jesus died for your sins and rose again. All you have to do is believe in Him. Submit your life to him. It's more of a heart thing. But peace can be yours, Dad. God promises us that when we rest in Him, death doesn't have to be scary. The doctors say you're going to live. I expect you to be around a long time."

His eyelids sank. When they rose again, his eyes were brighter, and she thought he tried to smile. "I love you, Dad. I'll bring David up later, after school, to see you. OK?"

He blinked several times, and she grinned.

"Get some rest." She kissed his cheek and left.

Katie rushed through her shopping. She ordered a bed she liked and one for David, as well as an air mattress. She purchased bedding and new towels and a shower curtain and rugs. She was grateful the apartment had blinds so she didn't have to worry about that. She ran down to Goodwill and found some dishes, glasses, silverware, and pots and pans. Nothing fancy, but it would do for now. Long-term, those were decisions she could make when she had time to really shop and look at reviews. For now, mismatched dishes and silverware would suit her fine.

She got everything into the apartment, along with the clothes, and used a small air compressor to pump up the bed. She hoped David would consider it an adventure.

She finished in time to pick up David from school.

~*~

"Mommy! I made Daddy a get-well card. Can we take it to him right now?"

"I think that would be wonderful, David. Let's go visit him."

On the way, Katie explained the burn and what he might see at the hospital.

They knocked on the door.

"Come in."

David bounded into the room. "Daddy!"

"Hey, buddy. Wow. Look at that cool sweatshirt."

Katie walked in behind David. Johnny sat on the edge of the bed, and the nurse on the other side was applying a large gauze bandage to his back. The nurse peeked over his shoulder. It was Greta from this morning.

"Hi, Greta. Do you need some help?"

"Could you get this hunk here to stop moving?" She smiled as she worked the bandage around the front of his chest.

"Greta," Johnny whined, "You're covering up the best part. How am I to woo a woman like this?"

"You'll have to try to get by with your charm for a while." Greta fastened the bandage and then helped work a shirt on one arm and then the other.

Johnny winced.

"Daddy, does it hurt?"

"Yeah, son, it does."

"This is your little boy?" Greta asked.

"Yes, ma'am. My daddy saved me in the fire. He's a hero." David plopped on the chair and tilted his head as if he dared the nurse to contradict him.

Katie bit back a giggle as her eyes met Johnny's. He grinned too.

"Well, I suppose we'd better get this hero home. Does the hero want me to button up his shirt, have the pretty lady do it, or does he want to do it himself?"

"As much as I would love a pretty nurse, meaning either of you, to rub my chest, I'll manage."

"You, my boy, are too sassy for your own good. Now behave, and your ride will be here soon." Greta walked out of the room.

Johnny buttoned up his shirt, but Katie had gotten an eyeful and was grateful. Yup. Johnny had definitely matured over the years. She shook her head to get her mind back on track and catch what David was saying.

"Card? You made this for me? This is cool." Johnny was reading the card, and David now perched on the bed beside his father, who had one arm around his son, his shirt not fully buttoned yet.

"Yeah, see you're Batman with a black cape. I know it was really your jacket, but it was black, so kind of the same thing."

"And I'm flying out of the window?"

"Yup, and you're holding me, and you get me safely to the ground."

"Oh, and here's the explosion?"

"Yeah. That was so cool. But Dad?"

"Hmm?"

"I'm not so fond of that kind of adventure. Can we do something else next time where you don't get hurt?"

"Sounds good to me."

Katie wiped away a tear. The two of them were so new to each other but already so bonded. It was going to be hard to get David to leave.

Niko walked in and gave her a smile. "Hi, Katie. David. How are you?"

David promptly showed Niko the card he made and explained it. Niko grinned. "That's so cool. I hope someday you can help Apolo draw as well as you."

"He's too little."

"Right now he is, but he'll grow. Did you know that Apolo's middle name is Jonathon, after your dad?"

David's eyebrows scrunched. "Mommy, isn't my middle name Jonathon too?"

Katie nodded. "I guess that's something you have in common with your cousin Apolo."

"He's my cousin?"

"I am too, buddy." Niko offered. "It gets confusing with first and seconds, but we'll keep it simple. Apolo calls your dad Unka Johnny. It was one of the first phrases he ever spoke."

"But Daddy is mine," David whined.

"He is, buddy, but lots of people love your dad. Not just you," Niko said.

"I can't be selfish?"

"Nope." Katie ruffled her son's hair.

The little boy frowned. "I just want Mommy and Daddy to live together with me."

"We can't do that, honey," Katie said. "Remember I told you I found a place for us to live?"

"Why not?"

"We're not married, David. We've talked about

this before," Johnny said.

"How do you get married?"

"You go to church and have a wedding ceremony," Niko offered.

"Let's go!" David jumped off the bed and reached to tug at Johnny's hand.

"David, you're hurting your dad. We have to agree to get married, plan a wedding, which takes time, and we'd need to apply for a license. It's not happening today."

"When?" His arms had dropped to his sides, and his shoulders drooped.

"David?" Johnny's voice was a whisper.

"Yeah?"

"Your mom and I both love you, but marriage is a really big deal and not something to be rushed into. We will do our best to love you and care for you, but I cannot live with you. You'll come and visit with me at times and maybe even have sleepovers at my place."

"Can you sleep over in my new home?"

Johnny shook his head. "No. I can't."

David ran to Katie. She picked him up and held him close as he buried his face in her neck.

Niko frowned. "Katie, the doctors asked if you, as a nurse, could check in on Johnny every day. I know you won't be staying with us, but when they found out you were a nurse..."

"Yeah, I can do that, maybe after work. That way David can see his daddy more, too."

David perked up. "Really?"

Johnny nodded.

"Let's go, Johnny." Niko brought out a new leather coat and draped it over Johnny's shoulders.

"You found one?"

"Well, yeah, but nice, not at all like yours."

"If I weren't in so much pain, I'd slug you."

"Be grateful I won't hit an injured hero."

Johnny turned to David. "I'll see you tomorrow evening?"

Katie nodded, and David smiled. "Yes. I love you, Daddy."

Johnny stepped close to give David a kiss on the cheek. He was close enough to kiss her too, and his eyes glanced down to her lips for a second. Niko cleared his throat, and Johnny winked at her. "Thanks for the card, David." He followed Niko out of the room with an orderly pushing the wheelchair behind him, just in case.

"Let's go visit Grandpa. He misses you."

"OK, Mommy. I can walk now." She put him down and treasured the small hand in hers, all the while wondering if Johnny's kisses were better than she remembered. She had a spectacular experience with those lips after the fire, but was that just the heat of the moment? She longed to find out.

~*~

The phone rang as Niko drove, and he handed it to Johnny, who was resting face-down in the back seat.

"Yeah, Tia?" Johnny asked.

"Johnny?"

"Niko's driving. It's kind of slick out."

"I wanted to warn you the press is outside the house. Do you still have that blanket you took with you to the hospital?"

"Yeah."

"Cover yourself with it until the garage door is

closed."

"How bad is it?"

"I've called the police, and they are trying to keep them off the property. Neighbors have complained. I've got all the drapes and blinds closed. The phone's been ringing off the hook for interviews and exclusives. You're a hero, Johnny. No longer the bad guy vilified in the press."

"Seriously?"

"Yes. We'll talk more when you get home. I'm putting everyone off for now to give you time to heal. That's my excuse."

"Tia, it's not an excuse. It's the truth. Thank you. See ya in a few. Covering up now."

Johnny grabbed the blanket and tossed it over his head and torso. "Niko, press outside, I'm hiding. You might have trouble getting in, but the police are there."

"How quickly the tide changed. I'm surprised they didn't hunt you down at the hospital."

"They might not have realized I was injured."

"Oh, but you could milk this good..."

"No. I'm not exposing David or Katie to that kind of scrutiny."

"Agreed. Here we go. Wow. Wish you could see this, Johnny. Cops must have been warned by Tia. They're flagging me into my own driveway. How weird is that?"

The car parked and turned off. "Wait. Garage door is closing...now. You're in the clear."

"Good, it was getting warm under there, and I'm already running a fever."

"Totally normal. Give it a few days, and you'll feel better."

"I sure hope so." Johnny folded the blanket while

trying to keep his back away from the seat. He got out and followed Niko into the house.

"We're home!" Niko called.

"Here's your phone." Johnny handed it to his cousin. "Can you take the jacket off? I'm going to need help with the shirt once I get to my room."

"I can call Katie to come and assist." Niko wiggled his eyebrows. "I saw how she looked at you…"

"Just how is that?"

"Like you're her favorite dessert, and she hasn't eaten in a week."

"Right…I can always ask Tia…"

"You'll be back in the hospital if you do. Come on, smarty pants." Niko followed him to his room. In spite of his words, he was gentle in helping Johnny get his shirt off. "Do I need to take the bandage off too?"

"I think it can stay on for now. Katie will remove it tomorrow."

"Thought so."

"What?"

"You want to impress Katie with your manly torso."

"What do you know?"

"I'm a man too, remember? I would be doing exactly the same thing if it were Tia. Now stop sassing me and get some rest."

Johnny crawled onto the bed and hugged his pillow. It smelled like her. *She's going to be the death of me.*

That night, he slept without any nightmares…only sweet dreams of holding Katie in his arms. He was disappointed to wake up to only a pillow he had managed to drool on.

11

I have found the paradox.
That if you love until it hurts
there can be no more hurt, only more love.
Mother Theresa

The day was slow and boring. He tried to watch television while lying on the sofa—first on his stomach and then on his side—but he quickly grew tired of the tripe he witnessed on the screen. He wrote a letter to Katie to give to her later. He went to the basement, cranked up the heat a little, picked up his guitar, and played.

Footsteps alerted him to someone descending, but he continued. When the steps stopped in front of him, he opened his eyes. *Katie.*

"You came."

"I promised I would. You ready for me to take off those bandages?"

"Where's David?"

"Upstairs begging for a root beer."

"That's my boy." Johnny rose and put the guitar on its stand. He stood toe to toe with Katie. "You're a beautiful sight."

"You on drugs again?"

"Nope. I'll take some before bed but trying to avoid them during the day. Did you have trouble getting in?"

"Nah, the media are gone now. They pulled up old video footage and photos to create their story."

"They lack patience."

"It's not as exciting if it's too far past the event, I guess."

He reached up to touch her cheek. "I wouldn't know about that. I think the time apart has only added to the wonder and excitement when I see you."

He leaned down, and his lips brushed against hers. She responded by arching toward him, and his arm wrapped around her back. A tremor of delight shot through his veins. It was as if seven years had never passed. The desire she stirred in him was still there.

Her hand came up to caress his head, and she pulled herself back. "Why do you shave it?"

"Lost the locks to cancer and grew used to it. You don't like it?"

"It's fine, but I miss running my fingers through your hair."

"Niko suggested a wig."

Katie giggled. "He would."

"I could grow it out if you like."

"It's your head."

"It's been over three years. I hardly remember what it feels like any more to have hair, much less a woman's fingers running through it. If it would tempt you more, I'll let it grow."

"I wonder if it would come in as curly as Niko's."

"It was wavy before."

"Sometimes chemo changes things. Might be interesting to see."

"Might be." He pulled her close and kissed her

again. "I know we can't return to the past, Katie, but can we start fresh? Could we date and get to know each other again?"

Katie pulled back. "What's your end game?"

He frowned. "I don't understand."

"What do you really want? Long term?"

"If I can beat this cancer, I might want to marry you."

"Why would you have to beat the cancer before that happened?"

"It wouldn't be fair to leave you a widow."

"Isn't that my decision to make?"

"I don't want to rush into anything."

"I do." Katie put her hand up to her mouth and stepped back as his arms dropped to his side. "I can't believe I said that. I'm sorry. I'm—"

"—honest. But why now? Nothing is different. I'm still a musician. You're a nurse. I'm not good enough."

"I've changed. I've grown up, Johnny. I'm tired of comparing every man I date to you and finding them wanting. I'm tired of being alone. I'm tired of carrying the responsibility for our son on my shoulders."

"I'm trying to help with that."

"I know, but it's not the same. David's wish is mine too."

"I'm not in the best position to make life-altering choices."

She frowned.

"I'm on meds and in pain. As much as I want you right now, I'm too incapacitated to act on it any more than I have. I'm not thinking clearly."

"Either you love me or you don't."

"I do love you, Katie. I never stopped. But the girl I fell for seven years ago has changed, and I need to get to know her now. We didn't grow up together, and who knows, there might be things you need to understand about me too."

"I don't want to lose you again, Johnny."

"I have no control over that."

"Daddy?" a little voice called.

"Coming! Save some root beer for me." He grabbed Katie's hand. "Let's go have dinner, and then you can remove my bandages."

She nodded and followed him back up the stairs.

He struggled into an oversized, zippered hoodie before settling at the table.

~*~

All through dinner, her body throbbed in response to his kiss. Seven years were gone, and she was a teenager again, impatient for more. More than was right or good. She glanced over at David as he sat next to his dad, chattering away about school and trying hard to belch and receive a grin from his father.

"Katie? You OK?" Tia asked.

"Just too many memories haunting me."

Tia followed her gaze to the father and son. "Give him time. He really is gaga over you."

"Life is too crazy right now for decisions like that anyway."

"Is it? Did Johnny ever tell you how Niko and I came to be married?"

"No."

Niko piped in. "She was attacked and almost killed trying to save my life. It wasn't until then I realized how much I loved her."

"Really?"

"And the best part? It was Johnny who forced me to face the truth."

Katie's eyebrows rose.

"He's a romantic at heart. Donna crushed his spirit when she abandoned him after he announced his cancer diagnosis," Tia whispered.

"What are you whispering about over there?" Johnny asked.

"Just telling your darkest, dirtiest secrets as any well-intentioned friend would do," Niko bragged.

"Enough of that. I'm done eating. Katie? We ready to do this?" Johnny rose from his chair.

"I guess so. David, you OK staying out here?"

"Yes, Mommy."

"David, I'm going to say good night now. I think I'll be resting after this."

"OK, Daddy." Katie watched her son wrap his arms around Johnny's slightly burned and uncovered neck. She saw Johnny wince, but he wrapped his arms around his son and held him tight. "I love you, buddy."

"Love you too, Daddy." David let go, gave Johnny a kiss on the cheek, and settled back in his seat.

"He'll be fine out here with us," Niko assured her.

Katie rose and followed Johnny to his room. After removing the hoodie with her assistance, he uncapped a water bottle, swallowed a pill, and sat on the edge of the bed. "Go for it, but be gentle."

"I'll do my best." Katie slowly undid the bandages securing the gauze on his back. She peeled back the bandage soaked with the weeping from the wound. Thankfully, it pulled free with little stickiness, but Johnny's muscles contracted anyway. "I'm sorry."

"I know." His voice was hoarse and low.

She winced for the agony he suffered. The bandages were off, and she wound everything up and took off her gloves as he crawled to lay down on the bed, hugging a pillow under him. His head turned, and she spied the tears he tried to wipe off on the fabric.

"You going to be OK?"

"Yeah. Just a shock to feel the air on the skin again."

"It'll heal soon. A couple days of this and you'll be more comfortable."

"Thanks. Katie?"

"Hmm?"

"I promised you a letter. There's one on the dresser for you."

She walked over to get it. It sat in front of their photo. She picked up the necklace. "When did you finally take it off?"

"My wedding day." His eyes followed her.

"I'm surprised you kept it."

"It reminded me of you. Donna didn't like it, but I replaced it with this..." He held out his left wrist, where he had a tattoo matching the design. "It hid under my watch. She never knew it was there. See, even when I got married, I couldn't escape you. The photo and necklace lived in my guitar case for years...you were with me more than my wife ever was."

"I feel sad for her. It had to be hard to fight against a dream."

"Don't. She pursued me. She pushed for the wedding. My bruised ego agreed, and she was soon, unbeknownst to me, having affairs when I was out of town. I was clueless until she filed and served me papers."

"And she did that when you announced your diagnosis?"

"Bad timing. She had already put things in motion with no clue, but it didn't change anything. She didn't care. Never had, unless it came to attending an awards show on my arm in an expensive dress."

"I'm sorry."

"It's not your fault. I went willingly enough. I might have been naïve, thinking I could move past us, but I tried hard to be a good husband to her."

"I'm sure you did." She swallowed the jealousy and anger. The thought that he kissed and did even more with another woman boiled her blood, but the fact that his wife couldn't cherish the wonderful man he was angered her.

You mean like you cherished him? How was her betrayal any worse than yours?

The truth hurt, and the knife cut deep and twisted as her conscience stripped away any delusions that Johnny had broken her heart. She had held on to that thought as a shield for years, but the truth now was irrefutable. He had been faithful. She was the one who had walked away. Sure, her parents were a roadblock to her happiness then, but they weren't anymore and if she hadn't let them keep her from her dreams. If only she'd been strong enough…

"Katie?"

"Sorry, just lost in thought."

"Obviously not happy ones. You asked. I don't want to hide from you. I'm sorry if my past hurts you."

"Not in the way you think…"

"Then how?" His voice pleaded.

She sat down on the bed. "You're an amazing

man, Johnny Marshall. I failed to recognize that and trust you years ago. I was a fool."

"We were both young and foolish."

She shook her head. "Sure, we made our mistakes, but Johnny, you were always faithful. Even your letters…"

He reached up to wipe away a tear. Moving like that had to hurt. She tapped the letter on her other palm. "I'll read this tonight. Thank you, Johnny."

Katie bent over to kiss his cheek. His eyes watched her closely, begging for more, but she pulled away. "Good night. I'll return tomorrow after work. Rest, drink lots of fluids, and try to let it heal."

"Sweet dreams, Katie."

She rose and left the room, shutting the door behind her.

She collected David and went home.

~*~

After David snuggled into bed, Katie shuffled into the kitchen and flipped on the light above the sink so as not to disturb her son. She took out the folded paper Johnny had given her and started to read.

Dear Katie,

I've never thought of you as anything other than dear. All these years later and it is as if my heart doesn't recognize that time passed. But I look at you and you are more beautiful than you were in high school. I was the envy of all the boys in our class. I realize you could have dated a quarterback or some other jock. You could have easily been homecoming queen. Why you ever even said yes to me, I'll never understand. Beauty and brains paired with the loser musician who could barely pass some of his classes. We made no sense then. Do we now?

You love the Lord. It was one of the things that first drew me to you. And you could sing even though you never wanted to be in the choir. Tia never did either. Just warning you. She sings one song with us.

You've been an amazing mom to David. Thank you for that. Thank you for being open to sharing him with me. He is a gift that is dear to my heart. The best gift because I thought all hope was lost with being a father. But I am one and I'm glad I can be in his life with peace between us.

Yours forever,
Johnny

Katie folded the letter and held it to her heart. She knew she had hurt him deeply. How did he not hold that against her? Maybe that was why he hesitated to move more quickly in a relationship.

Seriously. If he proposed tomorrow, would I say yes?

She nodded. The adult needed to right the wrongs of her teenage self. Wanted David to have a family. Desired more of Johnny's mind-numbing kisses. Longed to be the one to walk through this cancer journey with him, with the right to care and see after his needs.

If he asked…she would say yes.

But is that what God wants?

She wasn't sure.

12

The only thing that truly heals people is unconditional love.
Elisabeth Kubler-Ross

March 2014

A week had passed, and Johnny was able to put on a cotton T-shirt without pain. He was playing his guitar more and still wrote letters to Katie. She had pulled back a bit in pursuing him. David was eager to see him, and they would play checkers when he visited. Johnny started to teach him Chinese checkers, and the boy was a good loser but a tenacious game player. When they played Trouble, he was no-holds-barred and out to take his father down. Johnny grinned.

He had missed church with his healing process but figured it was better to heal and prevent infection as much as possible. Tia wouldn't even let him change Apolo's diapers for the time being. Not that he minded escaping that. He had missed some opportunities to travel too, but more would come. It was a season. A season of healing, not only his body but hopefully his relationship with Katie.

David's birthday was less than two months away. He wondered what he could do for his son. The phone rang.

"Hello?"

"Hey, Johnny, it's Roberto."

"Yeah, what's up?"

"Just wanted to let you know Pamela's camp has paid rather than go to court over her slander."

"How much?"

Roberto named a number that made Johnny gasp.

"Seriously? Do I have to pay taxes on that?"

"That would be up to your accountant. Probably, but even so, you'll have a nice chunk of change left."

"Thanks, Robbie. I appreciate it."

"Your overall coverage since the fire has had the media—social and music industry wise—back-tracking in their comments. Looks like things are good. Has the insurance from the fire covered your medical?"

"I don't know anything about that yet. I think Katie's brother, Ken, is Power of Attorney, and I've not talked to or heard from him."

"Ken Bailey? If you want, I'll give him a call. He might not even realize what happened."

"That would be great. But none of that 'pain and suffering' type settlement, OK?"

"Have you lost work with your recovery?"

"Sure. A few gigs in Atlanta and Nashville."

"Medical bills and lost wages. Tia can fill me in on the lost income from those. We'll get you taken care of."

"Thanks, Roberto. And make sure you're paid too?"

His attorney laughed. "But of course. You're making my house payment for the next few months."

Johnny laughed. "Glad to help out."

He disconnected and hung out with Apolo, watching him crawl all over the place and start to pull himself up on furniture. "Yeah, buddy. I know why your mom wanted me to move in here. It wasn't to help me out—it was for free babysitting. Well, I'm not complaining at all. She's turned into a pretty good cook. It's my turn tonight, though. What'dya say? Should I do something fancy or simple?"

"Unka! Unka!" the little boy said as he slapped Johnny's face and squeezed his cheek.

Johnny chuckled. "Spanakopita is a specialty of mine. I suppose I could do that. Wonder if Katie and David ever had that?"

He wondered how Katie was. He settled Apolo down for an afternoon nap and went to the kitchen to begin some preparations for dinner later. His phone rang again.

"Yeah?"

"Johnny Marshall?"

"That'd be me."

"This is Dr. Osgood. I wanted to let you know we found your match for a transplant. Now all we need to do is schedule the procedure."

"Can you tell me the name of the donor?"

"Nikolos Acton."

Johnny closed his eyes and sat down. Niko. They'd been closer than brothers growing up. It was only right that they share this too. "Great."

"I want to start treatment in a few weeks, just enough time for your back to heal before we begin the chemo and radiation to prepare your cells for the operation."

Johnny gulped. "Fine. Do I need to check with Niko on timing?"

"No. We'll contact him and arrange it. I'll keep you informed."

"Great. Thanks."

He set his phone down and stared off in the distance. Did Niko even realize he had matched? How soon would they let him know?

Tia walked in with bags of groceries. He hated that he couldn't help with them and had to even fight to do dinner tonight.

"Johnny? Is everything all right?" Tia came and put a hand on his arm.

"The doctor just called."

"And?" She sat down.

"They found a match."

"Oh, Johnny. That's wonderful. When will you get the transplant?"

"It'll be a few months. There's chemo and radiation first. You're not curious as to who the donor is?"

"Do I know the person?"

"Yes."

"Does the donor know?"

"I'm not sure."

He watched her bite her lower lip. "Will they tell me?"

Johnny nodded.

"Let me wait to hear from them, if that's OK." She stood and went back to putting away the groceries. "Did you decide on dinner?"

"Apolo asked for spanakopita, so I said I would make it."

Tia laughed. "I've not managed to master that dish yet."

"But you can make a mean lasagna."

"True. So will you serve root beer with that meal, or will it be water?"

"Water. Root beer is not an everyday kind of thing, but I do suspect root beer floats would be a fabulous desert."

"Fine, I'll put some in the fridge to chill." She laughed.

The whir of the garage door opener alerted them to Niko's arrival. Johnny stood but held on to the chair. Niko stormed into the kitchen. "Johnny! Did you hear the news?"

Johnny nodded.

"What news?" Tia asked.

"I'm the match." Niko's grin was wide. He rushed toward Johnny, who put his hand up.

"I'd love a bear hug, but my back can't handle it yet." He blinked away the tears. "Thanks, coz."

"It's an honor and privilege to get to do this for you."

Tia was in tears as she came up to hug Niko from the side.

Johnny didn't know what else to say, so he left to go to his room and collapsed on the bed and cried. Grateful for Niko's match and dreading the upcoming challenges of chemo and radiation. While his family understood there was a potential cure, they didn't understand the painful months ahead. Tears of despair, gratitude, and yes...hope.

~*~

"OK, while they enjoy their floats, let's go look at that burn." Katie rose from the table and accompanied Johnny to his room.

Johnny pulled up the T-shirt so she could inspect his back.

"You're healing well." She tugged the T-shirt down and checked his vitals. "Everything looks good. Are you excited about the match?"

Johnny shrugged. "I'm grateful, but now the reality of what the next few months will look like scares me."

"What's scary?"

"I'm going to be really sick from the chemo and radiation. The peach fuzz growing on my head is going to fall out again. I'll be in so much pain it makes me wonder if it's even worth it to go there."

"But on the other side?"

"Everyone says it's worth it."

"Yeah, they say that about childbirth."

"Was it hard? Were you alone?" Johnny asked as he clasped her hand.

"Yeah. It hurt, and the nurses were great. I didn't want my parents there. I wanted you, and that made it worse because you had no clue. And then I was holding this beautiful boy and no one to share it with who cared. I fought my parents to keep the baby. They wanted me to give it up."

"Why didn't you?"

"David was all I had of you to hold onto. I'd let you go and regretted it, but then I held this precious boy, and I couldn't...there was no way I could give him up."

"I'm sorry I wasn't there for you."

"It was my own fault."

"You need to stop blaming yourself."

"I love your letters, by the way."

Johnny smiled. "I'm glad. I have another for you." He pointed to the spot on the dresser where he always left them. "You know what'll be really hard?"

"What?"

"I'm going to be so alone."

"Why? Tia, Niko, your parents...me and David."

"You've not worked long in oncology, right?"

She shook her head.

"My immune system will be destroyed. I'll be in isolation after the transplant if not before. Only immediate family, so maybe my parents will get to see me, but they have their own lives. No children. Not Niko or Tia, either. Whoever comes has to be healthy and wear head to toe coverage. I'll be in the hospital for weeks."

"This didn't happen last time?"

"No. I got sick, and it was awful. I had surgery and recovered well. Niko hung around some of the time, and Tia was in and out when she could be. The guys would visit. This is an entirely different ballgame."

"A wife could be there."

"I thought of that, but you have David to care for and a job. Even now, we can't see each other much alone without David being close by and watched. How is he going to react to not being able to see me for a long period of time?"

"Video chats?"

"I'll lose weight, and my appearance will be altered. It'll probably terrify him. But it might be possible."

"You're borrowing a lot of trouble from tomorrow."

"What?"

"You are anxious about things that haven't even happened yet."

"I prefer to think of myself as realistic."

"Me too. So what do we do? I want to be there. For the here and now, through the cancer and its aftermath, and the years beyond."

"I don't deserve you, Katie. I can't burden you with more than you've already carried."

"I would rather have two or ten weeks with you than forever without. I'm lonely. I think about you night and day. Nights are the worse. I re-read your letters, picture you resting here hugging your pillow and wishing it were me. You already live in my heart— I want you in my whole life."

"It's going to get nasty."

"It'll be you and me fighting together. We'll fight 'till victory."

"But what if I lose?"

"Then I will at least have the comfort of knowing I was able to love you and treasure you."

Johnny shook his head. "I've been praying about it."

"I know. And you proposed once."

"It wasn't a very good proposal. I hadn't even picked up the ring yet to do it properly. By the time I had it, you were long gone."

"You bought me a ring?"

Johnny nodded. "Kept it all these years too. Traveled in my guitar case so Donna wouldn't find it."

Katie shook her head. "You amaze me."

"You tempt me." He turned to face her and leaned over until their lips met. She returned the kiss, and his blood fired. He pulled back as if burnt. He was in no condition to act as a husband even if he were one. "You should take your letter and go. I'll see you tomorrow."

Katie stood and grabbed the envelope. She turned and bent over so her face was before his. Her eyes searched, but he wasn't sure what they looked for. He met her gaze, trying to swallow equal parts fear and need. She kissed him, and his eyes closed. She let go and was gone before they opened again. He sighed. *God, what am I to do?*

~*~

After he heard Tia take Apolo to bed, Johnny wandered out to the living room and sat by the fire.

"Want company?" Niko asked.

"Sure."

"I thought you'd be happy."

"I'm grateful and scared."

"Why? It's a cure."

"It's also chemo, radiation, pain, isolation, and months of recovery for me. With no guarantee of a cure."

"Different from last time?"

"Yeah. Except…" He sighed.

"What?"

"Katie wants to take the journey with me."

"So one woman leaves when you get cancer, and another woman wants to stay."

"Yeah. But, Niko, if I propose and we marry…"

"Wait. We're talking stay as in getting married kind of stay?"

Johnny nodded.

"About time."

"What?"

"It's clear you adore each other, but you tiptoe around each other, afraid to really express things. Maybe that's out of consideration for David. You don't want him getting his hopes up. But I see Katie after she leaves your room. I know you don't do anything improper with the door propped open and your healing back, but it's clear that she struggles to leave you. When she comes in at the end of the day, you light up."

"I love her as if seven years never passed."

"But you love her now, as a man seven years older who was hurt by his ex-wife. You've both lived a lot in those seven years."

"That's what holds me back."

"Why?"

"I don't know. It's not like you and Tia, who had been around each other and knew each other well before you finally realized you were in love. You were well-acquainted."

"Negative. She knew me better than I did at times, but I had many things to learn about her. We had our rough spots."

"Yeah, but neither of us really knows much of anything about the other...except for the past two months."

"What's God telling you?"

"That He's redeeming my pain. Giving me a son, a faithful wife, my dream of a family. But how much of that is just my own flesh—my heart's desires?"

"You've prayed and asked God."

Johnny nodded.

"And His answer has been..."

"Yes."

"So why aren't you on your knee before her? You still have the rings."

"It doesn't feel fair."

"Life's not fair, and she needs her own answer from the Almighty. You have to give her the option to say yes…or no."

"She indicates she's willing, but what if she says no?"

"You're worrying over nothing."

"Borrowing trouble from tomorrow."

"What?"

"That's what she accused me of. I think it comes out of the New Testament."

"I think in there, it's phrased with a 'do not' at the beginning."

Johnny grinned. "You're probably right."

"So what're you gonna do?"

"I guess I need to plan something special."

"I'm glad, Johnny."

"So, if she says yes, can my bone marrow donor also be my best man?"

"That could be arranged."

13

Every moment is a fresh beginning.
T.S. Eliot

She answered the phone. "Hello, this is Katie."

"Hey, beautiful." Johnny's voice purred.

"Johnny? Why are you calling? Are you OK?" Her heart raced.

"I'm fine. Are you available on Friday night? I need to get out of the house, and I thought a date would be fun. Haven't had one of those in a long time, and you're the prettiest girl I know."

She glanced at the calendar. "A—a date? Wait. That's tonight."

"I realize it's short notice. Thought we'd go to DeLuca's Cucina for dinner. Remember our dinner there?"

"Homecoming." A happy memory flooded her mind.

"Yup. A guy at church owns it."

"I'll need a sitter for David."

"Niko and Tia said he could hang with them. They mentioned something about Lightning McQueen and popcorn."

"David's wanted to see that movie."

"So, is it a date?"

She grinned. "Yes. What time?"

"Can you be here by six?"

"Yes." She could hardly wait.

"Great."

~*~

Katie fidgeted through the rest of the afternoon and rushed to get David from the day care after school. He played as she dressed up. How long had it been? She freshened her makeup and slipped on a white blouse and green skirt with a little flair that looked great with her new boots. She was glad she had splurged when buying new clothes. She rarely had a reason to dress up. She walked out while putting on her last earring.

David looked up from his toys. "Wow. Mom. You're pretty."

"Thanks, sweetheart. Dad and I are going out to dinner tonight. Will you be OK playing at Niko and Tia's?"

He shrugged. "Sure. Apolo's kind of cute. If they need help, I can be there."

Katie smiled. "That's my boy. Grab your coat. We should hustle."

~*~

When they entered the house, David shed his coat and ran to play. Johnny emerged from his room and walked toward her.

"Johnny?"

He winked. "Yeah, the lowly musician can clean up like a real human being."

She shook her head. He wore a dark gray suit that

appeared tailored and a crisp, light green shirt, but he still didn't do a tie. His shirt was unbuttoned at the top, and she spied the Celtic Trinity knot hanging from its chain. Black dress shoes completed the ensemble. She swallowed hard. His soft, dark hair on top hadn't grown in much, but it gave him a different look. "I like what I see."

He grinned. "You do?"

"Very much."

"I'll have to wait till the restaurant for your unveiling, I think. We're going to be late if we don't leave now." He grabbed for a red scarf and a longer leather coat. "Bye, David." The little boy gave a quick wave. Johnny pulled out his keys. "Since I invited you, I drive."

"Are you sure?"

"Come, my lady." He took her elbow and steered her back outside.

At the restaurant, he helped her out of the car and held her hand as they walked inside.

"Good evening, Stephanie," he said to the hostess.

"Johnny. It's good to see you. I reserved the table you requested."

Johnny helped Katie with her coat. He let out a low whistle as he removed it and whispered in her ear, "You are gorgeous."

They followed the hostess. Katie paid close attention to the curvy blonde who seemed to know Johnny. The woman sauntered through the tables and led them to a cozy corner booth.

"Maggie will be with you in a few minutes. Here are your menus."

"Thanks."

"Who is she?" Katie asked.

"Stephanie? She's married to my attorney, Roberto, and she's one of Tia's friends."

She swallowed her jealousy. She scanned the menu but already knew what she wanted. She glanced at the candle-lit visage before her. Johnny didn't look like a musician tonight. He was as dapper as any attorney or banker.

"How do you happen to own a suit like that? It looks like a name brand, custom—"

"It is. Got it for our first award ceremony, and I've only worn it twice since. I wanted you to have the best of me tonight. I'll warn you, though. I'm a jeans and T-shirt kind of guy most of the time."

She grinned.

They ordered their meal, and she sipped her ice water.

"How are your parents?"

"They've both moved to an assisted living facility in the Falls, but they are already more into the nursing home part of the facility. Mom rarely recognizes David or me anymore, and Dad needs help with everything since the fire and his last stroke. My brother has the responsibility of taking care of all that. I visit as much as I can."

"Can your dad talk?"

Katie shook her head. "No. I read Scripture to him and pray over him. Mom tries to interrupt. She doesn't like it when I pay any attention to him. They still share a room, although they have separate beds. Neither of them are there for me. I'm an orphan even though they are still alive and I'm a grown woman."

"That has to be hard. Tomorrow I want to take you and David over to my parents' home, if it's OK with you. They are eager to meet David and long to see you again too."

"That'd be nice. I always liked your family."

"I like them pretty well myself, and I'll be more than happy to share."

Their food arrived, and Katie spent the next few minutes enjoying the savory flavors of the classic Italian wedding soup. The wilted spinach salad with the warm raspberry vinaigrette was heaven. When the more traditional ravioli came, she was almost too full to enjoy it.

"The pasta is all homemade."

"It's amazing."

"Room for dessert?"

"No way."

"Something to share perhaps?"

"You can go ahead if you want, but I just can't."

"Katie..." He was fidgeting now. "I've been praying, and God keeps telling me what to do, and I've fought this because I don't feel it's fair to ask this of you."

"Ask me what?"

He pulled out a jeweler's box and flipped it open. "I've waited seven years to do this right. I've loved you that entire time. Will you marry me?"

Katie's hand covered her heart. "Oh, my. That has to be the most unique and beautiful ring I've ever seen." She reached and picked it up.

"I designed it especially for you. You wondered why I was working so hard that summer. I had to pay for it."

"It's perfect. Yes."

"Is that a yes to the ring or to me?" He set the box on the table.

"To both, Johnny. Yes, I will marry you and wear

your beautiful ring."

"This is the engagement ring and wedding ring in one. Is that OK?"

"Absolutely." She leaned forward, their lips met, and the kiss was sweet. She pulled back. "When?"

"Soon? I'd like to get married before I have to start all these treatments."

"As soon as you want."

"You need a dress and attendants. Oh, your parents…"

"Why don't we keep it small? My parents cannot come, but I would like my brother and his wife there."

"My entire family will want to be there, and they can be a bit overwhelming."

"Let's just enjoy this and let the planning wait till tomorrow?"

"We could get married by the justice of the peace and do a bigger wedding later."

"Why not at church?"

"I would love to do it at church, but they prefer months of premarital counseling, and we don't have time for that."

"That kind of counseling could be invaluable." Katie frowned.

"Why don't we meet with Pastor Andrew and talk about it before we decide how we want to proceed?"

"OK. I do love you, Johnny. I've waited too long to say yes to that proposal."

"I've been waiting a long time myself. I love you, Katie."

She glanced at her phone. "It's getting late. I'm not sure how much help Tia and Niko need from David tonight."

"Let's go share our news."

Johnny paid the bill, and they headed back home to Niko's house. Johnny followed her inside, and David ran to greet them in a stage whisper. "We have to be quiet. The baby is sleeping."

Katie waved to Tia and Niko, who sat on the loveseat with the TV on pause and a bowl of popcorn between them.

"Come in and sit down," Niko said.

Johnny once again helped her with her coat and handled his own. She turned to him. "I didn't get to check your back tonight."

"It's probably better to skip that this evening," he whispered in her ear and sent shivers down her spine.

His hand on the small of her back propelled her forward. "Should I take off my boots?" she asked.

Tia waved the question away with her hand. "No, we're fine. How was dinner?"

"Wonderful." Katie blushed.

"Stephanie says hi." Johnny offered, and Tia grinned.

"We have news," Katie started and sat down on the couch and pulled David next to her. Johnny came to sit down too, with the little boy in between them.

"Oh?" Niko asked.

"I asked Katie to marry me. As soon as possible."

"Let's see this ring I've heard about." Tia rushed forward, kernels of popcorn finding their way to the floor. "Oooh, Johnny. Well done."

"He said he designed it for me seven years ago. He told me it symbolized our relationship together with Christ—a chord of three strands is not easily broken."

"I have a similar one for me waiting for the right time. Just lacks the rocks."

"Welcome to the family, Katie," Niko said.

David yawned. "Does this mean Daddy will live with us?"

"Yes, David. Daddy will live with us after the wedding."

"That makes me happy." The little boy leaned in to Johnny and closed his eyes. Soon he was asleep.

"I'll take him and let him snooze on my bed."

"No, you cannot carry him. No stretching your healing skin," Niko chided. "I'll take him in there for you. I'm assuming he'll spend the night?"

"Would that be OK?" Johnny asked.

"Funny, I'm the one who got engaged, but David is the one who gets to sleep with you?"

"I'm not making any more mistakes. I won't sleep with you till our wedding night."

Heat rushed to Katie's face.

"Can I get you anything? Soda, water, popcorn?" Tia offered.

"No, thanks. I guess I'd better go home."

Johnny rose and helped her up. "I'll bring David by in the morning to change clothes before we go to meet my family."

Katie nodded. He walked her to the door.

Tia scooted by. "I'm going to make myself scarce."

Katie couldn't help but giggle. Johnny pulled her close and bent his head down for a long, lingering kiss. He broke away. "Soon. Please let it be soon," she whimpered.

He helped her with her coat. "Good night, Katie."

"Sweet dreams, Johnny."

She saw him standing at the door watching as she drove away. Someone loved her.

~*~

She entered her apartment building and climbed the stairs. It was weird to be coming home alone. In all her years as a mother, David had always been there with her.

Katie went into her apartment and locked her door. She dropped her coat and purse and headed for the bedroom to change. She flicked on a light there and glanced again at the new weight on her left hand. The ring was like nothing she had ever seen and stunning in its woven, multicolored bands. The stones were gorgeous too. She had always wanted pink diamonds, and he had given her two—one on each side of a slightly larger white diamond.

She prepared for bed and climbed in, shivered, and pulled the covers close around. Her hand slipped over to the empty side of the bed. Soon, Johnny would be there with her, and the nights wouldn't be so lonely or cold.

She fingered her ring again and wondered. What kind of ring had Donna received? Did she dare ask?

~*~

The next morning, the question still bothered her. She logged onto her computer and typed in "Donna Marshall." She found wedding photos online and looked closely. Donna's ring was a basic solitaire. Nothing unique or special about it. And Johnny. She looked at him as a young groom. Handsome, but not as handsome as he was now. His smile wasn't genuine. His eyes didn't have the twinkle she was used to seeing. He was stiff, not the fluid musician, the man who liked to belch with root beer and joke with friends. Johnny had gone through a lot, just as she had.

Now the question on her mind was whether she was the person to make him happy.

Is that your job?

Maybe not...but it was a good goal, wasn't it?

14

Every life is a pile of good things and bad things.
The good things don't always soften the bad things,
but vice versa, the bad things don't always spoil the good
things and make them unimportant.
The Doctor, "Doctor Who" (Vincent and the
Doctor)

I'm getting married.

He hugged his pillow as the sun came into the room through the cracks in the blinds. His son snored softly next to him.

My son.

He had never dreamed he could experience such joy. Peace.

Like maybe, just maybe, God liked him after all.

Yeah, he knew God loved him, but cancer sure seemed like a low blow when coupled with betrayal, divorce, and the loss of any hope to have children of his own. When the cancer came back, he wondered how else he would be afflicted.

Instead, he was blessed. With David...and now Katie finally becoming his wife.

Well, there had been the car accident and the fire...but in both of those, God used him to save his son. He did not regret his choices.

Pamela. He didn't regret her either...only that he ever accepted the job.

No. Regrets were a thing of the past.

You still have cancer.
Shut. Up.
You still have cancer.
I said, shut up.
It's not going away.

Johnny groaned. How like the enemy to remind him of his painful future battle. Was his present happiness a wisp of smoke to be grabbed only to find it evaporating in the wind?

He finally rose and prepared for the day. He was making his cinnamon toast when David wandered into the kitchen. "Did I stay overnight with you, Daddy?"

"Sure did. Want some toast?" He waved a plate with a stack on it, and the boy eagerly grabbed it and headed for the table. "Hey, David?"

"Yeah, Dad?"

"You need to share with me. It's my favorite too."

~*~

After breakfast, they drove to Katie's apartment. She buzzed them in, and Johnny followed David up the stairs. He remembered when Niko lived in this complex. Katie opened the door to welcome them in.

"David?"

"Yeah, Dad?"

"Why don't you go put on fresh underwear, socks, pants, and a shirt."

"OK." The little boy scuttled away.

Johnny smiled. "Now. A few minutes to have you to myself." He kissed her, delighting in her response to him as her fingers caressed his fuzzy scalp.

They broke apart, and Katie giggled.

"I was hoping more for a sigh of contentment,"

Johnny defended.

"I just recalled a childhood poem."

He raised an eyebrow. "Let's have it."

"Fuzzy Wuzzy was a bear. Fuzzy Wuzzy had no hair. Fuzzy Wuzzy wasn't fuzzy, was he?"

"Great. I suppose I'll be hearing that one for months now."

"You've been bald for years. Why would it bother you now?"

"Because my future wife wanted to run her fingers through my non-existent hair." He moved farther into the apartment and looked around. "Where's your furniture?"

"I haven't had time to purchase any."

Johnny walked over to her laptop on the kitchen counter. Out of curiosity, he tapped a key, and the screen lit up to pictures of him and Donna from years ago. He shook his head and closed the monitor.

Katie was about to say something, but David bounded back into the room. Johnny was grateful. He didn't want to hear a defense. He couldn't blame her for being curious. If she had been married before, he'd have looked up more than photographs.

"He has more energy than Tigger in the morning," Johnny stated as he ruffled his son's hair. "Ready to go meet Grandma and Grandpa Marshall?"

"Are they *my* Grandma and Grandpa?"

"Yes, they are."

"Great!" David grabbed one of Johnny's hands and one of Katie's.

"Wait, son. You and your mom need to put on coats."

"Good point, Dad." The little boy said with all seriousness as he grabbed his mother's coat and held it out for her.

Katie gave Johnny a wink. Good. Whatever possessed her to peek into his past didn't interfere with her affection for him. He let out a sigh of relief as he followed them out the door.

They were in the car and David safely in his booster seat in the back. Katie had expressed surprise he had purchased one. She didn't realize he'd done that the same day he'd talked to Roberto.

"Johnny, about the photos…"

"You don't have to explain. I assume you were curious. You can ask me anything."

"I—I wanted to see if her ring had been as special as mine."

Johnny grinned. "And were you satisfied with what you found?"

"Yes. Very much so."

"Good. She selected her ring. I designed yours. She got what she wanted, and you got what I wanted. Really, I guess that makes me selfish."

"Selfish for knowing exactly what I like and making sure you made something one-of-a-kind just for me? I think that makes you special and unique, and me—blessed."

"I prefer your version."

They entered his parents' home, and Mrs. Marshall rushed up to give Katie a hug and a kiss. Then she dropped to one knee and opened her arms. "Oh, David. You look so much like your father when he was your age. I'm your grandma. Can I give you a hug?"

David ran into her arms and allowed Grandma to smother him with a hug and kisses on his hair.

"Katie, he's beautiful. You have given us such a

blessing."

"Mom, Dad. We have some news for you."

Grandma stood and ushered them into the living room. When they were all seated, his dad spoke up. "You found a match?"

Johnny nodded. "Yeah. Niko. It's going to be a few months before we can do the transplant, though. The other news is that I proposed to Katie and she accepted. We hope to be married soon."

"Why so fast, son?"

Katie jumped in. "The treatment for his cancer is long and painful, and he's going to be in isolation for much of that time. Only immediate family is allowed to visit. We didn't want to wait and have him go through that alone when I could be there by his side to encourage him."

"Johnny tells me you're a nurse," Mrs. Marshall said.

"Yes. For now, I work at the oncology clinic Johnny visits. I'm looking for a switch so there's no conflict there."

"I think she should quit and stay home to take care of me," Johnny said softly.

Katie gaped at him. "You've never mentioned this before."

"We only got engaged last night. There's a lot we haven't said yet. I can support us while I recover. I'm not without resources."

Katie grasped his hand. "Your own personal nurse?"

"What could be better than your pretty face when I'm in agony?"

She smiled.

"So, there's a wedding to plan?" his father asked.

"We need to meet with our pastor to discuss the details. Tia and Niko got married quickly, but normally, the church requires a series of premarital counseling appointments. I'm not sure we have time for that."

"Well, let us know, and we'll do everything we can to make your wedding day special."

"It'll be small, Mrs. Marshall. I don't have much in the way of family."

"I'm sure our brood will more than make up for the lack." Mr. Marshall chuckled as he spoke.

David tugged on his grandma's shirt. "Can I see the house?"

"Well, aren't you're a curious boy. Of course. You want to check out where your daddy grew up. Let me give you a tour." She rose and escorted him from the room.

"How are you really doing, Johnny? I've been worried," his father asked.

"My back is healing well. I'm scared about what the next few months hold, and I'm grateful this beautiful woman is willing to walk that road with me."

"A good wife is a wonderful blessing when life is hard. I'm happy for you both. How are your parents, Katie?"

"They are in a nursing home now. Dad had a stroke and can no longer care for himself, and Mom has Alzheimer's."

"I'm sorry to hear that. They were much older when you were born, right?"

"Yeah. I have an older brother."

"You will be our daughter now. We understand what a schmuck our son can be, so don't worry about us taking sides with him just because he's ours."

Katie laughed, a light tinkling music that denoted joy, as she leaned against Johnny and kissed his cheek. "I appreciate the support."

Johnny wanted to frown but couldn't fight the grin spreading across his face. "I'm really happy, Dad. I always loved Katie. And I'm thrilled I get to be David's father too."

"After you get through this cancer, you work on giving us more grandkids."

Johnny squeezed his hand joined with Katie's and looked up into her face. "I'm sorry, Dad. My last cancer battle removed the possibility of me fathering a child."

"So adopt. I don't care how you get the kids, just have kids. Lots of kids. David can't be an only child."

"I guess that's something we'll have to talk about when Johnny recovers," Katie said.

"If I get well."

"When. This is going to work," Katie assured.

Johnny's dad frowned, and their eyes met. Johnny realized his father understood the uncertainty of the months ahead. There were no guarantees.

Katie's phone rang.

"Yes?" She said. "What? How could you let her leave? Have you called my brother? Fine. I'll be there soon. Keep looking. Did you call the police? OK." She hung up and looked to Johnny. "My mother left the nursing home, and they can't find her."

"I thought they had some kind of system to keep her from escaping?"

"Yeah, an alarm goes off if she leaves her room. It went off, but they didn't notice."

David and Grandma returned.

"David, we need to leave and go find Grandma."

"She wandered again?"

"Yes."

Johnny interrupted. "Again? So she's done this before?"

"Twice that we know of before we moved in. Ken installed an alarm system at the house to alert us if she tried to leave."

"But what about when you worked?"

"I locked the doors and hoped she wouldn't figure out how to unlock them."

"Which almost became deadly when the fire happened."

Katie looked away. "It was my fault."

Johnny wrapped an arm around her. "No. It wasn't. A lot of things could have been changed about that day, but at some point, something was bound to happen. You couldn't know."

"Mommy, can I stay with Grandma and Grandpa? They have Legos."

"We would be happy to keep him here for you," Mrs. Marshall offered.

"OK. We'll be back as soon as we find Grandma Bailey."

"Great!" David turned to his Grandma. "Can I play with the Legos?"

"You go right ahead. I'll mix up a batch of cookies for us to enjoy in a little while."

David's eyes and smile grew big. "Thanks!" He ran to Katie, gave her a hug, and planted a kiss on Johnny's cheek. "See ya later, Mom and Dad!" His little footsteps sounded as he went up the stairs.

"He's a delightful boy."

"Thanks." Katie rose, and Johnny did too. "I'm sorry we need to leave."

"We'll see you soon. We will pray you find her

safe."

"Thank you."

~*~

Johnny held the car door for Katie and went around to his side. "Just tell me where to go." She gave him the address, and they took off. Katie pulled out her phone and dialed.

"Ken? Yeah... We're on our way. Johnny and me. Yes, Johnny Marshall. I had planned to call you and let you know that we're getting married. I don't know the date yet. No. I don't care what you think about it. I'll call you when we find Mom." She dropped the phone in her purse with a growl.

"What'd he say? Or don't I want to know?"

"You can probably guess anyway. He's not happy that I'm getting married."

"Getting married or getting married to me?"

"Same difference."

"Come on, Katie. Your parents disapproved years ago...and aren't in a position to have much of an opinion now, but this is your brother."

"No. We're not talking about this. He doesn't matter. He's always been perfect. The favorite son. They never wanted me, because I wasn't him."

"Why would they have ever complained? You were a great student in school. You got me through some of my classes with your tutoring."

Katie giggled. "Is that what you called it? Tutoring? I remember a lot of kissing."

Johnny grinned. "Those are great memories, aren't they?"

"Yeah. They are." She reached over, placed a hand on his knee, and squeezed. "Now we have the opportunity to make new ones."

"Mother hunting was definitely not on my list of things to do on a date with you."

"We'll make the best of it. I'm glad you're with me."

"Me too."

~*~

With the melting snow, tracking down an older woman was a challenge. The cold was a concern as well. Johnny left Katie at the nursing home and got in the car to drive around. He found his future mother-in-law almost a mile away from the nursing home. He called to tell Katie but wasn't too sure he'd be able to coax his future mother-in-law to come with him.

"Mrs. Bailey?" He strode up to her as she rested on a bench for a bus stop.

The older woman squinted up at him. Her white hair was a rat's nest, and her coat misbuttoned. "Who are you?"

"I'm Johnny. Remember?"

"Johnny."

"Johnny Marshall."

"No matter. You're a handsome enough man. Come and sit with me."

"Kind of a chilly day to be taking a walk."

"I need to get home. My mother is probably worried."

"Where is home?"

She shook her head at him. "Mill Street, Philadelphia."

"Where are we now?"

"I'm not sure."

"Are we even in Pennsylvania?"

"Are you lost, young man? Of course we are." She tapped his knee.

"Sorry, I'm so confused. Where did we meet again?" he asked.

"You're a teacher at my school. Surely you remember me, Mercy McKinley. "

"Right. I thought you were familiar. Could I give you a ride home?"

"I can take the bus just fine."

"Well, the bus that comes here cannot get you to Mill Street."

"It can't?"

Johnny shook his head. "I can drive you there, though."

"You don't even know where we are."

"Well, I do, but see, I'm the Doctor."

"Doctor who?"

"Exactly."

"You don't look like him."

"Regeneration."

"Ah. Where's your blue box?"

"Hidden. I borrowed a car to search for you. I need your assistance."

"Really?"

"Yeah. Can you help me?"

"I would be delighted. Have aliens attacked?"

"Any threat is possible. We just need to be prepared." Johnny helped her into the front seat of the car and buckled her in. He came around and started it up to head back to the nursing home.

"OK, Mercy, you are undercover at a nursing home. So I need you to stay there, and I'll pop in to get reports from you when I can."

"But I'm not old."

"They will think you are. It's a funny trick I learned."

"No Daleks?"

"I sure hope not. So, Mercy, are you in? You'll help me?"

"Yes, Doctor."

Johnny glanced at the older woman sitting there with a huge smile on her face, heading into what she thought was an adventure in a science fiction show. Was he wrong to have duped her to get her in the car? He wasn't sure. He just figured he had to find a way to connect with her, and the *Doctor Who* reference was a total shot in the dark. She might hate him later.

They arrived at the nursing home, and Johnny escorted Mrs. Bailey in. "They think you are Mrs. Mercy Bailey, and you share a room with a man they think is your husband. Don't worry. He's had a stroke and won't hurt you."

She smiled and nodded as she gripped his arm and held him close. Katie approached. "Mom. Are you OK?"

Mercy glanced at Johnny, who nodded. She glanced back to Katie. "Why of course, dear. I'm fine. This nice young man…"

"Johnny."

"Johnny—has been helpful."

He continued to lead her to her room and helped her settle into a chair. "Would you like to watch some television or take a nap?"

Mercy searched his face for a clue but finally said, "I think I'll take a nap here in this comfortable chair." She leaned over to whisper in his ear as he crouched next to her, arranging an afghan over her lap. "I can keep an eye on things outside this way."

Johnny whispered back, "Good work. I'll try to return in a few days for a report."

Mercy snuggled into her blanket and closed her eyes after giving him a wink.

Johnny grabbed Katie, and they left the room. Farther down the hallway, she stopped him. "How did you get her to come back with you?"

He bowed his head. "I'm not sure you'd believe me if I told you."

"She acted like she was half in love with you."

"She's not in love with me, but who she thought I was."

"And just who did my mother think you were?"

"The Doctor."

"A doctor?"

"No, *the* Doctor."

"Doctor...Who?"

"Exactly."

Her eyes grew wide, and she started to giggle. "Seriously?"

Johnny nodded. "I'm sorry I lied to her, Katie. I just couldn't figure out how to get Mercy, who lives on Mill Street in Philly, to agree to take a ride with me and come willingly into this place in Menomonee Falls, Wisconsin."

"You remembered from years ago how she loved *Doctor Who* as a kid?"

"Yeah, but I think God reminded me. My brain isn't that sharp."

"It's brilliant. Wow. Didn't know I was marrying a time lord." She squeezed his hand as they walked to the car.

15

There are divine things more beautiful than words can tell.
Walt Whitman

Katie dropped off David at his classroom on Sunday morning. "Johnny can't be in there while his back heals." She didn't bother going into how cancer treatment might impact Johnny's ministry. She doubted Johnny had even thought of it.

"I want to be with you and Daddy."

"You can sit in the service with us, but Daddy can't carry you or pick you up yet."

"I know. His back is still healing. I'll behave."

Katie frowned. "Fine, but if you don't, you'll have to be taken out."

David nodded.

Katie walked down to the sanctuary and found Tia sitting alone, as Niko led worship. "Where's Johnny?" she whispered.

"The electric guitar player got ill last night, so Niko asked Johnny to step in. He's been here since before seven this morning, making sure he knew the parts."

"From what I understand, he could have probably done it cold and he still would have been amazing."

"This isn't a concert though... he plays differently when he's on a worship team like this," Tia said. "Just watch. You'll see."

Katie sat with David next to her. "Daddy's on stage this morning helping Uncle Niko lead worship." Her son had never heard Johnny's music, much less his guitar playing. It had been a long time for her too, and she promised herself to listen to every recording as soon as she could. This was his livelihood, and she needed to be interested and supportive.

David squirmed in his seat until the worship team appeared. He waved to Johnny, who winked at them. He sat on a stool since he couldn't put the strap around his back yet. She suspected he hated that restriction.

The service started, and the congregation stood. The first song was upbeat, and everyone clapped. Niko was in his element leading the congregation. She watched Johnny as he played. Such intensity. David was thrilled. The congregation turned and greeted each other, and soon the next song began, but the opening riff was Johnny.

Katie gasped and covered her mouth. He had thrown the strap on and stood, jamming the intro with Niko. Everyone started to sing, and it was electric. Tears were in her eyes as she worshipped God and watched Johnny pour himself out through his guitar. The next song came down a few steps to a ballad, but the intricacies he brought to the song added such beauty. Finally, they had a slower song, a modified hymn, and Johnny's guitar sang.

The congregation sat for the message, and Johnny soon appeared beside David to listen.

Katie had a hard time paying attention to the message. She had never realized how gifted Johnny was. Even years ago, she heard all about his dreams and plans, but she had rarely attended any of his gigs with Specific Gravity. They were just a garage band like many others around the Milwaukee area or any other larger city. She had never recognized how special Johnny's gift was, or the dynamic that existed between him and Niko.

As the message wound down and the pastor started to pray, Niko, Johnny, and the rest of the band took the stage. Johnny picked up the guitar, threw the strap on, and started to play. He stood up to the microphone and led the song with Niko providing an echo. There was joy and passion, and she thought she heard angels singing.

As the service ended, she sat in awe.

"Can I see Daddy?" David asked.

"Yes. Let's both go." Katie followed David out of the row and to the stage. Johnny set down his guitar and came to sit on the edge of the stage.

"Hey, buddy. Decided not to do Sunday school?"

"No. I saw you play. You're really good."

Johnny smiled. "Thanks. I'm glad you think so."

"How come you haven't been on the worship team before?" Katie asked.

"I love the kids and couldn't see how I could do both. I've been asked, repeatedly. I couldn't be in David's room this morning…and may not for some time, but this opportunity came up, and I couldn't say no."

"You couldn't stay seated, either."

Johnny frowned. "I'm going to pay for that."

"Does your back hurt?"

"Not yet. I sat through rehearsal."

"But you have another service."

Johnny nodded. "I need to get some coffee and meet with the team. Will I see you later?"

Katie stepped forward to give him a kiss.

He slowly pulled away from her lips. "Is that to make it better?"

She shook her head. "No. It's an apology for not recognizing how wonderfully God has gifted you...and for not supporting that gift seven years ago."

Johnny gave her a half-smile. "Thanks. Apology accepted."

"See ya, later, Daddy."

Johnny slid off his stage perch and dropped to a knee to give his son a hug. "Love ya, buddy. I'm glad I got to see you this morning." The little boy wrapped his arms around his daddy's neck. Katie blinked back tears. Tears of regret that she had denied them both this for the past six years, but also of deep love.

Johnny rose. "Gotta go." He leaned forward and placed a kiss on Katie's cheek before he headed back on stage and out behind the curtain.

Katie nodded and grabbed David's hand as they walked to the café.

Tia met them there with Apolo. "Katie, did you want to stay for second service to watch Johnny? I can take David home with us, and you could join us for lunch."

"I'd like that."

"You've never seen him play live?"

"I barely remember him playing seven years ago. I had no idea."

"He's pretty special. He was instrumental in helping Niko and I get together."

"You mentioned that before."

"The man has hidden depths in spite of the wounds he's carried. The next few months are going to be brutal, aren't they?"

"Yeah."

"Well, I'm glad he's getting a chance to shine right now. He glorifies God with his music, and when he and Niko are together, it's pure magic in my mind."

"I agree." Katie bent over to David. "You OK going home with Auntie Tia and Apolo?"

David nodded. "She likes me to help. Then I'll see Daddy sooner."

"Smart kid." She gave him a hug, and he followed Tia as they left.

~*~

Johnny's back itched like crazy and only hurt a little bit. Katie's blatant admiration of his playing humbled him. His heart sank at the thought that she had focused on him instead of the God who had gifted him. He did a quick gut check. Had his ego risen to the surface as he played? He hoped not. He wanted God honored by his music and really didn't care for anyone to notice he was there.

People noticed Beethoven too…

Right. As if I'm anything like him.

You're exactly how I created you to be.

Thanks, Lord.

He met with the team for prayer before they headed back out on stage. He picked up his guitar and glanced out at the congregation. Faces of people he knew but more he didn't. He blocked them out much as he did at any concert. *Father, this is for You.* He glanced over to Niko as the lights came up, and they joined in together on the first song.

Deep joy filled him as his fingers worked the notes, and the band became one sound raised to a holy

God, the Triune God. Father, Son, and Spirit. He glanced out briefly over the crowd and wondered if angels gathered in the corners, defending this group of believers against the evil one. As the last song's notes rang out and evaporated into the atmosphere, he became aware of a sacred hush in the room. Niko let the silence hang for a moment, and Johnny slowly let his fingers move across the guitar strings, softly filling the space with sound. Niko prayed, and the pastor came to the front, hand raised, to join in the prayer. As the prayer ended, Johnny continued to play as the band slowly stepped off the stage. He ended and set the guitar down and slipped off the stage so the pastor could begin his sermon.

He knelt backstage in the dark, alone, listening to Pastor Andrew's message again. If God could hug him, it could come no closer to the Presence he experienced as he prayed and listened. All pain was forgotten. When the pastor ended, Johnny joined the band back on stage for a final song. The congregation responded with passion, and the band stopped playing to let the room ring with the voices of only the people. Chills ran up his spine at the beauty of the moment.

How did one create this? Obviously, it was beyond human ability to orchestrate such a time of worship, but it was one he wanted more of. After the service, he packed up his guitar in its case and set it aside. Pastor Dan Wink waited for him.

"Johnny. We finally got you on stage."

"Niko called in a favor."

"And...?"

"I've never experienced anything quite like it. I'm in."

"I think we'd want to keep you with Niko...or do

you want to try with Amy or some of our other leaders?"

"I'm willing to play on different teams. I'm flexible."

"Good. I'll be in touch. I need to talk to Niko."

Johnny was about to walk down the aisle of the sanctuary when he spotted Katie off to one side. She stayed? He set his guitar down and went over to her.

"Katie?"

There were tears in her eyes. She shook her head. "I've never experienced anything so beautiful."

"Me neither."

"I stayed because I wanted to listen to you again...but I don't know how to describe what that was like."

"Good."

She frowned.

"It wasn't about me anyway."

"Yes."

He stretched out his hand. She took it and rose from her seat. They walked over to his guitar and made their way down the aisle together. In the lobby, they ran into Pastor Andrew.

"Johnny. You sent me an intriguing email. Am I to assume this is Katie?"

"Yes. Katie, have you met Pastor Andrew?"

"Not face to face. I was convicted by your message today."

"I was convicted by the worship. It was hard to get up to preach after that. Thanks for being on the team, Johnny. I heard you were a last-minute addition. I'm thinking it was God's divine appointment."

"Thank you. I was honored to be a part of what happened here."

"So, you want to talk about getting married."

"Yes."

"Do you have time to meet for a few minutes right now?"

Johnny looked to Katie, who nodded. "That'll work."

They headed to the pastor's office and sat down. Johnny explained the desire for a wedding as soon as possible.

"We realize you normally have great premarital counseling, though, and we don't really want to bypass anything that would give us a chance at a good marriage."

Andrew glanced at his calendar and tapped his chin with his pen. "Would two weeks be sufficient time?"

Johnny's mouth dropped open. "Really?"

"On one condition."

"What is that?" Katie asked.

"I want to pair you up with an older couple for mentoring for the first year. Do you think you could agree to that? Of course you are welcome to come see me too, but this is a new ministry we're trying."

Johnny turned to Katie, who nodded. "Yes. We would be grateful for that kind of help."

Pastor Andrew smiled. "OK, so let's put some specifics on paper and meet again next week for final details...and we'll get you guys hitched and ready to face your future, the good and the bad, together."

After they had the basics hashed out, Johnny stood and stretched his arm out to Andrew. "Thank you."

Andrew smiled. "I've known you a long time, Johnny. I wouldn't be doing this for just anyone." He pulled Johnny in for a gentle hug. When he finished, he shook Katie's hand.

"Let's go get some lunch, beautiful." Johnny smiled at Katie as they grabbed his guitar and headed to the parking lot.

"Where's your car?"

"I came with Niko. So if you won't give me a ride, I'm stranded here with my guitar and my thumb."

"I suppose I could give you a lift."

"Thanks."

Johnny leaned against the seat of the car as pain seared through him. After the high of the morning, why now? He couldn't even put a finger on it as his temple beaded with sweat in the cold.

"Johnny? You OK?"

He could only manage a groan.

Niko helped him out of the car. Johnny could barely open his eyes. As he collapsed on his bed, someone's hands stripped off his shirt and rolled him over to his stomach. Something cool touched his back. Ahh.

"Daddy?" A soft voice penetrated the darkness, and a rank odor assaulted him. He cracked open an eye to see his son standing there, furrows on his brow and a frown on his face.

"Hey, David," his voice scratched out. Hadn't he just sung this morning?

"Are you sick?"

"I...don't...know." A marching band was doing a routine in his head. He wished they'd shut up so he could focus.

"Mommy's really worried."

"She is?"

"She's crying, Daddy. Why is she crying?"

"I don't know."

"Are you going to die?"

Johnny had no strength to move. His bones were like gelatin. "We all die at some point. We don't usually know when."

"I mean now. Soon. Are you dying?"

What could he tell his son? He felt like death in this moment, and cancer was crusading for that outcome in his body. He would be violently ill in the near future with treatment. "I don't know the answer to that."

"I have to go to school now. Uncle Niko said he would take me."

"It's Monday?"

"It's Tuesday, Daddy."

"Mommy's been taking care of me?"

David nodded. Whoa. That meant she wasn't going to work. He must be really sick.

"Where have you slept?"

"I sleep in Apolo's room. He has a bed in there, but he's too little for it yet."

"And Mommy?"

David pointed to a chair in the corner. "She sleeps there or on the sofa in the living room."

Must be serious. "Have a good day at school."

"Get better, Dad. I want you to teach me to play guitar."

"It'd be an honor to give you lessons." Johnny tried to smile, and his cracked lips added to his agony. He closed his eyes.

Soft hands caressed his forehead, and fingers drifted through his short stubble on his head. "Johnny. Come back to me, please?"

He wanted to, but his eyelids were too heavy. Coffee? Maybe a cup of Joe would help him wake up.

His stomach growled and threatened to expel its contents. A light touch on his back brought cooling relief, and he almost sighed in pleasure as every joint ached, and his muscles, filled with lead, refused to respond. A soft scent permeated the foul air. So good. Katie. She had to be the one touching him. He longed to hold her. Kiss her and let her know how good her touch was to his tortured body. Darkness enveloped him. *Katie*...his heart cried out in vain.

Soft guitar music played. Finger picking. Niko. Only Niko played with that unique style. He pried open one eye and saw his best friend and cousin sitting in the chair next to the bed.

"Hey," he croaked out.

"Getting tired of you lazing about like this, dude," Niko said softly, concern lacing his words.

"Am I sick?"

"Very. I don't think you were even this sick when we were on tour."

"Can't be sick. Getting married."

"Yup. In a little over a week."

" —need—house."

"You need a house?"

"Married. Need practice space."

"Why don't you wait until after your transplant to worry about a house?"

"Katie deserves a house."

"She needs a husband who's well enough to walk down the aisle."

"How sick?"

"We've considered calling an ambulance several times."

"Stinks in here."

"Vomit and sweat will do that. I'll help you get a

shower if you think you can manage it. Tia will strip and change your bed."

"So weak."

"Not surprising. You've not eaten in days, and getting fluids into you has been a challenge."

Johnny tried to roll to his back and lay there gasping. He realized he was only wearing his pajama bottoms. He struggled to sit up, and Niko set his guitar down. The world rocked back and forth. "Let's do this."

"You sure? You don't look too good."

"I stink."

"Yes, you do."

"Help me, Niko?"

His friend grinned. "Anything for you." Niko half-dragged Johnny to the bathroom and helped him get in the shower, standing guard lest he topple. Johnny's minute burst of energy traveled down the drain with the soapy water. After fresh clothes and the liberal use of deodorant, he was almost ready for a return to humanity. Niko helped him back to the bedroom and the freshly made bed. The entire room had a crisp, clean scent.

"How'd she do that?"

"I don't know. Tia's a miracle worker."

"Where's Katie?"

"She had some errands to run."

"She'll be back?"

"Yes. She hasn't abandoned you. She's barely left your side, and David's been really worried too."

"OK." Johnny rolled to his side and hugged the pillow. "Thanks, Niko."

"Get well, Johnny."

"Tryin…"

"Try harder, will ya?"

16

Think not on what you lack as much as what you have.
Greek proverb

Katie picked up her last paycheck. She couldn't keep a job when she was rarely there. Johnny said she didn't need to work, and right now, she had enough money to survive for a short time if she needed to…if…

Don't go there. Johnny will be fine. With a deep sigh, she walked into the bridal shop Tia recommended. She was so new to the area that Tia was her only friend so far. She hadn't had time to connect and make new friends over the years. School, working, and taking care of David had consumed her life.

Who was Katherine Bailey? Mother. Nurse. Dutiful daughter. There had to be more, but she couldn't find it. No hobbies. No friends. No favorite movies. She was vanilla. Boring and plain. "Can I help you?" The woman's nametag said "Leah."

"Yes, I'm getting married next week and need a simple wedding dress," Katie stated.

"Long or short?"

"I'm not picky."

"Lace, beading, tulle?"

Katie shook her head. "No clue."

"Let's go look at some of the racks and see what catches your eye."

Leah walked Katie through trying on several dresses. Katie knew she wasn't a skinny-minny. She never had been, but that had never mattered to Johnny. He had always said he loved her curves—that she looked like a woman should. Her parents had never been happy, though. She had worn nurse's uniforms. She preferred darker colors for her regular clothes because they were more flattering to her figure. And white? It was obvious she wasn't a virgin.

She finally decided to expand her search outside the traditional and found a sweetheart neckline bodice in a deep rose with a flared skirt that swished and swayed. Embroidery in a light green gave the illusion of vines, and the sleeves were long with lace. The mid-calf length dress and a pair of simple heels added elegance. Imagining Johnny next to her in his charcoal gray suit made her heart flutter. *Get well, Johnny.* The dress fit, and she purchased it on the spot and left with it and the shoes to match.

She ran home to put it in her closet.

Katie skipped back down the steps. She yawned as she slid into the driver's seat and sat there for a few minutes. She lost her job. Her fiancé was seriously ill. She was getting married. Had she really just volunteered to be his personal nurse? What did she get out of this?

A home. A family. Someone who loves you just the way you are. Stop trying to think like your mother.

Mother. She hadn't visited her parents since her mother had run away.

~*~

"Hi, Mom," Katie said as she sat in a chair across

from her mother in the day room. Her mother's hair was meticulously combed, and her eyes darted around. She leaned over. "Where's that nice young man?"

"Johnny?"

"Yes."

"He's been really sick. He will hopefully be here to visit you soon."

"Don't blink."

"Mom?"

"There's an angel statue in the far edge of the garden. I stay away from there. Tell him. Don't blink."

Katie stifled a giggle. "OK. How's dad?"

Mercy Bailey shrugged. "He doesn't talk to me, so I leave him alone."

"He can't talk. He had a stroke."

"Something very strange is happening here."

"I agree. I'm going to talk to Dad for a few minutes."

"Don't forget to tell the Doctor. Don't blink."

"Got it. I'll remember."

Katie walked around the other edge of the curtain to where her father rested. His eyes flickered open.

"Hey, Dad. I'm sorry I haven't been able to come and visit. A friend has been sick. I also wanted to tell you I'm getting married next week to a wonderful man. I hope you'll be happy for me. I'll be taken care of and loved."

A tear leaked out of one of his eyes.

"I didn't mean to make you cry." She reached down and squeezed his hand, and he weakly squeezed back. She gave him a kiss on the cheek. "I love you. I'll be back to visit you soon. Maybe I'll bring David next time."

She walked out of the complex to her car. *Why do I*

try so hard to win their favor? Even now she wanted their validation, but it had never happened. They were not capable of giving her that now.

Maybe they never were.

She arrived back at the house to find David sitting with a guitar in his lap and Niko guiding him on finger placement. Sadness pricked her. Johnny was supposed to do that with their son. She wanted to rush over and tell them to stop. Let Johnny have that opportunity. But David was content and focused intently on the strings, and she didn't have the heart to end it. She walked over to Johnny's room, and with a slight rap on the door, pushed it open.

Her eyes grew wide as she surveyed the scene. The wretched stink was gone, and in its place was the scent of clean linen and springtime. Johnny had shaved and was wearing a fresh T-shirt and pajama bottoms. A lazy smile curved his lips, and his gaze followed her to the chair.

"I missed you," he croaked.

"You woke up."

"Barely. A dream."

"I'm glad I can be the focus of a dream. I hope it's a good one."

"I dreamt you agreed to marry me and the ceremony is only a week away."

"Yeah. We need to get to the courthouse soon. We don't have much time."

"Let's see how I feel tomorrow."

"Only if Niko comes to help you."

"I'm not that weak."

"Right. And you skipped into the shower on your own and made the bed too."

"Fine. I'm a noodle right now."

"I like pasta."

"I did take you out for Italian, didn't I?"

"Yes. It was lovely."

"Where were you?"

"Ran some errands. Stopped to visit my mom. She told me to let you know there is a statue of an angel out in the far garden and...don't blink."

"I didn't think she would remember any of that."

"Well, she remembered the Doctor when she can't recognize her own daughter."

"I'm sorry."

Katie shrugged and ran her fingers through her hair to push her long bangs out of her face. "My dad doesn't seem to be doing well. I'm a horrible daughter to leave him."

"You can't do everything. I think you and David need to go home tonight and get some sleep. You can return to work tomorrow."

"I lost my job."

"Because you were caring for me?"

"Yup."

"I wish I could say I'm sorry. I hoped you would quit so we could have some good times together before I get sick."

Her eyebrow rose. "Oh, and what have the past few days been? Practice?"

"I hope none of you get it."

"Me too."

"Thanks for taking good care of me."

"I had some help. Niko and Tia have been wonderful."

"I'm glad you like them. They're really important to me."

"I can understand why."

"Sleepy."

"Get some rest. Maybe I will go home tonight."

"Before you leave, I wrote you a letter."

Katie turned to take the folded note off the dresser. "I look forward to reading it."

"I look forward to marrying you."

"We have much to talk about."

Johnny yawned. "Not tonight dear. I have a headache."

Katie leaned over to kiss his cheek and swatted his butt partially buried under the blankets. His chuckle was the last thing she heard as she headed out the door.

~*~

Her phone rang as she drove home. It was her brother, Ken. "Hey, Ken."

"You're not really going through with this wedding, are you?"

"I am. I love Johnny, and David needs his father."

"You might be forfeiting your inheritance."

"I'm not going to have my future held hostage anymore by our parents."

"They acted out of love for you."

"No. They acted out of a need for control and to have everything perfect. I never measured up. The only time I defied them was in keeping David instead of giving him up for adoption."

"They told everyone you adopted because you loved kids so much."

"I really don't care what they told people."

"You should."

"Why can't you just support me in this?"

"Because he's a musician, that's why."

"Do you know anything about Johnny Marshall?"

"He's Greek, divorced, plays guitar, flirts with women, and gallivants all over the world."

"He was vindicated in that scandal. He saved the life of my son twice. He has more talent in his pinky finger than you do in your entire body. The man is a phenomenal artist, and he makes money doing it."

"And he has cancer. Katie, he might leave you a widow soon."

"I'd rather have one day with him than none at all."

"I won't be there to see you destroy your life."

"That's your choice, Ken."

The line went dead. Katie struggled to contain her emotions until she got inside. She settled David in front of the laptop to watch a video, locked herself in the bathroom, and cried.

~*~

That night, Katie collapsed onto her bed. The apartment was quiet. In a week, Johnny would share this bed with her. He'd bump into her in the tiny kitchen. He'd have no place to sit in the living room. Her heart sank. So many things to accomplish to prepare for their life together. He'd need a dresser, and she'd have to share her closet…

But he'd be here. Her mom was gone to another place and didn't even recognize her anymore. Her father was stuck in silence, holding onto life by a thread. Her brother had practically disowned her.

She flipped on the bedside lamp and unfolded the paper Johnny had left her.

Dearest Katie,

My letters burned in the fire and I realize you read the first horrible poem I originally sent. This is one I wrote after seeing you again.

Lost. Alone. Without You
No one to call my home.
God's grace, ever perfect,
But not I, for I lost my best friend and soul-mate
My past haunts me with mistakes made
All my longings buried in the aftermath
Because you weren't there
Abandoned by you but not by God
Thankful but lonely
My heart lingers and longs for things I can never have
A family of my own to see me through the pain
The struggle of life
I wander alone, without you
Could you ever see a way to a past love?
To overlooking my mistakes?
To see the man who adores you?
To give me what you once withheld?
Your heart could heal mine
Restore me to life and give me hope
And reason to go on.

I am beyond selfish in wanting you for my wife. I gain everything but what do you get? My love doesn't seem like a sufficient enough prize for the difficult challenges that lie ahead. I want you to understand that I am very aware of the imbalance and I hope you never regret taking a chance on us.

Forever yours,
Johnny

Katie slowly folded the letter, set it on the nightstand, and flicked off the light. What did she get?

A husband who adored her. A complete family. A father for David. A partner in parenting. A purpose. The opportunity to be a mom in ways she never could before. Comfort. Companionship.

No, Johnny. I'm the one who is being blessed.

~*~

Katie stayed with Johnny on Sunday morning while Niko and Tia took David with them to church. Johnny had wanted to go, but they had all fought him. He was still too weak.

Once they were alone, Katie prepared his toast and brought it to him at the table. "You sure you don't want some eggs? I can make them sunny side up or down, scrambled, or even an omelet."

"No. You can go ahead and make your own, but I'm not a huge fan of eggs. I know the protein would be good, but toast is fine for now." He picked up the coffee cup and inhaled. "Tia's flavor of the day. Let me guess—Highlander Grogg?"

Katie laughed. "You're good." She was at the stove making her eggs. Arms snaked around her waist from behind, and a raspy beard tickled her cheek.

"You are wonderful." He nuzzled her neck. She finished her eggs, placed them on the plate, and turned off the burner. Everything inside of her sizzled. She rotated in his arms, placed hers around his neck, and drew him in for a kiss.

"Hmm. Johnny, you taste good." She licked at his lips, and he captured her mouth again in a possessive kiss that seemed to go on forever. She finally slipped her hands between their bodies to gently push him back. "My eggs are getting cold."

He chuckled and walked back to the table. She noted his stocking feet. No wonder he had been so quiet in sneaking up on her.

"Tomorrow we'll go get the license," Johnny said. "When we finish here, I'd like to talk to you about where we'll live."

"I thought you'd move into my apartment."

"Temporarily that might work, but it's not a good long-term option."

"After you're done with treatment…"

"No. You deserve a place now. And I need a space to work too."

"So, what were you thinking?"

"Buying a house."

"I'm not employed, and you're not working. How are we going to afford a mortgage payment?"

"Same way we make a rent payment. I have a residual income and more money coming in. I think we can do this and stay solvent."

Katie finished her food and picked up the plates. Johnny went to his room and returned with his laptop. He settled down on the loveseat and patted the cushion next to him. "Come on. Let's at least peek, OK?"

Katie talked with him as they looked at various homes for sale. He really wanted to stick close to Menomonee Falls to be close to his family and Niko. They found a few possibilities and sent some emails to his cousin who was a realtor to ask if it was possible to arrange a time soon to see the properties.

Johnny yawned, set the computer aside, and wrapped an arm around her.

"You should really lie down."

"David will be back soon."

"You need to sleep."

"I need to be with my fiancée."

Katie snuggled into his shoulder. "I need to be with you too. By the way, I loved your letter."

He kissed the top of her head. "I love you."

Katie closed her eyes. Inhaled the scent of soap and something that was just Johnny. Yup. She was one blessed woman.

~*~

Johnny awoke Monday morning and stretched. He had slept most of yesterday after Katie and David left. Something about laundry...

Five days. Friday afternoon, Katie would be his. His parents would watch David for the weekend.

Every day that passed, Johnny grew stronger. He sat in the basement for hours while Katie shopped. They had toured several houses and finally extended an offer on one the day before the wedding.

Friday morning, Johnny rose early and wrote another letter to his bride-to-be. He had purchased a special card to put it in. He showered, shaved, and dressed in his expensive suit. Niko met him in the kitchen.

"Ready for today?" Niko asked as he took his coffee mug to the table.

Johnny had eaten earlier and grabbed his own coffee. "I think so. I'm eager to get this over with."

"Why?"

"I'm afraid she'll change her mind."

"And run away like she did before?"

"Yeah. I don't know that I could survive that."

Johnny's cell phone rang. "Yeah, Katie, is

everything OK?"

Her voice choked on the other end. "Daddy died this morning."

Johnny sat down. 'Oh, baby, I'm so sorry. What do you want to do?"

"I want to marry you, Johnny. Kenny has threatened to disown me for going through with the wedding, and he hurled more threats at me this morning if I fail to meet him at the funeral home at noon."

"We could go over there after the ceremony and return for the reception. People will wait for us."

"He said if I come as Mrs. Johnny Marshall, I might as well stay away."

"What do you want, Katie?"

"I want to marry you."

"We could postpone the wedding." Johnny looked over to Niko. His cousin set his coffee down and listened.

"No. I've waited over seven years to do this. I'm not letting my parents, or my brother, dictate to me now."

"If you're sure."

"I love you, Johnny. Please be at the church."

"I wouldn't miss marrying you for anything. I'll see you soon. I love you."

"I love you too," she whispered and ended with a kiss before hanging up.

Johnny stared at the phone.

"Who died?"

"Her father. He had a terrible stroke the night of the fire and never really recovered."

Niko nodded. "I'm sorry."

"Yeah. Her brother's trying to coerce her into

standing me up for money."

"He has no idea, does he?"

"Of what I'm actually worth? No. Neither does Katie...yet."

"That'll be a nice gift."

"She was concerned about a mortgage. She doesn't realize I can pay cash for that house. I won't, but the down payment will make our monthly costs pretty low."

"Let me grab my guitar, and we can be off."

"I'm eager to get there."

Niko grinned. "I remember being that way with Tia."

"I'm glad she can help Katie and that my parents are keeping David for a few days."

"Apolo is going to be so spoiled by my parents by the time we get him back."

Johnny grabbed his suitcase and guitar and tossed it in the trunk for the honeymoon.

~*~

Tia rushed into the room. "Katie. Niko and Johnny are here. David is with them. Johnny wanted me to give this to you." She handed over the envelope. "Do you want to be alone?"

Katie caressed the letter as she sat in the rocking chair in the classroom they had appropriated. "Yeah, if I could."

Tia smiled. "Love letters are special and best read in private."

Katie waited until the door closed. She traced the script on the front. Johnny's unique brand of half-writing, half-printing. Still, there was something beautiful in his penmanship even if it wasn't textbook. She opened the card and read the words of love. Inside was a handwritten note on a separate page. She unfolded it.

Dearest Katie,

If God is smiling on me, I will soon be able to claim you as my lovely bride. My wife. My forever love. I've waited over seven years for this opportunity and I can hardly believe the day is here. It's like a beautiful dream and I'm afraid to wake up to find it dissipate like mist in the light of the sun.

You have brought hope and a future to me that I thought was lost forever. The future includes challenges and uncertainty but I want you to know one thing I am sure of. I love you and have since our first date in tenth grade.

I love you. I love you. Don't ever forget that God loves you more. I'm thrilled to become your husband today and I will do my best to cherish you for as long as God allows.

Forever yours,

Johnny

For as long as God allows.

Katie thought about the brevity of life. Her father was gone. Johnny seemed to have given up before she and David came into his life. Every day they delayed starting the chemo to prepare for the transplant was a day closer to death. She chuckled to herself. As if they had the power over that anyway. But they would move forward, encourage, and cheer him on to health. Within the next thirty minutes or so, she would gain the right to speak life and light into his journey. She would have a home. She would have love. *Lord, allow us a long time. Please...*

There was a knock at the door. "Katie?"

"You can come in, Tia." Katie rose and went to check her makeup. She dabbed at some of her moist mascara.

"They are ready and waiting for us." Tia handed her the bouquet of blush pink roses.

"I can't believe I'm really doing this. Following through on my heart's dream. God led me to this place, but I'm still amazed to be here."

"Let's go make that dream a reality." Tia gave Katie a hug, and they left to meet her groom.

17

There is no remedy for love, but to love more.

Henry David Thoreau

Johnny stood at the front of the café area, where they had chosen to have their ceremony. For a small wedding, the place teemed with people. All the Specific Gravity members had come, including Sam from Nashville along with his family and Niko's family. Johnny's legs quivered. He wanted to think it was because he still wasn't one hundred percent recovered from his virus.

"You holdin' up OK?" Niko whispered. He stood up as his best man. He wore his guitar hanging around his neck, waiting to play the processional.

Johnny nodded. *Where is Katie? Had she changed her mind?*

Soft guitar picking caught his attention. Niko must have gotten the cue. Tia stepped into the doorway and made her way gracefully down the aisle in a soft pink dress. She stood on the opposite side of the aisle, but Johnny didn't miss the wink she gave Niko. He hoped to be that disgustingly in love as a married couple.

He gasped as Katie stood in the doorway. She had warned him her dress was unique, and it was. The pretty deep pink with a brighter pink bow falling past her knees, the skirt swished and swayed with every step. The light green embroidery caught his eye. She knew it was his favorite color. David held her hand. He looked handsome in a charcoal-gray suit that matched Johnny's. He had a solemn look on his face even though Johnny was sure their son was as excited about this day as he was. Johnny grinned at him, and the little man cracked a smile.

Katie stood before him, and David went to stand by Tia. Johnny was so entranced by the beauty before him that he barely heard a word Pastor Andrew spoke. He was aware enough to repeat his vows and was thrilled to hear Katie pledge hers. He slid her ring over her finger, and she reciprocated with a ring he had waited over seven years to wear. And then the moment came.

"I pronounce you Mr. and Mrs. Jonathan Marshall." Andrew winked at him. "Johnny, you may kiss your bride."

Katie's arms flung around his neck and pulled his head down to hers before he could move to respond, and his arms found their way around her to hold her close for the kiss. They all heard David ask Tia, "Are they going to be doing a lot of this?"

They broke off the kiss with laughter. Johnny held out a hand. "Come here, son." David came over, and they both bent down to kiss his cheeks. The little boy blushed and tried to wipe the kisses off his cheek as the congregation laughed. Johnny walked Katie down the aisle with David holding her hand on the other side.

They took David off to the side.

"Honey, we wanted to give you a special gift," Katie said.

Johnny dropped to one knee before his son. "I hope you'll like this."

"What is it?" The little boy bounced.

Katie and Johnny grinned at each other.

"Just now, your mommy's last name changed from Baily to Marshall. Because you are my son as well as hers, your name is going to change too."

The little boy's eyes grew wide, and he sucked a deep breath before yelling, "Waa Hoo! Thank you, Daddy!" David wrapped his arms around his father's neck, almost tipping him over.

"I'm glad you're happy about that. We wanted it to be a surprise since we will be together as a family now." Katie ruffled her son's hair.

Johnny stood as soon as David released him. "What do you say, should we go eat some cake?"

"Lunch first, then cake." Katie admonished.

"Aww, Mom." Both Johnny and David whined in unison as laughter erupted around them.

Every chance he got, Johnny would grab Katie and kiss her.

The crowd moved to another room for a buffet luncheon. A photographer snapped a few posed photos before they joined the rest of the guests.

After eating and mixing with people for some time, Johnny pulled Katie to his side. "I'm done sharing you. Can we go now?"

"You sound like a little kid."

"I want to play with my new toy," he whined and made a sad pouty face.

Katie laughed and kissed his lips. "I long to get away with you too."

They found David hanging out with his grandparents. "Hey, buddy. We're going to leave now. But we'll be back in two days. You behave for Grandma and Grandpa, OK?"

"Yes, Daddy. I'm glad you get to come and live with us now."

"I am too." Katie added. Exchanging hugs and goodbyes with everyone took time, but soon they were out the door and on the road to Chicago.

"You looked absolutely beautiful today, Katie. Even more lovely than you were at eighteen."

"I'm glad I got to marry a man with a little bit of hair. You really can work a suit." Katie rotated in her seat to be partially facing him.

"How are you really doing?" Johnny asked.

"I'm sad that Ken wouldn't come and that he threatened me. I'm sad my daddy didn't get to see me married. He was more inclined to like you. He would have wanted me to be happy."

"Are you sad that your mother couldn't be there?"

"The entire thing would have confused her. I mean, the Doctor marrying some strange woman? She's half in love with you."

"Jealous?"

"A little."

"You know you don't have to be."

"I'm jealous of Donna too."

"Why?"

"Because she got three years of life with you when I was alone and missing you."

"Was that why you looked her up?"

"I wanted to see what she looked like."

"She isn't competition for you."

"Right. She's remarried and has kids now. But I still don't understand how she could have walked away from you."

"I'm no saint. I traveled a lot, and she refused to come with me. She had dreams of big money and wanted to hang on my arm at awards banquets. In the beginning, Specific Gravity wasn't as big a deal as she hoped, but maybe that's why she left too. I didn't give her the riches some artists acquire in the business. I've earned better money since then with some of my studio work."

"Christian music isn't known for making people wealthy."

"There are some who have done well for themselves, but I don't think they would describe themselves as wealthy. I've done OK. But tragedies hit all of us, whether we have a lot of mp3 downloads or not. Anyway, Donna is not a threat. I haven't seen hide nor hair of her in the past three years."

"I'm glad I can be yours alone."

"You are my first and my last love." Johnny sailed through the automated toll checkpoint with his I-PASS.

"So, can we really afford a house with me not working? You've been so sick, and with wedding preparations, we've not discussed it."

"I forgot to bring my financial reports with me. I didn't realize that was honeymoon fare. Katie, I have royalties coming in, and there's a slander lawsuit settled out of court that is paying up, but I'm not sure of the actual amount after my attorney is paid. Add that to my pay for studio work, and we should be fine for as long as it takes me to get well and back to work again."

He paused as he scanned the highway to change lanes for his exit. "I don't want you to feel that you have to be my personal nurse, either. If you want to work because it makes you happy, I'd support you in that. I'm sorry you lost your job because of me and that I wasn't in any position to ease your mind about all this."

"I think for right now, I will do what your ex-wife refused to do. I want to be there for you through this painful journey. If money becomes an issue, I'll go back to work, but Lord willing, we'll be fine."

"I'm sorry I can't give us more kids, Katie. You're a great mom."

"When we get through this, we could consider foster care or adoption."

The smile started deep in Johnny's gut and burst out upon his lips. "Really? You would want that?"

"Yes. Absolutely. I love being a mom, and if we have the resources and the love to share, why would we keep that to ourselves? We could start looking into the process while you're recovering. It might give you something to do to keep busy."

"To be honest, I'm probably going to be too sick to do much of anything."

"I realize that. My heart aches for what lies ahead for you."

"We can only hope for the best, right? I have more reason than ever to live and fight this. Niko's a match, which shouldn't surprise me. I'm closer to him than my own brothers."

"Both Niko and Tia have been so gracious in welcoming me, as have your parents."

"They love you because I do."

Katie blushed. "I hope they love me for myself too."

"How could they not?"

"I don't know. All these years, I've just done what everyone else wanted. Keeping David and marrying you were the only two choices I've ever really made for myself. Part of me wonders who I really am."

"I'm not sure I understand. You are smart. You're a great mom and a caring nurse. What more is there?"

"That's mostly stuff I do. I don't have hobbies. I don't have many friends. I don't even have a favorite food. But you, Johnny. You have a passion for kids and music, and you've traveled, and you love cinnamon toast for breakfast, and you pour out your heart beautifully in letters…"

"What do you want, Katie? Do you need encouragement to try some new things to see what you like? I'm OK with that. Cooking classes, quilting, missions…whatever your passion might be, I would want to support you in pursuing that."

"Thank you. I have no clue where to even start."

"We can pray about that and see what opens up. It is entirely possible your nursing is really just who you are, a compassionate woman who has a talent to comfort and serve those who are hurting physically. That's a wonderful gift. Mercy. You have mercy and offer hope and dignity."

"We'll pray. And maybe you're right. Still, it might be fun to try some new things too…or maybe we could try some things together."

"Like what?"

"Ballroom dancing?"

"Really?"

"Square dancing?"

"Katie…"

"Swing dancing." Katie giggled.

"Fine, tease me. You remember I have two left feet. Prom was a nightmare for your toes, and I haven't improved since, so I stay off the dance floor."

"I was teasing you. My toes remember homecoming and prom. Even when I tried to teach you a basic waltz, you couldn't manage it. Not sure how a musician could have trouble counting to three."

"I can count...I just couldn't get my legs to move in a box. Do you regret not having a dance for our wedding?"

"No. I loved the way everyone visited with each other. The laughter, the music, and just the fact that we had support for this journey."

"We do. I'm miffed at your brother, though. How dare he put you in that position?"

"He thinks he is acting as my father would. It's fine, really. Any inheritance will likely be eaten up by my mother's medical bills. I won't even get a payout for the belongings I lost in the fire."

"Why not?"

"My brother says since I didn't pay rent, I didn't deserve compensation."

"Providing care for your parents wasn't a fair trade to him?"

Katie shook her head. "No. But it really doesn't matter. God brought me back here and led me to you again, and I'm so glad he did." She ran a hand over his short hair.

Soon they were in downtown Chicago, parking and hauling their luggage to their hotel room.

Katie flopped on the bed.

"Tired?" Johnny asked.

"Very. The last few weeks have been exhausting."

"Why don't you snuggle in and take a nap? I'll just play around on my guitar if that won't bother you?"

"A nap sounds heavenly, especially to your guitar playing. We'll get dinner later?" She yawned and kicked off her shoes. She headed to the bathroom to change. Then she came back out and slipped under the covers. "Some newlywed I am, huh? I'm finally alone with my husband, and all I want is a pillow and a blanket."

"I'm not complaining. We still have tonight."

"Oh, wait. I almost forgot." She reached into her bag and pulled out an envelope. "This is for you." She placed it on the table near his chair and leaned over for a kiss. "Hmm. Tempting, but maybe later." She crawled back into the bed.

Johnny closed the blinds and grabbed the envelope and his acoustic guitar to go sit in the living room area of their suite.

He sat and tapped the envelope. All this time, he had been the one writing letters, and now he received one. He had waited over seven years for this. He slit open the envelope and pulled out the card. It was a cute card declaring her love for him. Inside was a folded piece of paper. He took it out and unfolded it.

Dearest Johnny,

I'm too many years behind in writing to you, but since you were so faithful, I figure I owed you a letter.

I want you to know I always loved you. Even when I had submitted to my parents' authority. Even as I gave birth alone. I held David in my arms and longed for you to be there to share that moment. To rejoice in our perfect little boy.

I see so much of you in him and I drew comfort from that. I had a little bit of you in my life. It wasn't you but it was something.

I admired you years before you ever asked me out. You were so swoon-worthy. I was the envy of many girls in our class. And you always treated me like a lady. You're even more swoon-worthy now and I can hardly believe you love me too.

I was beyond shocked when I realized it was you who had thrown yourself between a car and the son you didn't even know you had. Then you walked into the clinic and my suspicions were confirmed. Johnny Marshall was back in my life. A long-lost love. A hero. The champion of our son's heart. You should know that of all the men David has met, you are the first he has ever connected with. The only one he ever talked about.

I'm so glad he gets to know his father and that you will be the one to speak truth into his life and show him what it is to be a man of God.

I'm thrilled beyond belief that I get to walk into the unknown future with you by my side. Yes, I know we have some dark days ahead of us, but I am hopeful. There will be an exit to the tunnel we will enter, and when we emerge into the sunshine of the other side, there will no longer be the specter of cancer hovering over us.

But even so, I am honored you chose me to walk this path with you. I am grateful that God has given us this time together now. All the sweeter for the years we lost and the heartache we both endured.

I love you Johnny Bear.
Always and forever yours,
Katie

Johnny slowly refolded the letter, put it back in the card, and slid them both in the envelope. He tossed it in the guitar case under his acoustic. Closing the lid, he rose and went to change out of his suit. He spied his sleeping wife, slid under the covers next to her, and pulled her close.

She was hot. Her face was flushed, and she shivered as she sweated.

His wife, who had cared for him so faithfully, was now sick with what he had.

"Oh, Katie..." he whispered in her ear as he spooned her and drifted off to sleep.

~*~

Welcome to marriage. Katie rolled onto her back and heard a moan. Wait. Was that her? Where was Johnny? They were supposed to go to dinner. Right. Honeymoon.

The room was dark although streaks of light penetrated the space where the drapes didn't quite come together.

"*Shh...*" Johnny soothed as the bed dipped under his weight. "Here, try to drink this." He lifted her up at the shoulders and put a glass to her lips. She sipped the blessedly cool water and swallowed shards of glass.

She looked up at her sweet husband as he lowered her back to the bed. Her head throbbed.

"Sweetheart. I think we need to pack up and go home. You'll feel better in your own bed."

She tried to talk, but all that scratched out was, "Sorry."

He smiled. "You've nothing to apologize for. You cared for me, and now you're sick. It happens. Do you think you can handle the car ride home? I could buckle you in the back seat, where you might recline more on your side with a blanket and a pillow."

She shook her head. "Front...with you. Recline seat back."

"OK. I'll go get everything ready after we get you changed for the journey. Then we'll check out. Navy

Pier will have to await our exploration another day…maybe with David."

He helped her up to dress, and when she awoke next, she was buckled in the car as they headed north, back to Wisconsin and home.

Some honeymoon. She looked over at Johnny as he focused on navigating the traffic. He glanced at her and smiled. Some bride she turned out to be. Getting sick on their wedding night. She had so longed to satisfy her longing to be intimate with him…

When she awoke again, she was in her own bed. She heard movement in the kitchen. She tossed back the blankets and slid her feet to the carpeted floor, shivering as the cooler air hit her sweat-drenched pajamas. Had he changed her clothes? She shook her head with a sad smile and instantly regretted the action as a jackhammer went to work behind her forehead. She closed her eyes against the pain.

"Katie?" Johnny's hand was on her back.

"Bathroom." Her tongue was thick.

He put an arm around her and helped her to her feet. It was humiliating that he had to help her to use the toilet. Without complaint, he took care of her with efficiency. Before she realized it, she was back in bed. Toasty warm and with a sweet kiss to her hair, she heard, "Rest. Heal. I'm here."

~*~

Katie had no idea what day it was. She stretched, and even though weakness infused her bones, she was finally free of her headache and fever. The room was dark. She rolled over, and her eyes adjusted. Johnny was asleep on his back next to her. He slept on top of the covers with a fleece blanket thrown over him. He still wore his jeans and socks and a thermal-knit long-sleeved shirt. One arm rested across his chest on top of the blanket.

Why had he not climbed in with her? She noted the growth of a beard. Funny how that hair grew so much faster than the stuff on his head. Dark and scruffy.

And he was hers.

She snuggled up to him, moving his arm around her as she cozied up to his side. Her hand rested on his chest, and she listened to the steady thump, thump, thump of his heart.

His arm squeezed her tight, and his other arm wrapped around her. A kiss landed on her hair.

"Hey, sweetie. How're you feeling?"

"Better, but weak." She tilted her head back to gaze up at him. "How come you're fully dressed and not even under the covers?"

He cleared his throat. Was that a blush coloring his cheeks?

"I returned from taking David to school and didn't want to disturb you. Besides, we've not, um…"

"Consummated our marriage?"

"Yeah. I didn't want to make you uncomfortable."

"I don't think that would have happened, but it was sweet of you to be so considerate."

His head moved toward her. He obviously intended to kiss her. She pulled back, escaping his embrace.

"What?" he asked.

"I need to brush my teeth." She jumped out of bed and headed into the bathroom.

"Katie?" Johnny knocked on the bathroom door.

"What?"

"I have some towels fresh from the dryer for you."

She opened the door to take them, and he pulled her to him and kissed her lips. As he pulled back, he grinned.

"Bad breath or not, I still love you." Johnny winked at her and let her close the door.

18

*Having cancer gave me membership in an elite club
I'd rather not belong to.*
Gilda Radner

May 2014

The sale of the house went through, and the next Saturday, Johnny, Katie, and some friends painted and prepared their new space to move into. Sunday afternoon, what few belongings Katie had were moved out of their apartment, and Johnny's few items were brought in.

Pizza containers filled the table as Niko and Tia sat with them after everyone else was gone. The grandparents dropped off David, and he happily explored his new room.

"I'm still confused as to why you felt you needed a four-bedroom house?" Niko asked. "I mean I know you can't…"

Johnny shrugged. "After we get through with this cancer thing, we might consider foster care or adoption. And one room could be used if I need to sleep apart due to my treatment. Sometimes I can't sleep at night, and this way I won't disturb Katie."

"You are not sleeping in another bedroom." Katie frowned and shook her head. "Silly boy."

Johnny frowned. "We'll be talking."

"Sounds like we'll be fighting," Katie retorted.

"Well, um, perhaps we should head out. We need to pick up Apolo at his grandparents' house. Try to enjoy your new home?" Tia grabbed for Niko's hand.

Niko leaned toward Johnny. "Just remember, get through it fast. The making up is the best part."

"Niko," Tia warned. "We love you guys. Keep in touch and let us know if you need anything."

"Thank you," Katie said.

Johnny locked the doors and turned to his wife. "Are we going to fight?"

"I didn't marry you to sleep in separate rooms. In sickness and in health, Johnny."

"You don't understand what chemo is like. Sometimes I just can't sleep. I fidget, and sleeping in a different space, even on a sofa, helps. It's not just so I won't disturb you..." Johnny sighed. "I'm back at the clinic tomorrow. Blood work...and probably starting the pills."

Katie wrapped her arms around his waist. "It doesn't feel like we had enough time..."

"I agree. But maybe I won't be as sick as I suspect." He let his fingers glide through her silky brown hair. "As bad as I fear this will be, I'm worried about how it will affect you."

"I'm tougher than I look." Katie pressed her body to his.

"Yes, you are. But I would spare you any hardship if I could."

"There are so many things out of our control. We should enjoy this day. Tomorrow will come, but we don't need to be anxious now. That's a waste of time."

"Agreed. Let's get our little man to bed so we can enjoy what's left of the day...alone." He wiggled his eyebrows.

Katie reached up, placed a kiss on his lips, and lingered there. Johnny moaned. As she pulled back and away, he growled. "Girl, you don't know what you do to me."

Katie winked at him with a sly smile. "Oh, but I do…"

~*~

The next morning, Johnny dropped David off at school and headed to the clinic. He stepped inside and checked in before sitting down. A little girl with springy curls knelt at a low table, coloring.

"Hi, I'm Johnny. Are you here with someone?" He hadn't seen another adult.

"I'm Khloe with a K." Startling brown eyes looked up at him, and she brushed a curl off her forehead. "I'm by myself. I have cancer."

"I'm sorry to hear that, Khloe with a K. I have cancer too. You look like you're about my son's age. How old are you?"

"I'm six."

Johnny knelt down at the table. "Mind if I color with you?" He grabbed a piece of paper and a blue crayon.

She shrugged. "Nah, that's fine."

"You're six, have cancer, and are here alone. Why?"

"You're here alone."

"True, but I'm an adult."

She tilted her head as she considered him. "And you have a little boy. Are you a good daddy?"

Johnny gulped. "I hope I am."

"Good. Little kids need good mommies and daddies."

"Are you saying yours are not good?"

"Never knew my daddy. Mommy didn't either. She liked drugs more than me. I'm in my third foster home now."

"I'm sorry. Are your foster parents nice?"

"They're OK, but they're old and really don't like little girls to make any noise or ask questions."

"Why aren't they here with you?"

"My foster father dropped me off this morning and went to work. My foster mom is busy with other kids."

Johnny grabbed some other colors and continued to draw. The girl looked over at what had been a blank page.

"Who is that?" Khloe asked as she pointed to the drawing he had made.

"This is Princess Khloe, who is loved and adored by the King of the universe and is going to beat cancer and go on to live a wonderful life." He shoved the page toward her as her name was called. "I hope I get to see you again, Princess Khloe."

"Thank you, Prince Johnny." She skipped after the nurse holding her paper tightly to her chest.

Johnny pulled himself back up to a chair, his legs still stiff from kneeling on the floor. *Lord, a little girl all alone in the world. Please help her see how much You love her even when she feels all alone. Heal her, Jesus.*

They called his name, and he followed the nurse to his own appointment.

~*~

He came home with some preliminary medications. He changed and met Niko for a jog.

"Hey, things work out OK last night?" Niko asked.

"Yeah. Avoided a meltdown, but I'm sure it will come to a head at some point. Katie didn't work in oncology long enough to really understand what it's going to be like for me."

"What did she do before she moved back here?"

"She worked at a clinic for a general practitioner. She has such a soft heart, and I worry how she's going to cope with what's coming."

"We'll be there too."

"Thanks. Get all your stuff done in preparation for the transplant?"

"Yeah. How about you?"

"I'll be starting some chemo and possibly some radiation. Bye, bye, fuzzy head. For a while anyway."

"Scared?"

Johnny stopped to lean over and catch his breath. Niko stood nearby and sipped his water. Johnny looked up. "More than ever. I have so much more to lose this time around."

"You had a lot to lose last time too. And we helped you through."

"I never would have made it if it hadn't been for you and Tia."

Niko shook his head. "I can't believe I had been so clueless about how she had been helping you and how rude I'd been. We could have helped you more if I hadn't been so pig-headed."

"You're still pig-headed, Niko. Good thing she loved you all that time anyway."

"Unexpected blessings."

"Took you long enough to figure it out."

"I think she's still ticked that I read her journal."

"You told her I insisted you do it...but she finally figured out I peeked."

"I never pushed the blame on you."

"Niko, you were a good friend to keep that secret...but she figured out long after she could have poisoned me for it."

"Her cooking has come a long way."

"It has." Johnny gave his cousin a nod and took off again with him by his side.

"David's seventh birthday is this week. Not sure what to do. I've never bought my son a birthday gift before."

"I think you got him the best gift when you became his full-time daddy."

"Yeah. It scares me that I might not beat this disease."

"You'll beat it."

"You know what really ticks me off?"

"What?"

"I met a little girl, Khloe, this morning at the clinic. She has cancer. No parents. She was there alone, Niko. She is David's age, and she's alone as she battles cancer."

"Ouch."

"I sat and colored with her. I talked with the nurse, who wouldn't give me any information but was willing to schedule all my appointments when Khloe would be there. I just can't stand the thought of her not having someone there."

"Similar treatment?"

"Best I can tell."

"I'm glad she'll have you there. Maybe that's the reason God allowed this...so that Khloe wouldn't be alone at a scary time in her life."

"It's not enough."

"It's better than what she had this morning."

"Yeah. But it's still not enough. Would you join me in praying for her?"

"Sure. I'll ask Tia as well."

"Thanks. Something about this little girl tugs at me."

"I'm not surprised. You've always loved children."

"Yeah. And I had so looked forward to having a big family like our own parents had."

"Defying Greek tradition?"

"That part doesn't bother me. I don't care if it's tradition or not. It was just what I wanted."

"I know, just razzing you."

They had reached Niko's house, a block away from Johnny's new place. "Thanks for the run, and the chat."

"My pleasure. We both need to be ready for this."

"You know you're my hero, right?"

Niko frowned. "Why would that be?"

"You're a leader. A shepherd. I hope I can be at least half as effective in leading Katie and David as you were with Specific Gravity."

"You do remember we will tour again when you're through this."

"I hope so. I miss our adventures on the road."

"It'll be different with an extra wife and two children."

Johnny grinned. "Yeah, but how wonderful."

"Something to hold on to when you're feeling down."

"You know me too well."

"I was there last time, remember?"

"How could I forget? This time is likely to be worse."

"Don't scare yourself before you've even begun."

"One day at a time." Johnny sighed.

"And let tomorrow worry about itself." Niko strode up the driveway to his house. "See ya."

"Yeah. Have a good one, Niko. Love to Tia and Apolo."

Niko waved, and Johnny took off at a slow lope to home. The spring air chilled him with his sweat, and he stunk. He needed a shower.

~*~

Thursday came, and Johnny dropped David off at school with a container of sugar cookies. He was glad their school didn't get legalistic about treats like that. As long as they were nut-free, they were OK.

"Dad?"

"Yeah, son?"

"What are we doing for my birthday?"

"That's a surprise. Was there something special you wanted?" Johnny was curious.

David smiled. "You. I had prayed for a daddy for my birthday, and God answered. When I met you, I asked him to let you be my daddy."

"I gave up hoping for a son, David, but you are that and more. I love you. I'm glad God answered your prayer."

"Me too." David leaned over the front seat and planted a kiss on Johnny's cheek. "Have a good morning at chemo. Say 'hi' to Khloe for me."

Johnny watched his son run to meet with

classmates as the bell rang, and they filtered into school. He had been amazed at David's soft heart for a young girl he hadn't met. The first night he had told Katie and David about Khloe, they began to pray diligently that God would give Khloe a family to help her.

Later, he picked up David and took him home. They collected Katie along with several wrapped packages and headed over to his parents' home. Soon the house filled with kids and adults alike.

Johnny was already experiencing the side effects of the chemo. He had had radiation today as well. He had to wear a mask now just to be with his family, but it was worth it to see David laughing and giggling as he ran wild with his cousins. Maybe someday, he'd be as close to one of them as Johnny was with Niko. He prayed his son would be blessed with a friendship like that.

After a dinner of hot dogs, bratwurst, and hamburgers, everyone sang to David and he blew out candles. With ice-cream cake devoured, he eagerly ripped into package after package of presents. Finally, he got to Johnny and Katie's.

He opened the card and read it. "It's from Mommy and Daddy." He opened up the smaller of two packages, peeled back the wrapping, and stopped. His mouth dropped open, and he glanced up at Johnny, moisture in his eyes. He leapt onto Johnny's lap and wrapped his arms around his neck, the gift still in his hands. David sobbed, and Johnny settled him in his lap.

"Why the tears, David?"

The little boy stared at the colorful frame that contained a photo from the wedding of Johnny, Katie, and David. The frame said "my family."

"God answered my prayers."

Johnny hugged him close and whispered in his son's ears, "He answered mine too. Ones I thought were impossible. You have one more gift to open, and then we're going to have to go home and get ready for bed. You still have school tomorrow."

David nodded and swiped his eyes with his sleeve. "Thank you, Daddy." He climbed off Johnny's lap and set about unwrapping the next package. The room gasped as he opened it up and revealed an acoustic guitar in a hard case. David beamed as he lifted it out and began to strum.

"You told me you wanted me to teach you how to play. I figured you should have your own guitar if we're going to be giving you lessons. Uncle Niko promised to help when I'm in the hospital."

David leapt into his father's arms again and planted kisses over the part of his face not covered by the mask. "You're the bestest daddy ever!"

"I'll remind you of that in a few years when you're angry at me for grounding you."

"What's grounding?"

"We'll worry about that later. Let's get your stuff and head home. Make sure to thank everyone, son."

Katie snuggled close as they watched David flit from one cousin and uncle or aunt to another and finally give Grandma and Grandpa big hugs and kisses. Johnny helped get all the presents to the car and soon followed with a sleepy little boy.

As they tucked him in that night, David prayed, "God, thank You for my mommy and daddy and for making us a family. Please let Khloe have a family just like ours. She really needs someone to love her and show her who You are."

~*~

Every day that week, Johnny bumped into Khloe at the clinic. They sat in a room together and watched cartoons. Or played Trouble. Or Uno. Johnny found out she was an avid reader and challenged her to hangman.

"Brutal game, isn't it, Khloe?"

"Why do we have to kill him?"

"I'm not sure," Johnny answered honestly. "Maybe we should play something else."

She tilted her head his way. "I like you."

"Thanks. I like you too. Do you miss school?"

She shrugged. "Yeah, but they said that my body won't handle infections, so I can't go right now. I do homework by myself at home, and it gets dropped off at school. Classes will be out in a few weeks, and I'll have had my transplant by then."

"Me too. Kind of a bummer that we'll both be dealing with this just as the weather finally gets warm."

Khloe brightened up. "Yeah, but if a mosquito bites me, I bet there's enough poison in me to kill it."

"I hope so." Johnny laughed. It was Friday. "Hey, we're almost out of here soon, and I probably won't get to see you for two whole days. I brought you something." He handed her a gift bag.

"For me?"

"Yes. From me, my wife, and our son, David."

Khloe pulled out the tissue paper. Inside the bag was a plush teddy bear wearing a gold necklace with the letters of her name. "Can I put this on?"

"It's yours. Would you like me to help you?"

She nodded, and he unclasped the necklace from around the bear and put it around Khloe's neck. Above her name was a little crown.

"We want you to remember that you are God's princess. And the bear is to hug and hold whenever you feel lonely. So you can remember that someone is praying for you."

"You are?"

"We all are."

"Who's all?"

"My family and some friends."

Her voice held a hushed awe, and tears filled her eyes. "I've never had a present before. Thank you."

Johnny wiped a tear away from her cheek. "It's all right, sweetheart. God stores every one of those tears, and He knows your dreams and desires, and He delights in you."

"Then why did He take my mommy and daddy away and give me cancer?"

"I don't know, but maybe He has something better in store."

"Maybe."

The nurse came in. "Come on, Khloe, it's time to head out. Your ride is here."

Khloe looked back at Johnny, and he read the longing in her eyes. He wouldn't encourage a hug at this point, although he suspected she really could use one. He was afraid he'd be seen as a predator. He gave her hand a squeeze instead. God knew he had no designs on the girl...but she had quickly wormed her way into his heart, and he wondered if he would ever recover if he had to walk away from her when this was over.

19

*Love is not an affectionate feeling
but a steady wish for the loved person's
intrinsic good as far as it can be obtained.*
C.S. Lewis

Johnny insisted she sit down with Roberto Rodriquez, and Tia also highly recommended him. Katie had seen him in church with his wife and young son.

She sat in the outer offices at the law firm and fidgeted with her purse strap. A petite secretary came to call her. "Mrs. Marshall?"

Katie rose.

"Follow me. Mr. Rodriquez is ready to meet with you now." The woman led her down the hall to a side office. She opened the door and stepped back to let her in. "Can I get you something to drink? Water, coffee, tea, a soda?"

"Water would be nice. Thank you." Katie turned to look at Roberto, who motioned her to a chair across from his desk. To one side was a large window and a view of trees outside and a busy birdfeeder.

She sat, and before they could begin, the door swung open again. A bottle of ice-cold water was set before her and Robbie's coffee mug refilled. "Thank you, Shelby," Roberto said as the woman nodded and departed.

"I keep telling her I can take care of that stuff, but she's an intern and eager to serve." He grabbed a pen and legal pad. "You intrigued me with why you were coming in today. I've worked with your husband on a variety of issues. What can I help you with?"

"Well, you know Johnny is undergoing cancer treatment."

Roberto nodded. "We've been praying for him daily."

"Thank you. While the outcome is hopeful, it is in no way guaranteed."

"Not much in this world is."

Katie smiled. "True. Well, the thing is, Johnny loves kids, and so do I. Due to his previous cancer, we are unable to have any more children. So, we were considering foster care as possibly a path to adoption."

Robbie's eyebrow rose. "Interesting. Most people jump to seeking adoption, usually of an infant. Foster care opens you up to children of many ages and backgrounds."

"The agency might be more willing to accept us in spite of Johnny's cancer treatments."

"Once you've come out the other end. You certainly don't need to add foster care on top of all you have going on."

"Well…normally we wouldn't, but…"

"What is the child's name?" Robbie winked.

"How'd you guess?"

"Because I've known Johnny long enough to understand how much he adores kids and how they gravitate to him. He'd have made a great grade school teacher if he hadn't pursued music, which, fortunately for him, has been profitable."

"There's a little girl, six years old. Her name is Khloe, and she's undergoing cancer treatment. She's in the system but pretty much abandoned in her treatment. No one comes with her. Johnny's taken her under his wing, schedules his appointments to coincide with hers, and plays with her. We've been praying for her too."

Robbie scratched his head. "I'm not sure what I can do for you. Foster care has a process they go through, and you have to submit an application and possibly a home study. They are desperate for foster parents, so why don't you try? Are her parents around at all?"

"No. From what I can tell, she would be adoptable."

"Well, that's in your favor. A kid that age with cancer is not a highly adoptable kid. What do you want me to do?"

"Can you help us with the adoption?"

"I'm not sure you can jump to that right away. Talk to the Case Manager for the girl and see what you can discover. That is the person, along with the *guardian-ad-litum*, who advocates before a judge for the best placement of a child. But when it comes to representing you, I would be glad to help."

"Thank you."

"Is that all? Johnny had mentioned that there were some legal shenanigans done by your brother with your parents' insurance payout for the fire, along with a trust fund for you?"

Katie shrugged. "Apparently, there were funds held in trust for me to be released upon my marriage or at my thirtieth birthday, whichever came first. As Power of Attorney, he refused to release the funds if I married Johnny."

"Unless the terms are written up excluding someone specific, I'm not sure that's legal. Would you like me to look into that for you? We could possibly get you the money your parents designated for you."

Katie's shoulders drooped. "My parents always used money to manipulate me, and now my brother has tried it as well. My father died the morning of the wedding, and Ken forbade me to come to the funeral because of my marriage. I got really sick, so it was a moot point."

"I'm glad you're better. I'm sure your parents loved you, even if they struggled to show it in a healthy way. Maybe the trust was one of those ways."

"Go ahead and investigate. Let me know if there's any action we can take."

"Will do." Robbie took down the pertinent information.

After they had finished, Katie rose to leave. "Thank you, Mr. Rodriguez."

He thrust a hand out. "Robbie. Please. Or Roberto if you must."

"Robbie. Thanks. And you can call me Katie."

"We'll see you at church. Tell Johnny I said 'hi.'"

"I will."

~*~

Katie picked up groceries, focusing on organic fruits and vegetables to help Johnny stay healthy. He still loved his cinnamon toast in the morning but was already struggling to eat as much of it with the nausea that accompanied the medication he took. She unloaded the groceries at home and heard music coming from the basement. Johnny usually left for a jog at this time of day. Maybe he'd gone and returned already?

She headed down the stairs to his little music studio, where he hoped Specific Gravity would resume practice sessions after he was well again. She watched him from the foot of the stairs as his fingers flew over the strings making intricate melodies as he hummed along.

He paused and looked up, finally noticing her presence leaning against the wall. "Hey, Katie. How'd your meeting with Robbie go?"

"He's looking into some things and gave me steps to take."

"For what?"

"For possibly adopting Khloe."

Johnny set down the guitar. "You haven't even met her. You never said you wanted to adopt her."

"You don't want that? I figured with the way you and David had been praying for her every meal and at night, that your heart leaned toward..."

He held up a hand. "It's my fondest dream, but I have never considered pursuing it now."

"Why?"

"Duh. Cancer?"

"And that precludes you from loving and nurturing a lost little girl who desperately needs a family to support her through and beyond her battle with cancer?"

"You would take that on?"

"Why wouldn't I? It's the desire of your heart, and having this little girl to care for and focus on has helped you tremendously. I think you both are a blessing to each other more than you realize. I just want to explore if it could be a more permanent thing, for all our sakes."

Johnny rose and strode across the room to her, placing his hands on her shoulders as she stood away from the wall, facing him and placing her hands on his waist. "Have I told you lately that I loved you?"

Katie smiled. "Yes. You did. But you need to show me more." She wiggled her eyebrows.

"We're all alone."

She nodded and smiled.

"It's the middle of the day."

"So?"

"Niko is coming over in an hour."

"I didn't think you were that slow."

Johnny growled, and Katie giggled. She broke free and ran up the stairs with Johnny hot on her heels.

Afternoon delight, indeed.

~*~

Katie accompanied Johnny the next day to his appointment, as he wasn't feeling well enough to drive himself and she was eager to meet the sweet girl who had captured his heart.

She was terrified of falling in love with the child. What if she fell in love with the little girl, but they weren't able to adopt? Or worse yet, what if Khloe didn't survive? Could she handle that?

What if Johnny doesn't survive? How would she cope with losing him after all these years? A deep anxiety rooted in her heart as she walked in beside the man she had loved for so long. When they were finally alone with Khloe, Katie sat down by the little girl.

"Hi, Khloe. I'm Katie. Johnny's wife."

The little girl with the stuffed teddy bear gazed up at her with bright brown eyes. "Johnny was right. You're beautiful."

"And you are too. He told me your hair had been really fluffy and curly." Katie nodded as she glanced at a bald head.

The little girl frowned. "Yeah. My foster parents shaved it. I didn't want to. Not yet, but they said I had to so they wouldn't have to keep cleaning up my clumps of hair."

"It happened to me last time...I only just shaved mine. It will grow back more beautiful than ever," Johnny reassured her. He relaxed in his chair, fatigue written large in his features.

"We brought you something special, though, to help," Katie offered as she pulled a bag from behind her back. "Our son, David, helped pick it out for you."

Khloe took the package and opened it wide. A big smile erupted on her face as she dragged out the soft-textured, bright purple hat with vivid pink and yellow flowers on one side. "I love it!" Khloe put it on and then rose to go find a mirror. She posed and looked at herself from every angle possible. She came back to sit down with a big sigh.

"What was that for?" Johnny asked.

"I wish you were my parents. Thank you for the hat. I don't ever remember anyone being this kind to me before."

"Can I give you a hug?" Katie asked. The little girl flung herself into Katie's arms, and Katie pulled her gently into her lap, careful of the line attached, and held her close.

"Is this what it's like to be loved?" Khloe asked.

Katie fought back her own tears as she looked at

the sorrow on her husband's face. "Yes, darling Khloe, this is what it feels like to be loved. And God loves you this way all the time, even when you can't feel it."

"I've been praying."

"For what?" Johnny asked.

"That God would let me come home with you."

"Are things that bad at your foster home?"

An involuntary shudder traveled through the little girl in her arms.

"Khloe? You can tell us if something is wrong. We'll do everything we can to help you."

Tears flowed from the little girl's eyes, and sobs racked her body.

"My foster brother…he…touches me."

Katie rang for a nurse to come in. Helen arrived.

"Can you show us where he touches you?" Johnny held up his phone to videotape the confession.

Khloe pointed to the areas she had been touched.

"Is this with your clothes on? Or off?"

"Both."

"This has happened more than once?"

The little girl nodded and burrowed her head into Katie's chest. Katie looked up at the nurse. "Can you call the police and the social worker?"

Helen had tears in her own eyes but nodded and left the room.

Katie hugged the little girl. She wanted to pummel anyone who would dare hurt a child. "Khloe, you have done nothing wrong. I want you to tell the police what you told me. They can help us so this doesn't happen again."

Khloe nodded. She had a death grip on her teddy bear. "He tried to take Teddy away too." She released her grip to show Katie a rip in the seam of one of the legs.

"I will bring a needle and thread next time, and we'll get Teddy sewn up good as new."

Khloe nodded.

Khloe told her story to the police and social worker, and when she was done, they took her away.

Katie helped Johnny to the car. They sat, and after turning on the air-conditioning, Katie let her head fall back. "I adore her."

Johnny clasped her hand. "I knew you would."

"I did everything Robbie suggested, and it still feels too little, too late."

"God knows." He sighed and pulled his hand away. "Can we go home? I need to recline." He pushed his seat back as far as he could.

"Sure, honey." She started the car and backed out of the spot to drive home.

~*~

Johnny rested, and David played in his room with a new set of Legos he had gotten for his birthday. Katie tried to get dinner ready, and a plate fell to the floor and shattered. She dropped her head into her hands and sobbed. Anger and sorrow overwhelmed her heart. *Lord, Khloe needs us. Why can't she be ours? Please protect her.*

After she calmed herself, she grabbed the broom and started to clean up the tile floor. She brought out a mop to make sure she didn't miss any tiny pieces. Well, the floor needed to be cleaned anyway, right? She shook her head as she put it away. She checked the casserole in the oven, set a timer, went to the bedroom, and stretched out next to her husband.

"You OK?" Johnny asked. "I heard something break."

"Just clumsy."

"Still thinking about Khloe?"

"Yes."

"Me too."

"As hard as it is to watch you go through this…my heart aches more for her. So alone. No one to care enough to be there. To protect her."

"Katie?"

"Hmm?"

"Is there something else?"

"What do you mean?"

"You seem more agitated than I would expect. Did something happen to you when you were little?"

Katie couldn't find the words. She nodded her head and let Johnny wrap her in his arms as she sobbed and received the comfort no one would give her when she was a little girl.

When she calmed down, she pulled back to her own pillow and faced Johnny. "It was Ken. When he came home from college. I was younger than Khloe."

"Why didn't you ever tell me when we were dating in high school?"

"We were just kids, and I was too ashamed to tell anyone."

"Did you ever try to tell your parents?"

Katie nodded. "They felt Ken could do no wrong and that I must be imagining things. He was already an adult when it happened."

"When did it stop?"

"When I finally kicked him in the most tender spot and told him the next time he touched me, I would use scissors."

"Ouch." Johnny winced. "Remind me never to cross you."

"I only got bold enough when he finally tried to go further. I had adored him. He was my big brother."

"What did he do when you threatened him?"

"Beat me up. Slapped me. Kicked me. Told me no man would ever want me anyway."

Johnny drew her into his arms. "Well, we've proved him wrong, haven't we?"

Katie nodded.

"Sweetheart, we need to trust God with this. It's hard, but He understands just what Khloe needs, and He knows what we need."

A beeper went off in the kitchen. "Right now, dinner needs to come out of the oven."

"Good, because your man needs to eat." He planted a kiss on her lips, and they both rose to take care of dinner.

~*~

After dinner, Katie found her men downstairs in the new studio. David had his guitar on his lap. The instrument dwarfed him. Johnny insisted learning on a full-sized guitar was best, and thankfully, their son had long fingers like his father. She sat in a chair and watched Johnny patiently teach. David stuck his little tongue out of the corner of his mouth as he concentrated.

She shook her head. Johnny should have been a music teacher. He was patient and encouraging even though she knew he was weak and tired from the treatment.

Soon. Too soon. He would be in isolation, and it

would be weeks before David could be with him in person. They could talk using the computer and see each other. Katie knew it would never replace moments like this with Johnny's arms around the little boy, whispering words of encouragement in his ears. She pulled out her phone and snapped a few pictures.

Lord, help him get through this. Help all of us get through this so we can enjoy more moments like these.

~*~

Katie tossed and turned that night as Johnny lightly snored next to her. Memories of her brother taunted her. She had been younger than Khloe. Ken had come home from graduate school full of himself and his dreams. He would drink with his buddies, come home, and find her. Even after she had threatened him, he would at times, in public, wrap his arm around her and whisper dirty things into her ear.

Katie shuddered at the memory. She shook her head trying to escape it. *Stop! I don't want to be thinking these thoughts. Lord, help me. Help Khloe.*

Her husband snuggled up to her, and she allowed herself to be enveloped in his warmth and love, given so freely even in his sleep. She was grateful she married this man.

20

*We all need someone who inspires us
to do better than we know how.*
Anonymous

June 2014

The day had finally arrived, and Johnny wasn't sure if he was ready. They hadn't heard anything about Khloe, either, even though they prayed for her all the time. They knew she'd been placed in another foster home, but it was a temporary solution. *Lord, don't let her be alone. Show her You are there.*

He spent the night in isolation at the hospital in a specific oncology unit. Niko arrived today to have his bone marrow harvested, and then it would be given to Johnny. The weeks following would be painful as his weakened body assimilated Niko's gift and fought the cancer. It was, in reality, the most dangerous period of his treatment. There was a risk his body would reject the donation.

He would miss hugs and kisses from his wife and son. Runs with Niko and handshakes that were skin on skin. He had his guitar, some books, his laptop...he'd probably become a social media junkie while here with little to do but troll the sites and interact with fans.

Maybe he should let them know. He pulled out his phone and snapped a picture of his bald head and gaunt face. He uploaded it to his social media sites. He could add it to Specific Gravity's page later. Or Tia could.

Johnny captioned the photo. *Bone marrow transplant today for this battle with cancer. Appreciate prayers. Love to you all.*

He thought about Khloe. Her time would be soon as well. Would she be in this same area? Maybe. *Lord, if we could see her and support her during these weeks, then let it be so. Even if You won't give her to us as a forever family, help us love her in her lonely, dark hours. Wrap Your arms around her, Lord.*

His phone rang. Katie.

"I have news."

"Yeah?"

"They gave us Khloe."

"What? Now?"

"Yes. I'm so thrilled and can't wait to tell her. She undergoes her bone marrow transplant tomorrow. I'll be picking her up today and accompanying her to the isolation unit. She has nothing, Johnny. What should I get for her?"

"Princess stuff. Her favorite color is purple. Coloring books. Maybe a tablet where we can download games for her to play and she could watch videos? Pretty pajamas and slippers. You're a girl—be creative. She comes in tonight?"

"Yeah, her transplant is tomorrow. They said she's in the hospital but not in isolation. She's been having a rough time with the chemo and radiation, just like you."

"I didn't end up in the hospital, though. Was it because she was that sick or that they didn't want to deal with her?"

"I think it was a little of both."

"Get someone to paint the walls in her room and make it a magical place while we are here."

"But what if…"

"The worst happens? Then we provide her with the best life and love she ever had right now, but let's not think that way. Decorate the room. Take pictures so she'll be able to see. Give her something to live for."

"Robbie is looking into the adoption, but he says it's better to wait until you are home before we pursue that."

"Even if I don't survive"—he could hear her weeping—"Katie. Stop. Would you still want to take care of her and love her?"

"Yes," came the choked reply.

"Then have Roberto start the process now. It might take a long time, and I want to be assured she's going to be cared for. Do this for me?"

"OK. How are you today?"

"Tired. Scared. Praying it goes well for Niko."

"He's strong and healthy," Katie assured.

"Yes, but it's going to knock him off his feet for a while."

"Not as much as it will you."

"True, and he gets to go home today when it's all over."

"You'll come home too, eventually. We'll get through this. Khloe will end up next door or across the hall from you, so neither of you will be alone as you recover."

"Thank God for that. I had been praying…"

"We all have and will continue."

"You are a wonder, Katie. Not only taking on me but now Khloe."

"This is what God called me to do."

"Where's David?"

"In the basement practicing his guitar. He is working through the book you bought him. He said it's stupid and you are better than a book, but I think he wants to learn well so he can show you when you get home."

"I hope he'll show me over the next few weeks. We'll attempt a few lessons over the computer. I'm sure Niko would help too."

"David is going to be so spoiled."

"Good, because he'll have a sister to share us with soon. Let him enjoy this while he can. His only-child days are ending."

"I like the way you think."

"So, once we adopt Khloe, do we search for other kids?"

"You can't save everyone, Johnny."

"Why not?"

"Let's get Khloe settled first and see who else God brings our way."

"OK. It makes me happy to watch our family grow."

"Me too. I'm going to go. I promised Tia I would sit with her through Niko's donation. She adores you, but she's a little nervous."

"I'm glad you'll be there for her."

"Oh, and Pastor Andrew called. I almost forgot. We got assigned our couple. Dale and Terri Walker. I'll shoot them an email to let them know what's going on, but Andrew said he thought we could even start some of our contact with them via computer too. They are grandparents, but apparently tech savvy."

"Wonderful. I'll let you go, Katie. Tell Tia I'm

praying for Niko."

"I will, and I'll also share our news about Khloe. I plan to visit her while I'm there. Maybe take Tia to meet our newest addition."

"That'd be great. I love you, Katie."

"I love you too."

~*~

The day stretched on, and with the chemo and radiation, Johnny was worn out. He kept his phone by his side, waiting for any news. He finally got a text later that afternoon.

Niko's in recovery. It went well. Love you. Katie.

He smiled. *Thank you, Niko.* He'd miss his jogs with his best friend. And the jam sessions. They might try that via computer video links too. He hoped he'd have lots of contact. It was sad to think that even ten years ago, it wasn't available. He rolled over but couldn't stop his mind from racing. Cancer. Katie, David, fire. Khloe. His parents and siblings. The fans over the years who had cheered and applauded.

And here he was. All alone. It would be easy to slump into despair as time became as thick as molasses in January. He rose and forced himself up to lean against the windowpane. The sun shone on a beautiful June day. Everything was green. Was it only five months ago that David swooped into his life, knocking him off his feet? He grinned at the exuberant love of a little boy. The son he never thought he could have. A family he had longed for. God had redeemed the past and given him his wildest dreams.

And now, Khloe. A sweet little girl with brown eyes and a bald head. A girl used to loss and having no one there. He looked forward to filling those empty places in her heart with the love of a family. He laughed aloud at the thought of how his parents would react to this sweet girl. As much as they were thrilled with David, how much more so would they gush over Khloe? His mom would enjoy baking cookies with them, and this year, Christmas would be...

He stopped himself. There were no guarantees of tomorrow, much less Christmas. He'd been blessed to beat cancer once. His doctor had given him supplements to help boost his system, especially his thyroid, suspecting that hypothyroidism might be at the root of his tendency to cancer. It didn't make sense to him, but he had never been good at science. If taking a few extra pills for the rest of his life could spare him this again, he would gladly do it.

As lonely as he was in this moment, he recognized how blessed he was. Katie was probably with Khloe now and would be bringing her here later to settle into her own isolation room.

The nurse came in. "We need to get you ready."

He nodded and walked away from the window. Time to embrace the tough stuff and pray God would see Him through to the other end. He knew God could. Just wasn't too sure what the end would be.

~*~

Katie had shopped for all kinds of wonderful items and rushed home to throw the clothes in the washer and drier as she prepared the bags for the hospital. She finally reached Khloe's room after supper.

"Hi, Mrs. Marshall. How's Johnny?" Khloe

Susan M. Baganz

struggled to sit up in bed.

Katie leaned over to give Khloe a hug. The poor girl was skin and bones. "Johnny was doing fine this morning. He's having his transplant now. He was thrilled to hear you were coming there tonight and having yours tomorrow. Hopefully you'll be able to keep each other company some of the time."

"You'll visit me?"

Katie smiled. "Of course. Our prayers were answered just in time. Foster care placed you with us. Let's get you ready to go, shall we?"

"Really?" The little girl blinked rapidly, and a lone tear trailed down her cheek. "Thank you."

~*~

At the isolation ward, Katie helped bring in all kinds of goodies after getting suited up in the protective gear. Protective for Khloe. And Johnny, who she hoped to visit soon. She was grateful for grandparents eager to entertain a little boy for the day. She brought in the bags of clothes and toys with her as Khloe settled into her bed.

"What is all that?"

"These, dear Khloe, are yours. There are fun pajamas for you and fuzzy socks. A pretty robe and some toys, books, coloring books, crayons, and games...oh and a tablet loaded with some movies and games for you as well."

"For me?"

Katie nodded. "You'll tell me if there's anything you need, and I'll see what I can do to get it."

"A hug would be nice."

Katie embraced her. It took some time before the

254

little girl let go.

"I'm scared."

"I'm sure you are, sweetheart. Even after I leave, God is with you. I also bought you a phone programmed with my number and Johnny's too. You can call to talk any time you want."

"Really?"

"Really."

"Even in the middle of the night?"

"If that's when you need us, yes. Even then."

"Is Johnny OK?"

"I hope so. I would have heard if he wasn't. The process is simple and goes in through the central line they've placed here in your chest. It's supposed to be painless."

"Then why am I so sick now?"

"You're reacting to the chemotherapy and radiation. They needed to get your body ready to accept the transplant. You're fortunate that a match came up through the registry, but we don't know who it is. I don't know what they told you, but after the transplant, you'll be weak and might feel sick for some time. You'll be here in the hospital for several weeks while you recover and your immune system rebuilds itself."

Khloe yawned. "Tomorrow?"

"Yes, tomorrow."

"OK. Guess I had better sleep then."

Katie bent over to place a kiss on the little girl's cheeks. Even through the mask she hoped the love could be felt. "David, Johnny, and I are praying for you."

"Thank you, Mrs. Marshall."

"My hope is someday you'll call me 'Mom.'"

"I think I'd like that." Little eyelids framed with long lashes drifted shut, and Katie left the room. She walked over to Johnny's room and knocked.

"Come in," a soft voice answered.

"Hey. It's me." She walked in to find him in bed, resting on his side.

"Khloe all settled in?"

"Yeah. Just across the hall from you. She has your phone number."

"What is it so I can program it in?" He grabbed his phone and punched in the numbers. He was glad they were allowed in that unit of the hospital. "Great. How's she doing?"

"Scared, tired. Grateful someone cares."

"Good. You are a treasure, Katie."

"How did it go?"

"Anticlimactic. Painless. Boring. But when Niko's cells get to work, I'll be beat up and weak."

"Even more than you have been?"

"Yeah. Can you imagine?"

Katie shook her head. "No, I can't and don't want to."

"Care to snuggle with me for a little bit?"

"Until the nurses kick me out?"

"Sure." Johnny slid over to make room for her in her sterile suit. She snuggled into him as he rested his head on hers. "You smell good."

"I love your scent too. Thankfully, your pillow reminds me of you. It won't get washed until you're going to come home, just so I can hold it close at night and pretend."

"I wish I had yours, but that probably violates the whole idea of being sterile. I miss kissing you."

"You went seven years without kissing my lips."

"Well, true. There were other lips to kiss in the meantime, though."

"You do want me to visit you again, right?"

"Yeah." A chuckle rumbled in his chest. "Just picking on you. Humor a sick man."

"Fine. I'll humor you, as long as you remember who gets all your kisses from now on."

"I don't want to kiss anyone else but you."

"Good."

Johnny soon fell asleep, and a nurse came in to check his vitals. Katie rose to leave. She noticed an envelope with her name on it next to their picture he had brought with him. She grinned and picked it up to read at home.

~*~

After spending time with David and reassuring him both Johnny and Khloe were fine, she crawled into bed and turned on a lamp.. She pulled Johnny's pillow close and opened up his letter.

Dearest Katie,

You cannot imagine how much I miss you right now. It's only been one night and all I want is to be home, in our bed, in your arms.

Regardless of how this turns out, remember I love you. I've loved you from the day we first met. Your inner beauty shines through in everything you do.

Tell your mother that the Doctor had to go save another planet, Planet Marrow, but will hopefully return soon. She should stay away from the Weeping Angels and not blink.

I know you'll want to be here every chance you get, but it is summer, so make sure it's a great one for David. Take him swimming, to the Kettle Moraine, the zoo…make memories and take lots of pictures for me. Soon we'll be doing all those things together. And remind him every day how much I love him.

And remember how much I love you as well. Because I do. Very much. And I miss you terribly. I already know being apart from you is the worst part of recovery for me.

Forever yours,
Johnny

Katie folded the letter up and sent up a prayer for Johnny and Khloe. She inhaled her husband's scent on his pillow and fell asleep dreaming of him in her arms.

~*~

A few days later, David sat at the kitchen table eating his 'cimmamon' toast and talking to his daddy on the computer. Katie listened in the background.

"Did you do anything fun yesterday?"

"Mommy took me to Long Lake. She said you guys used to go out there to swim."

"Did you like swimming out there?"

"Well, the green stuff at the bottom tickled my legs. The water was cold. I had more fun building a sand castle."

"Wait a sec, David…" Johnny called off to the side of the room. "Wanna meet Khloe?"

"She's there?"

"Yeah, she had her transplant a few days ago, but she's doing well. Khloe, come here and meet David."

A little girl peeked at the screen and pulled back. "That's your son?"

"Hi, Khloe! I've been praying for you."

"Thank you. I wish you could come and visit with me."

"We'll play together when you get out. What's your favorite toy?"

"I like building blocks and ponies."

"The talking ones?"

"Yeah. You?"

"I like building blocks just fine...but prefer trains to ponies."

"I've never had a chance to play with trains. Is it fun?"

"Yeah. I have a small train set. I had a big one before the fire, but it all burned up. I can share it with you when you're better."

"I'd like that."

David grinned. "Cool. It'll be fun to have you live with us."

"Where will I stay?"

"Your own room. We are going to make it so cool. Mommy's working on it."

"Thank you. No one has done anything like that for me before."

"Why not?"

The little girl shrugged. "I don't have a mommy and daddy like you do."

"I only just got my daddy a little while ago. But you can share mine. OK?"

"OK."

"Cool."

Khloe yawned. "I'm tired but glad to meet you, David. I'm going to go rest." She climbed off Johnny's lap and walked out of the view of the monitor.

"I like her, Daddy."

"Me too. I'm glad she'll be part of our family."

"Are you going to teach her to play guitar too?"

"Only if she wants to learn."

David perked up. "Hey, we could start our own band."

Johnny chuckled. "We've a long way to go before that, and I'm still in Specific Gravity. Remember?"

"Mommy let me watch some videos of you. Will you have hair again?"

"At some point it'll grow back. Might be a while, though."

"Oh, OK. My hair is straight like Mommy's, though."

"Yes, it is, and I love your hair and Mommy's hair."

"You can't love hair." David giggled.

"Fine, I love the heads the hair grows on."

"You can't love heads."

"Can I love you? And your mom?"

"Yes."

Katie listened to some more silly talk before Johnny said good-bye and ended the connection. David ran off to play. It was going to be a long few months until everyone was healthy and home. She could hardly wait.

21

*Take care of your life
and the Lord will take care of your death.*
George Whitefield

July 2014

The weeks dragged on, and Johnny grew homesick. He had little energy to do anything, and both he and Khloe coped with nausea as their bodies dealt with all the changes. They were miserable. For a short time, the doctors worried Johnny might have Graft Versus Host Disease, but if he did, it resolved itself.

His marriage mentor called.

"Johnny, it's Dale. I know you're going through some tough stuff right now but wanted to touch base. Figured we needed to get acquainted somehow even while you're in the hospital. How are you?"

"Hi, Dale. Thanks for calling. I'm sick. Exhausted. Missing Katie and David."

"The first year of marriage is hard as you adjust. You've thrown a lot of extra variables into the mix with an instant family, new home, cancer, and pursuing foster care. Sorry to cut to the chase, but Pastor Andrew filled me in."

"It's all public knowledge, so no offense taken. I don't even know what to ask for prayer for anymore."

"How's your walk with God? That's the foundation that everything else will rise or fall on. You are the spiritual head of the home even though you are not there at the moment."

Johnny sighed. "You would think with all this time on my hands, I'd be pouring over God's word. Memorizing scripture. Studying. I can barely keep my focus to read anything, to be honest. I'm exhausted. I can play my guitar and worship Him. I pray as I toss and turn. To be honest, those prayers are more for relief from my own suffering than they are for others."

"All natural, I would suspect. How are things between you and Katie?"

"I don't know. She's used to being a single mom, so I think she's doing OK. She comes to visit every day, but lately there hasn't been much to discuss."

"So, what do you do?"

"Sometimes we play games with Khloe. Sometimes I just rest, and she sits and reads or watches a video with me. Pretty boring."

"You've been married, what, three months?"

"Yeah."

"And you reconnected in January after a seven-year separation."

"Yup."

"It would seem there would be plenty of ground to cover in getting better acquainted, wouldn't there?"

"I suppose…"

"Think about it, Johnny. What questions can you ask your wife? What things make her feel loved?"

"Besides physical affection? It's been hard not being able to touch without the barriers she has to wear to protect me."

"Yeah, what else?"

"She likes the letters I write her."

"Anything else?"

"Special, well thought-out gifts."

"Anything else?"

"I can't think of anything."

"Gifts are hard when you're hiding away like you are…but think about it. I know that right now, much of what is going on revolves around your needs. And that's great that you have support. Try to remember that Katie needs as much as you can give to her as well."

Johnny nodded. "I'll see what I can do. Depression has been a huge issue, and at times, that colors my perceptions and ability to look past my own nose to the needs of someone else."

"How about Khloe?"

"I think I'm pretty good about trying to meet her needs. But she's a kid and hasn't had much. Time and attention I can provide to a certain degree, and words of encouragement and love. It's easy."

"Take that need and think of Katie as having it times ten, and be as intentional with her as you are with Khloe. Yes. Khloe is important, but Katie is someone who signed up for the long haul. I know you have little energy. I realize you're going through a rough time physically and even emotionally. Just don't neglect the one relationship, besides God, that is most important to you."

"Thanks, Dale."

"Call me if you need anything. I suspect our next time will be face-to-face and maybe as couples."

"Sounds good. I do appreciate it, Dale. My first marriage didn't make it, and I would hate to lose Katie due to negligence on my part."

"I'll be praying."

"I appreciate that." He hung up the phone and sighed. Dale was right, and Johnny needed to stop being so self-focused, but some days that was so hard. Like today.

~*~

Life was in a holding pattern while he healed. He spent time with Khloe each day and tried to talk with David, and between that and regular checks with the nurses, he mostly slept.

The phone rang.

"Hey, Katie. You coming today?"

"I'm sorry. I'm not feeling well again, and I don't want to risk getting you or Khloe sick."

"You haven't seen the doctor?"

"What could they do anyway? It's probably just a summer cold virus. I'll drink lots of liquids, take some naps, and I'll be fine in a few days."

"I miss you."

"I miss you too, but honestly, Johnny. I come and visit, and you have nothing to say. I don't have anything to say. We're boring each other."

"I'm sorry I can't be more entertaining for you." Johnny sighed. Was he wrong to have hoped that marriage would have made this easier for him?

"I don't need to be entertained, but if all I'm going to do is color with Khloe and play a few games of Uno and watch you sleep...well, it doesn't always seem worth the drive there."

Ouch.

"I understand. Rest and get well. Tell David I love him." He hung up before she could respond and turned the phone off for the first time since he had been there. He retched in the bathroom, and with a sore stomach, he crawled into bed, curled up, and cried himself to sleep. Rejection and abandonment wrapped around him as a wet, scratchy woolen blanket.

The next morning, a nurse walked in, disturbing his sleep.

"Johnny? How are you today?"

He peeled open one eyelid and groaned.

She picked up his phone and looked at it. "I've been getting calls at the desk that you weren't answering your phone. Some people are worried about you."

Johnny shook his head as he rolled onto his back. He had nothing to say.

"Listen, I've been a nurse here for many years, and you need to know this is going to get better. Before you know it, you'll be home. You'll be traveling and playing your beautiful music for all and sundry. You will settle into a nice life with your wife and kids, and cancer will be a distant memory. God's already there, Johnny."

"I'm not in the mood for this, Linda."

"I realize you're not, but sometimes you need to hear the truth anyway." She pulled up a chair and sat down so she could look him in the eyes. He averted his gaze. "You and Katie have done something special taking in Khloe and pursuing adoption. I've never seen a child come through this process as well as she has. She glows because she is loved and not alone. Johnny, your cancer probably saved her life. It's hard. It's painful. You have a beautiful family that will be waiting for you when you get home. You have a future and a career, a ministry."

Susan M. Baganz

"A wife who is too bored to visit me."

"Well, you have to admit, Johnny, your witty repartee has been lacking of late."

"Et tu, Brute?"

Linda laughed. "There's that spark of humor we've been missing. Come now. Let me take your vitals." She checked him over, and he noticed her frown.

"What?"

"Your numbers aren't as good as we'd like. I'll have to call the doctor."

"He's already ruled out the rejection of the marrow."

"True. It's still possible, though, that in spite of all our precautions, you might be terribly ill. I suspect you'll not be allowed any visitors until we can see you are better." She closed her laptop where she took her notes. "Not even Khloe. I'm sorry, Johnny."

"It's just as well."

"Why?"

"I'm not in the mood for company."

"Mood or not, you'll do much better once you are able to escape these four walls. Rest now. Lunch will be in soon."

"Can you turn out the lights?"

"They are not on, Johnny, but I can close the blinds for you. Headache?"

He nodded. The room darkened, and he heard the soft steps of the nurse as she left his room and flipped a sign on his door. He was certain it was now saying he was in quarantine. Just as well. He'd rather die in peace. *God, are you ready for me? I'm so tired of all this now. I just want to go home. Katie and the kids are provided for. I can't take it anymore.*

~*~

The phone rang. Who had turned it on? Linda? She wouldn't do that to him, would she?

With a deep sigh, he reached for the device and looked at the number. *Niko.* He answered.

"Hey."

"Johnny? Katie had told me she wasn't feeling well and couldn't visit. I know I can't come but wanted to touch base. You don't sound so hot."

"I'm not. I'm quarantined."

"How much different is that from being in insolation?"

"No one can visit me but the doctors and nurses. Not Khloe. Not Katie. No one."

"Is it serious? What's wrong?"

"I don't know. Feel like crap, but how is that different from any other day?"

"Sorry my transplant is kicking your butt. Should have expected that since I've been doing that to you since you were knee-high to a grasshopper."

"Ha. Ha."

"No sense of humor today, either?"

"Nope. Just want everyone to leave me alone. Nurse must have turned my phone on."

"Johnny?"

"Hmm?"

"Have you given up? After all this...marrying Katie, finding your son, meeting and helping Khloe, getting the transplant. After all this, you're quitting?"

"I don't have anything more to give, Niko. I can't do this."

"You don't have a choice. I'm sorry Tia or I can't

be there for you. You know we wish we could. This is so not like last time, when we were able to see you and hug you and pray you through each day."

"Human touch. Now there's a novel concept."

"Pick up your guitar and play, buddy."

"I don't have the energy."

"Do it anyway. Pick it up. Turn on your computer and record whatever comes out. I want to hear it. By the end of the day I expect to see that file."

"I can't," Johnny whined.

"You can, and you will. I need you, Johnny. We're a team, and God has great things in store for us. Do it for me. Please?" The words hung between them, and Johnny struggled to sit up.

"You are a bully, and when I'm strong enough, I'm going to pummel you. I owe you a few punches anyway."

Niko laughed. "I'm sure you do, and I deserve every one of them. Now go. Play. I'll be waiting."

Johnny turned off the phone again and hid it under his pillow...disconnected from the chargers so the nurse couldn't find it so easily. He fired up his laptop and tuned his guitar. He usually played electric but only brought his acoustic to his jail cell so he wouldn't be messing with an amp. He turned on the video recorder software. He looked at his image reflected in the screen. His T-shirt hung on him, peach fuzz grew on his head, and stubble showed on his chin. His eyes had bags under them, and he lacked a smile. He couldn't even force the muscles to move that direction. He warmed his fingers up and hit *record*.

He closed his eyes and let his fingers move over the strings. It wasn't a tune he had played before. He strummed, he picked, and he hummed. A knock on the door shook him to awareness. Over forty-five minutes had passed, and it was dinner time. He stopped the recording and put his guitar away.

He caught a whiff of his body odor and hauled himself to the shower while the nurse brought in the food. He didn't want to talk to anyone anyway. When he had finished and changed, he came out to eat a few bites. He had no appetite for anything. Nothing tasted good. He clicked on the file he made and sent it to Niko. There. Now he'd have one person off his back.

Strangely enough, he was more at peace after playing. There was something in the divine when he sat with his guitar. It was just him, the guitar, and God. The music he played was not for an album. It wasn't to gain the praise of anyone. Sure, it was to get Niko off his back, but there was no pride in what he had done. It was raw, it was random, and it reflected the chaos and darkness of his heart. God understood. He doubted anyone else would.

He crawled under the blanket and hardly roused when someone came in later to hook something up to his central line in his chest. He didn't care what they put in him. Nothing they gave could cure the hopelessness and weariness in his heart.

~*~

Guilt tormented Katie. How dare she blame her husband for being boring? She practically told him it wasn't worth coming to visit him. What was wrong with her? Since their conversation yesterday, his phone had been shut off and she couldn't get through. She missed Johnny terribly. But she longed to be held and touched by him. Kisses and more. Just having him there. And she couldn't give that back? She had hated the sound of defeat in his voice. She hated that she couldn't rush to his side and hold him tight. She still wasn't feeling well, and now Johnny was in quarantine possibly sick with something, and even the slightest virus could have deadly results.

Khloe would be coming home in a few days. Her body accepted her transplant without Johnny's complications, so her discharge was coming sooner. David was excited to meet her in person. The room was ready, and grandparents were eager to shower their new addition with love and gifts.

Her phone rang.

"Hello?"

"Katie? It's Tia. Can you and David come to dinner tonight?"

"Sure. I've not been feeling too great, but I don't think I'm contagious."

"Five thirty OK?"

"Sure. Thanks, Tia. It'll be nice to spend some time with you."

"Niko has something to show you."

"Oh?"

"Yeah. See you in a few hours."

~*~

Katie and David arrived. David ran off to play with Apolo, who had moved from crawling to walking and climbing things.

"I'll keep him safe, Mom," David assured her.

Tia gave her a hug, and Niko did as well.

"How are you holding up?" Tia asked.

Katie shrugged. "I'm a horrible wife. I'm worrying

myself sick. All my dreams came true, and all I want to do is cry."

"Sit down at the table while I get the food on."

"Thanks."

Niko gathered the kids, and they all sat down to eat. Niko bowed his head to pray. "Lord, thank You for this meal and for Tia, who so lovingly prepared it. I ask that it would sustain us and that our conversation would also bring nourishment and hope. We love You, Jesus."

"Amen!" Apolo shouted with a slam of his sippy cup.

Katie laughed, and they all began to eat the chicken enchiladas Tia had prepared.

When the meal was done, Niko excused himself. "Katie, can you come with me?"

Tia got Apolo out of his seat. "I'm coming, too."

Curious, Katie rose and followed them to their living room. Niko turned on the big screen and clicked open his attached computer.

"Sit down. I want you to watch this."

Katie settled in, and David sat on the floor with Apolo, stacking blocks for the little boy to knock over. When Johnny appeared and started playing, David and Katie focused on the screen.

Katie saw the man she had fallen in love with. Passion. Creativity. Such stunning talent. It reminded her of the Sunday he played in church, and she could have sworn angels were drawn closer to God like she was. Tears flowed unbidden, and a box of tissues appeared in her lap, but she wasn't sure who put them there.

She didn't even know if Johnny realized he was singing as he played. Despair, agony, and love. She could barely make out the words, but she couldn't mistake the emotion behind them.

More than that, she could see just how sick he was. His cheeks were flushed, and he had lost more weight. His face held new lines, and a smattering of dark fluff appeared on his head. Sturdier hair was on his jaw, upper lip, and chin. Uneven growth. But it was something.

She fell in love all over again.

The music ended, and Johnny stared at the monitor. "Happy now, Niko?" Tears streamed down his face as he reached forward.

"He hasn't played for some time, I don't think," Katie whispered into the silence. Niko stopped the recording as Johnny had reached forward, so his face hung on the screen in stark definition. His eyes glassy from tears and dark circles more pronounced, as well as the shadows under his cheekbones.

"Music has a healing power. He wasn't happy when I demanded he do this. I wanted you to see it."

"Thank you."

Tia spoke up, her own voice choked from crying. "You never got to really see him and Niko in concert, did you?"

"I've seen videos online but not live. No."

"It's an amazing thing. The entire Specific Gravity band had something powerful when they played, but Niko and Johnny were the hub of it all. It was always out of their relationship and the complement of their voices and instruments that carried the spirit and power of the group. God has used them so powerfully over the years."

"I got a glimpse of that the last time he helped you lead worship, Niko."

Niko frowned. "Something was different with Johnny's second service. Something like we saw here. Like he stepped aside and let the Holy Spirit play the guitar using his fingers and singing with his voice."

Katie nodded. "Yes. It was that afternoon he got really sick too."

Tia giggled, and Niko looked at her with scrunched eyebrows. "What's so funny about any of this?"

"I'm sorry. It just hit me—maybe Johnny needs to be really sick to be his best. I know. Horrible thought, but it is as if when all is stripped away and he doesn't have the energy to pretend it's all OK, that his music becomes so holy. So other-worldly."

"He's really hurting right now. He turned his phone off. I don't know how to reach him." Katie crumpled up the wad of wet tissues into one clean one and rose to throw it in the garbage. She returned to her chair.

"We pray," David said. He'd been mesmerized by his father's performance and only now spoke. "God can help Daddy."

Niko grinned. "You're one smart cookie. How'd you learn so much?"

"Daddy taught me in Sunday school about trusting God and asking Him for help when we don't know what to do. He told us the story of Daniel in the lion's den."

"And cancer is your Daddy's lion," Tia whispered.

"Right," David said. "So, let's pray. I'll start. Dear Jesus, heal my daddy so he can come home, and care for Khloe, Mommy, and me. We love Daddy, but You love him even more. Thank You for letting him play guitar gooder than anyone."

Tia, Katie, and Niko all took turns praying, but when they left, Katie could only remember the words from her little boy's mouth.

She tucked him in that night. After his prayers, he patted her face. "Don't worry. God answers our prayers."

Katie nodded her head. "I love you, little man."

"Love you too, Mommy."

She flicked off the light and went to her room to prepare for bed. How would she get through to Johnny when she couldn't visit him and he refused to answer the phone?

~*~

Johnny moaned as the nurse fumbled for his central line. Were they taking samples or giving him something? He didn't care. A cool hand touched his forehead.

A soft, feminine voice penetrated the deep fog of his brain. "Hang in there, Johnny Marshall. God's not done with you yet."

Time must have passed, but how much time he had no clue. He cracked open his eyes to a darkened room. A sliver of light came through the edges of the closed door. He sighed. He was still in the hospital. He rose and used the bathroom, his legs as weak as noodles. He leaned against the vanity and glanced in the mirror, his eyes squinting in the blinding light above him. He looked like a hobo. Scraggly but short beard. Rank, sweat-stained T-shirt, a soft brown shadow on his head. He reached up. Hair. He fought dizziness and went back to his bed and sat. *I need a shower*. He wrinkled his nose. Eww. If he weren't in quarantine for being sick, he should be for how bad he stunk. He grabbed some fresh clothes and went to the bathroom to clean up.

Deodorant. Who'da thunk I'd need that to sleep? He applied it liberally after washing up. He pulled out his shaver and cleaned up his face. Brushed his fuzzy teeth. When had he last eaten? His stomach growled. *What time is it anyway?* He went to his phone to check, but it was turned off. When had he shoved it under his pillow? He waited for it to wake up, and with unsteady steps, walked to the window to peek through the drawn blinds. It was either dawn or dusk. Which way did his room face? He couldn't remember.

He turned on a soft light and surveyed the room. There was a four-pack of bottled root beer sitting by his bed. He smiled. His favorite brand. He grabbed one. It wasn't ice cold, but it would do. He used a spoon to pop the cap and took a sip. The fizz slithered down his throat, and the rich flavor shot through his veins. He shivered and grabbed a hoodie with a zipper. He put it on but left the front open as he stuck his legs back under the covers. He picked up the bottle again and took another sip. Ah, yes. This was the good stuff.

He glanced at the phone—5:00 a.m. He set it aside and noticed an envelope stuck under the root beer case. He slid it out and set the bottle down. *Katie.* He saw her handwriting, and a wave of melancholy swept over his mind. Well, might as well open it. If she was going to leave him with a letter, it would be no more than Donna had. Maybe she'd found someone else too...someone who could give her a family. Someone who might not die.

Everybody dies.

He flipped open the card and took it out. It was a

sweet, silly card, and he couldn't help the smile it brought to his lips. He opened the piece of paper.

Dear Johnny,

I'm sad that our last conversation was so hard on you. I'm sorry that I wasn't able to give you what you needed at that moment. I'm human and I struggle too. None of this is easy and you had warned me about that. I had so wanted you to not have to experience this pain—physical or emotional.

I love you more than you could probably ever realize right now. I'm not walking away. When I'm feeling better, and you are out of quarantine, I'll be back. And we will move on from here.

David is praying in full confidence of your healing. He says you taught him that. Khloe is struggling with not being able to see you. You should see the tiny, fuzzy curls on her head. Such a sweet girl. I'm so looking forward to the day when we can call her daughter, and change her name to Khloe Marshall. Our kids need their father. They adore you to pieces and we all long for the day when you are home again.

I long for the day when you are next to me in church. At the kitchen table. In our bed. I'm going to probably have a hard time keeping my hands from touching you to make sure you are really there. It seems like a dangerous fantasy, since you have been so sick.

Roberto is working on the adoption paperwork. Niko is already talking about the next tour. He's still pretty tired at times but doing well, and he started jogging again, but not far.

Niko showed me your video. It was so beautiful, I cried. God has blessed you with such a gift and I am once again sorry that I didn't recognize that seven years ago. I let the word "musician" blind me to the divinely gifted artist you are. Tia's been getting more studio requests and she has not confirmed them till we know you are ready to travel again. We all know that even when you come home, your healing will not be complete.

Your body has hard work to do and I pray this treatment will be successful in beating your cancer.

I've been so tired lately. Not sure why. Doctor at urgent care checked me over and said I was fine. No fever or sniffles so I suspect I'll be permitted to see you again when the quarantine is lifted. If you want me to come. Turning off your phone makes me wonder.

I hope you enjoy the root beer. David insisted that this was the best medicine and better than flowers, balloons, or a stuffed animal or even, gasp, building blocks! He's your son through and through.

I love you always and forever,
Katie

Johnny refolded the note and placed it in the card. She hadn't left him and had no plans to. She still loved him and believed in him. Him. He was nothing special. Just Johnny Marshall, guitar player and backup singer.

He picked up his laptop and surfed social media. It was far too early for a phone call. He was surprised at the pages of well-wishes on his fan page as well as the one for Specific Gravity. Some of the people he knew. Some he had worked with over the years. Old friends. Musicians and record company executives. If he didn't know better, he'd think he was some kind of special.

But you are, Johnny, because you are Mine.

22

It's not the strength of the body that counts,
but the strength of the spirit.
J.R.R. Tolkien

Late July

Katie stopped by as Johnny played Uno with Khloe. He was losing. She sat down to join them, in all her protective gear.

"You're feeling better?" Johnny asked.

"Yeah, some. Doctor isn't worried."

"Uno!" Khloe shouted. Katie placed her card down. Johnny played his card, and Khloe won again.

"You are a vicious player, Khloe," Katie declared.

"Johnny taught me."

"He taught you well. I might need to get David brushed up on his Uno skills to make a worthy opponent for you."

"Where is he?" Johnny asked.

"Visiting Niko and Tia for a little while. He said he missed Apolo. I think he wanted Niko to show him more chords."

"He was pretty disappointed when I didn't have the energy to show him yesterday."

"You've been really tired. What have the doctors said?"

"Things are looking better. I'll still have another few weeks unless my numbers show sudden improvement."

"Can that happen?"

Johnny nodded. "It did for Khloe, but she's younger. I'm glad she'll get to go home, but I'm sad I won't be there to welcome her."

"I can come and visit you though, right?"

Katie shook her head. "Sorry. No children are allowed. That's why David hasn't been up here."

"I don't want to leave Johnny." Khloe teared up, and Johnny hauled her into his lap.

"Aw, sweetheart, you still have some healing to do too, but you'll be able to walk in the sun, play with David, meet grandparents, and sleep in your own special room."

"My own room?"

"Yup. Katie, do you have pictures to show her?"

"I do." Katie brought out her phone and showed Khloe photos of her room.

"Wow. That's the prettiest room I've ever seen."

"I agree." Katie smiled as she put her phone away. "We planned it just for you. Johnny told me what to buy for you since he's known you longer."

"And I get to go to church?"

"Yes. You'll be able to go to church but probably not to Sunday school for a few weeks. When you do go, David will be with you, as you'll be in the same class. He's only a few months older than you," Johnny said.

Katie smiled. "And wait till your birthday! Oh, we have a fun party planned for you. It's hard to believe that is next week already and you'll be seven too. I'm going to feel like I have twins."

Khloe frowned. "But David and I don't look alike."

"You don't have to be identical. The fact that you are a girl and he's a boy means right there you are different. It doesn't matter. You'll look like you are ours, and we couldn't be happier. I don't know if I ever told you this, but I was a twin," Katie said as Khloe settled into her lap.

"You were?" Johnny was surprised.

Katie nodded. "My twin died at birth."

"And your parents loved boys..." Johnny said.

"Yup." Katie nodded. "Not only was I a girl, but I had lived when my brother Kurt had died. I was to blame apparently."

"You were a baby. You couldn't do anything about that." Khloe frowned.

Katie nodded. "You're right. And God has allowed me to have two precocious seven-year-olds to love. That makes me one very blessed mommy." She hugged Khloe close. "Just wait till you see some of the fun clothes I purchased for you."

Khloe's eyes grew big. "Really?"

"Really."

Khloe's arms wrapped around Katie's neck. "Thank you, Mom." She kissed Katie's cheek through the mask, ran to give Johnny a hug, and started to leave.

"Wait," Johnny said. "Where are you going?"

"I need to start packing. I'm going home soon." She waved to them both and was gone.

Johnny leaned back in his chair to look at his wife. Her eyes sparkled. He couldn't tell much else under her scrubs, hair cover, mask, and gloves. "You're feeling better?"

She shrugged. "Still tired, but life has been a bit crazy. I've been trying to visit my mom too, and she never remembers me or David."

"I'm sorry."

"It is what it is, you know? It's not like she ever really knew me when she had all her mental functioning. She's forgotten who Doctor Who is and now points to the angel in the garden and says how pretty it is."

"Wow. She's even forgotten me? Maybe that's for the better. She's not tried to leave?"

"No."

"Well, that's good at least." Silence hung in the air. "Listen. I'm really sorry about our last conversation. I shouldn't have said the things I did."

"I forgive you. I think I was more honest than I should have been. You weren't feeling well. Neither of us knew at the time how sick you really were."

Johnny shook his head. "That doesn't excuse my rudeness. And then shutting everyone out by turning off my phone."

"Niko got through?"

"Sneaky nurse, Linda."

He detected a smile under the mask due to the wrinkles that emerged by her eyes.

"Niko played us your video."

"Us?"

"David, Tia, and me."

"Oh."

"It was beautiful. How come you've never recorded your own album? I asked Niko for an mp3 of the recording, and he gave it to me. I've been listening to it all the time."

"You must be tired of it by now."

"No. Tired of you not being there with me, yes. Tired of listening to you play? I don't think that would be possible. Tia sent it in to her father at Jazzy Records."

"What? How could she? I can't reproduce that."

"She realizes that. She thinks they might be open to an instrumental album of your music. You could write your own songs to put on it. Maybe some of what was in there would be inspiration for it."

Johnny sighed. He knew Niko and Tia meant well, but it was like letting everyone read a personal journal.

Oh.

"Did Tia ever tell you how I got her and Niko together?"

"No."

"I found her journals. I read some and told Niko to read them."

"You read her personal diary?"

"Yeah, kinda."

"Was she angry?"

"Yeah, at Niko. She finally figured out that I read them too, and now this feels like payback. That video was like a private diary that I only thought Niko would see. I never dreamed…"

"You feel like your private thoughts are now exposed to the world?"

"Yeah."

"Isn't that what art is, though? Expressing emotions that people are too afraid to admit to. In listening to your music, they might find they're not alone."

"Maybe."

"Beauty birthed out of pain. Kind of like having a baby."

"I suppose. Tia's talked about how writing a book is like giving birth. She said the process is longer than having a child, though."

"I've read her first book. It was good."

"She's got a gift, but I'm glad she's a great manager too."

"I think we can trust her with this, don't you?"

"Yeah, but I probably need to talk to her. Apologize again."

"It all worked out, right?"

"They seem blissfully happy."

"And we will be too." Her phone beeped. She pulled it out to look at it. "I need to go. David seems to have taken a tumble, and Tia thinks he might need a trip to the hospital. No blood, though, and he didn't hit his head."

"Call and tell me how he is."

She rose. "I will. And Johnny...I really do love you."

"I love you too."

He watched her go and threw out a quick prayer for David. He'd had his own share of broken bones as a kid. He was surprised his mother didn't dress him in bubble wrap. Probably because he'd have had every bubble popped before he walked out the front door, making it useless. That would have been fun, though.

He rested and awoke when a text came through. A photo of David with his left arm in a splint.

Verdict: broken. Buckle fracture. Cast next week.

Johnny chuckled. He texted back. *That's my boy.*

He'll call you later.

Thanks. Johnny set the phone aside. Being a dad was going to be great.

~*~

Katie loaded up Khloe's belongings and came back to get her. The little girl had just finished saying good-bye to Johnny, and with tear-stained cheeks, she waited by the nurse's station.

"You ready to go home?"

Khloe nodded.

"Johnny will join us soon. You can still call him or talk to him through the computer, where you can see him."

"I know." Her little hand grabbed for Katie's, and they walked out together into the beautiful summer sunshine.

Katie placed a wide-brimmed floppy hat on Khloe's head. "You're more at risk for sunburn right now, so when we're outside, we'll put a hat on you. OK?"

Khloe nodded and climbed into the back seat of the car. "There are two boosters."

"Yes, the purple one is yours." Katie leaned in to help her buckle up.

Once home, Katie shepherded Khloe into the house. Grandma Marshall was there, having stayed with David, and wanting to meet Khloe.

Khloe looked around, doe-eyed. "This is a nice house."

"It's your house now, Khloe."

"Only until they find someone else to take me."

Katie set the bags and dropped to one knee. She placed a hand on each of Khloe's shoulders. "We don't plan on them taking you away. We are working to try to adopt you so you can be our forever daughter."

"I'll never be your real daughter."

Katie shook her head. "I don't think I could love you any more if you had been born to me, Khloe. Adoption will eventually make you our child legally, but to Johnny and David and me—you are already our child. We just can't change your name till the judge gives us permission." She hugged the little girl close. "We love you, Khloe."

David came up, fluorescent orange cast and black marker in hand. "Hey, sis. Wanna be the first to sign my cast?"

Khloe nodded, took the pen, and signed her name. David looked at it. "Cool beans. Wanna see your room?" Khloe followed him down the hall as David gave her the tour of the house. Katie and Mrs. Marshall traveled behind, sharing amused glances.

"Here it is." David motioned for Khloe to pass through the door first.

She stood in the midst of the pink and purple room and slowly turned around. She saw the dollhouse and went over to gingerly touch it. "This is all...mine?"

"Duh. It's your room," David said.

Khloe frowned at him, went to the closet, and opened the door. "Whoa. These are all for me?"

Katie nodded. "Yeah, I might have gone a little overboard. We can take back anything you don't like. I left the price tags on. I missed six years of dressing a little girl, so I think I overcompensated."

Katie brought in the bags from the hospital and set aside the toys. She took the clothes away to be washed, leaving Khloe to explore under David's watchful eye. She doubted he would let her fall into boredom and wondered how long it would be before they fought.

Mrs. Marshall followed her to the laundry room

and helped her sort. "You know, Katie. I don't care how you have kids. I'm just glad you do. Khloe is adorable."

"She's sweet. We pray she can heal from past neglect, abandonment, and abuse. It will be hard for her to feel like she's good enough to be loved."

"God can do that and more. No matter what happened, she will carry that past. You've given her the hope for a better future and a home filled with love."

"Thanks."

"How was Johnny today? I'm sad that our summer colds have kept us away. A sniffle turned into full-blown bronchitis for Dad and a sinus infection for me. Video chats are great but just not the same."

"He's lonely, of course. He'll really miss Khloe. They used to spend time together daily. He's been teaching her about Jesus and what it means to be a princess in Christ and adopted into His family. I don't know if she really gets it yet. Did you notice that princess drawing framed on the wall?"

"Yes, I thought it was an unusual piece of art."

"Johnny drew that for her the first day they met. She had saved it. He told her that was Princess Khloe."

Grandma smiled. "He always was a good boy."

"Except for when he wasn't?"

Anne Marshall laughed. "You learn fast."

~*~

Two days later, Katie took Khloe and David to Grandma and Grandpa's for Khloe's birthday party. She was overwhelmed with the number of people, but David stuck close and kept her up to date as to who was who. When she sat to finally open gifts, she didn't seem to know what to do.

"Khloe, don't be a dunce. Rip the paper open."

"But it's so pretty. It must be for someone else."

"No, silly, it's your birthday. They are your presents."

"OK." Khloe opened the package carefully and every package after and gushed her gratitude with tears and words of thanks.

At the end of the night, Katie asked, "Wanna call Johnny on the computer?"

"Can we?"

Katie nodded and dialed up to talk to Johnny on video camera.

"Hi, birthday girl! Big seven-year-old. David's going to have to watch out now." Johnny smiled.

"Hi, Johnny. I wish you could have been here. That would have been the best present."

"I wish I were there too, sweetheart. But hopefully soon. We can pray, right?"

Khloe nodded. "Everyone has been so nice. I got lots of presents."

"What'd you get?"

"Some dolls that Mommy says have to keep their clothes on."

"Good idea. I don't like naked dolls strolling around the house."

Khloe giggled, and David groaned in the background, dramatically executing a face palm. Katie fought back her own laughter.

"What else?"

"I got a journal, crayons, colored pencils, building blocks, and some ponies."

"Sounds like quite the haul."

"I've never had so much in my life."

"Enjoy it, Khloe. We love you."

"I love you too, Daddy."

A tear escaped Johnny's eye. "Sweet girl. You are loved more than you know."

"Are you OK?" she asked.

He nodded. "I'm fine. These are happy tears. That's the first time you called me Daddy, and that makes me very happy."

"Oh."

"Good night, princess. Happy birthday."

"Good night, Daddy."

David chimed in, "I love you!" before chasing Khloe down the hall.

Katie leaned down. "I love you, sweetheart. I'll be in tomorrow. Sleep well."

Johnny blew her a kiss. "I love you too. Hug my pillow close, and I'll pretend I feel your arms around me all night long."

Katie smiled. "Will do. Good-night."

"Night."

The call ended. Katie put the kids to bed and settled into her own. She hugged the pillow close and did just what Johnny had asked. She pretended she held him.

23

Even his griefs are joy, long after,
to one that remembers all that he wrought and endured.
Homer

August 2014

Johnny was still weak, but his numbers had been good, and he'd started to do some exercising. He slept a lot, but it looked like the transplant had been successful and his immunity was better. The real test would be fall with cold and flu season, but that was two months off yet before the nasty stuff surfaced. He'd still be playing it safe.

"No international flights for now." Doctor Osgood ordered.

"Nashville? New York?"

The doctor frowned. "With a mask during the flight and in crowds."

Johnny nodded.

Katie had already taken his things to the car, and the kids waited at home. She walked back into the room, and the doctor turned to her. "Take good care of our boy."

"I'll do the best I can. I'm invested in keeping him around for a long time."

"Good to hear."

As they walked past the nurse's station, Johnny reached to hold his wife's hand. Skin on skin. It was a wonderful sensation.

~*~

They arrived home to a small gathering. Tia, Niko, Apolo, his parents, and of course, David and Khloe. He knelt down to embrace all three kids. Apolo was stuck in the middle.

"Look. An Apolo sandwich. My favorite." He leaned down to pretend to nibble on the little boy's neck, making him giggle. He then attacked Khloe and David. Both struggled to get free and giggled uncontrollably. He finally released them and stood. His energy was quickly depleting.

He was enveloped by his mom and then his father. Tia hugged him and kissed his cheek, and Niko gave him a bear hug, lifting him off his feet.

"Welcome home," Katie said off to the side. She handed him a bottle of his favorite root beer. Soon everyone had one and raised them up.

"To whipping cancer," Niko said. The bottles clinked as everyone shouted, "Cheers!" and drank. Johnny found the nearest chair and slid into it. Soon Apolo was in his lap, and David and Khloe on each side.

Niko grinned. Johnny grew suspicious. "Look, kids. A Johnny sandwich!" The kids commenced trying to eat him, and he struggled to escape without spilling his root beer. He finally stood, out of breath. He growled at Niko.

"That was low."

"You deserved it."

"Probably. I don't have much energy. I need to rest. I wish I could handle more…"

"You don't offend us, son." Mr. Marshall patted him on the back. "Rest. Heal. There will be more time to connect later."

Johnny placed his bottle on the kitchen table. Katie had stood to the side, watching it all. "Before I do, I think I need to give this beautiful woman a kiss. It's been way too long since I've been able to do that."

David groaned. "Come on Khloe and Apolo. This is something we don't want to see."

Katie's giggle was cut off as his lips connected with hers, and he wrapped her in his arms. Her hands snaked up to wrap around his neck and rub along his fuzzy scalp. She tasted like root beer and smelled like vanilla, and in spite of his fatigue, he wished they had a night alone to get reacquainted. Perhaps a delayed honeymoon would need to be planned soon. He was grateful that even though his body was tired, some parts were still raring to go. He anticipated bedtime.

He released her and whispered, "I love you." One more quick kiss of the lips, a wave to his parents and friends, and he turned to seek his bed. He collapsed on top of the covers and hugged her pillow to him. Contentment wrapped around him like a fleece blanket, and he drifted to sleep with a smile on his face.

~*~

A week later, Johnny noticed Katie wasn't doing as well as she claimed. Nights were heaven as they tried to make up for lost time and reconnect. He had no complaint about her passion or response to him.

It was the little things. He caught her yawning a lot. He found her one day having fallen asleep leaned over the dryer, which was running. She wasn't eating much, either, even though she faithfully provided wonderful meals for the four of them. Some had been brought to the house by members of their church, which made life a little easier as they adjusted.

Today he guided her to the bedroom as the kids played together in David's room.

"I don't want to go bed…"

"You are tired and taking a nap. How long has this been going on?"

She shrugged as she allowed him to sit her down and bent to take off her sandals.

"I think we need to go to the doctor."

"Fine."

"Do you have one?"

"I haven't had time to establish a primary care physician. Last time, I just went to urgent care."

"I'll see what I can do."

He tucked her in, placed a kiss on her cheek, and closed the door behind him as he left the room. He grabbed his phone and called Tia.

"Hey, Johnny. What's up?"

"I think Katie needs to see a doctor. She's tired all the time."

"She doesn't have one?"

"No."

"Here's the number to mine. She's great, but it can take a while to get in. Might want to try urgent care."

"Great. Could I drop the kids off later? She's taking a nap right now."

"Sure. I'll be home, and Apolo will enjoy having them around."

"Thanks."

"Oh, and Johnny?"

"Yeah?"

"I'll be praying."

"Thanks."

~*~

He hung up and sat down at the table to pray. *Lord, please help us find out what's wrong with Katie. We need her, and I'm worried. Thanks for already knowing the future and that You are there with us.*

He sat at the table and flipped open his computer. He updated his status and checked out information online. It was a good way to keep busy, since he couldn't focus. He was too worried about his wife.

It wasn't more than a half-hour later that she walked in.

"Katie? Why are you up?"

"I couldn't sleep anymore."

"I want to take you to urgent care."

"Fine."

"I'll gather the kids, and you put your shoes on."

"Grab a mask, Johnny."

"Yes, nurse." He gave her a salute and called for the kids to get ready to go.

~*~

Later at the clinic, Johnny played a game on his phone while waiting to see the doctor for the results of blood work they had done.

"Katherine Marshall?" a tiny nurse called.

"You want me with you?" Johnny asked.

Katie nodded, and they rose together to follow the petite, lime-green-clad woman.

"You can wait in here. The doctor will be with you momentarily." She closed the door to the small exam room.

They sat, and Johnny sighed. "I'm so tired of doctors and clinics and hospitals."

"Good thing you didn't go into the field of medicine then, huh?"

Johnny grinned. "Yup. I only barely passed biology with your tutoring."

"Is that what you called it? If I remember correctly, you were more interested in my anatomy than the biology text we studied."

"Can't blame me, can you? You were hot." He gave her a wink. "Still are."

Katie grinned. The door opened, and the female doctor came in.

"Katherine Marshall? Mr. Marshall?"

"Yes."

The doctor sat down with her laptop open before her. "We got the results of the lab tests, and I think we figured out why you've been so tired."

"Yes?"

"Have you also been moodier lately?"

"Johnny's been through a bone marrow transplant, and we are in the midst of adopting a seven-year-old cancer patient. Life's been a bit overwhelming, so, yes."

The doctor nodded and smiled. "Well, your life is going to get crazier because, Katherine, you are pregnant."

Katie gripped Johnny's arm and blinked rapidly. Johnny gasped. "Pregnant? That's not possible. I'm not able to...I had testicular cancer well over three years ago. Radiation..."

The doctor nodded. "It was commonly believed that those treatments would render a man unable to have children, but research has shown that there is a healthy percentage who do go on to do so without medical intervention."

Johnny shook his head. "All this time I thought..." He turned to Katie, who hadn't said a word. Her eyes were wide as saucers. "Katie?"

"I'm having a baby? I'm having *your* baby?" She shook her head and bit her lip. "I'm a nurse. I never even suspected, but now that I think back... I've been so busy I missed my monthly. The first time I just figured it was stress...and then I didn't even think about it. I've been too busy...Johnny. We're having a baby!"

Johnny grinned. "Yes, we are. I couldn't be more thrilled." He leaned over and kissed her until the doctor cleared her throat.

"Here's a prescription for a prenatal vitamin. We have some good OB/GYN docs here. This one is new and taking patients, so probably the easiest to get into. I've heard he's one of the best. Congratulations." The doctor shook their hands and left.

Johnny helped Katie to her feet, and they floated home.

~*~

"How far along do you think you are?" Johnny asked.

"I don't know. I could be entering my fourth month. I'll have to go to the doctor. Probably have an ultrasound."

"I can't wait."

"Well, it's a good thing we have to. We just got one kid, and now we're going to introduce a baby to the mix?"

"It'll be wonderful—"

"—says the man who hasn't had to get up several times a night to nurse and change diapers or walk a colicky baby. The worst you'll have it is six weeks without, well, you know."

"What? Six weeks?"

"Yup. After the baby's born, no treats for daddy."

"Well, that's a bummer."

"No. It's a blessing. I'll be too tired to care anyway."

"Now who's borrowing trouble from tomorrow?"

"I thought it was my turn to do that. You already had yours." Katie elbowed him as they strode up to Niko's house to collect their kids.

"Can we tell them?" Johnny asked.

"You wanna crow?"

"Like a rooster. Yeah, baby, you bet!"

Katie shook her head. "Fine. Crow. You didn't get the opportunity last time. I at least owe you this one."

Johnny lit up. "That's right. You do."

They entered, and the kids looked up from the toys. Apolo got to his feet and toddled toward them. "Unka Johnny!"

Johnny swooped down to pick him up. "Hey, buddy. You being good?"

Apolo nodded and grinned. "Dabid. Ko-eee"

Johnny nodded. "Not bad. You're getting there."

"Tia. Is Niko here?"

"Yeah. In the basement working through a worship set."

Katie nudged him. "You go crow. I'll tell Tia."

"Thanks." He planted a kiss on her lips, handed off Apolo, and ran down the stairs with more energy than he realistically had. His excitement kept him afloat.

"Have elephants descended in my house?" Niko asked. He looked up from what he was working on.

"You're smiling and bursting with news. Cancer's gone?"

Johnny shook his head. "Too soon to know for sure on that score. Better news than that."

"Better than beating cancer?" He set his guitar down and found a chair. "I think I'd better sit for this. What happened?"

"We're expecting a baby." Johnny gave a big smile.

"You just adopted Khloe. You're adopting a baby too? Wow. That is a lot."

"No. Katie and me. We. Made. A baby. One of our very own. She's pregnant."

Niko's mouth dropped. "What? I thought you said you were shooting blanks. Really? She's pregnant?"

Johnny nodded. "Isn't it great? I couldn't believe it myself, but the doctor said infertility is no longer a certainty with treatment. Even with the kind of cancer I had."

"Whoa. All this time you grieved…"

"Yeah."

"That's amazing news."

A squeal was heard from upstairs. Niko smiled. "I'm assuming Katie just told Tia."

Johnny nodded.

"When is she due?"

"We'll have to go in for an ultrasound to find out.

Katie's not sure."

"There wasn't a huge window for you to get this accomplished."

"True. She could be in her fourth month. Does that mean a January due date?"

"Possibly. Congratulations, Johnny. I'm really thrilled for you."

"Thanks, Niko. I'm so happy right now I could burst."

"I remember that feeling when we found out about Tia. Total surprise there too, but what a wonderful one."

"Six weeks after the birth before we could...you know?"

Niko nodded. "Yeah, that part is not so hot, but to be honest, you will be too tired to care at that point."

"Seriously?"

"I'm lying to you. You will care, but when you see what she goes through, you'll be more than understanding of the need to wait."

Johnny sighed. "So get it while the getting's good?"

"That was my motto." Niko gave Johnny a gentle punch in the shoulder as they headed upstairs.

~*~

Back at home, they sat David and Khloe down.

"We have some great news," Johnny said.

"We're expecting a baby...possibly in January."

David's eyes grew big. "Cool!"

Khloe frowned.

"What's the matter, Khloe?"

"You won't want me around with a new baby."

"Why not? We are thrilled our family is expanding. This wasn't the way we anticipated it happening or as fast as we planned, but we longed to have more kids to love," Johnny said.

Katie sat down next to Khloe. "Listen. We are still adopting you, and if anything happened to you, I would be just as devastated as if it happened to David or this baby. You are ours. A child of our heart. We're in this for the long haul, Khloe. You're stuck with us as your mom and dad unless you object to being a part of our family. That's an option David or this baby never had."

"Why would I ever want to leave? No one has been as nice to me as you all have. Well, except for when I get yelled at for disobeying or fighting with David."

"And does David get in trouble too?"

Khloe nodded.

"Have we ever hurt you?" Johnny asked.

Khloe shook her head.

"So will you stay?" David asked. "I really like having you for my sister."

Khloe smiled. "I like having you for my brother too. Do you think we'll be in the same classroom this year?"

"Wouldn't that be fun? We could do our homework together."

Khloe grinned. "Wanna go play with your trains?"

David jumped up. "Yeah, let's." The two scooted out of the room.

Johnny looked over at Katie and started to chuckle. "Well, I guess we resolved that snag."

Katie grinned. "She's going to be a handful, but I love her to pieces."

"Me too," Johnny whispered as he sat down next to her and nuzzled her neck, trailing kisses up her neck.

"You're tickling me."

"I want to do more than that."

"Not until the kids are down for the night."

"Spoilsport." Johnny kissed her cheek. "But I suppose nothing would do more to cool my ardor than a little boy or girl walking in on us."

"Yup. My thoughts exactly."

They both relaxed on the sofa and sighed. "What a day this has been. When will you call to get an appointment?"

"Tomorrow."

"Good. Do you think they can tell the gender right away?"

"Might be too soon for that...I don't know for sure, though. You want to know?"

"Could be fun." Johnny squeezed her close.

"We'll see. I'm not sure."

"Might help the kids adjust."

"You really want to know, don't you, Johnny? Were you the kind of kid who peeked at his presents before Christmas?"

Johnny nodded.

"Well, we're doing something different that will foil that plan."

"We are?" Johnny wasn't sure he liked this line of thinking.

"Yup. We won't hide the gifts. As they are purchased, they will be wrapped and put under the tree. Anyone who peeks gets their gift returned."

"Hey, that's not fair."

"It is. It's good for the kids to learn delayed

gratification and appreciate the anticipation but also take the focus off the gifts because they are there."

"Does that really work? Put temptation out there the entire time?"

"I think it will. I've been doing it with David, and he knows to be patient. He'll get his chance to open his gifts when I say so, and he's content to wait."

"Khloe is so unused to anyone doing anything nice she'll be surprised to see anything under the tree with her name on it." Johnny frowned. "I wonder how long it will be till she feels like she really is a part of our family and that this isn't just another foster care?"

"Once she gets to change her name, that'll help."

"I hope so." Johnny checked the clock on the wall. "It's time for bed."

"Not trying to rush this, are you?"

"Me? No. Of course not. Why would you think that?" Johnny gave her a lingering kiss that promised more. There were some gifts he really did struggle to wait to unwrap. Katie was one of them.

24

Wonders will never cease.
Greek proverb

September 2014

Katie walked into the clinic with Johnny. It was the day for the ultrasound. He had been disappointed at the wait to see the doctor and then to get this appointment scheduled. He had been thrilled to hear the heartbeat, and it comforted her heart to hear it as well. She was starting to feel fluttering, and she wasn't so tired anymore, which was a huge relief.

They settled in and waited for the tech to return. Johnny's knee bounced, and he couldn't stop grinning. He was more excited than she was, and she had to remind herself that she'd been through this before, but he'd never had the opportunity.

The tech came in and squeezed the cold gel on Katie's baby bump. She wasn't sure if it had been a real need or psychological, but her pants seemed to be too tight almost immediately after finding out she was pregnant, and she had purchased some that were more comfortable for this phase of the pregnancy.

They heard the heartbeat right away. The tech frowned as he moved the ball over her tummy. He hadn't shown them the screen yet.

"I just need to snap some pics for the radiologist to

look at first. Then we can look closer. But..."

"But what?" Katie asked, fear causing her to grip Johnny's hand harder. She swallowed.

"Can you hear this?" The tech had moved the ball low to the right.

"Yeah. That's the heartbeat, right?" Johnny said.

"Right. But now listen to this." The tech moved the ball over to the left.

"Still the heartbeat."

The tech nodded. "No. Not the heartbeat. A second heartbeat." He flipped the monitor so they could see as he moved around. There wasn't just one little person in her stomach. There were two.

"Twins?" Johnny gasped.

"Do they run in your family?"

Johnny shook his head.

Katie answered, "I'm a twin."

"Well, that increased your likelihood right there, unless you did something to increase fertility?"

Katie shook her head. "We didn't think we could conceive and planned to adopt. This was a total surprise to both of us."

"And now doubly so." The tech smiled. "Congratulations."

"Can you tell if they are boy or girl?" Johnny asked.

"In another month I might, but not right now. All I'm focused on is how they measure and if they have the requisite numbers of arms, legs, fingers, and toes. And they do."

The tech gave them some pics of the babies and told them the full report would be forwarded to their doctor.

Katie dressed and ran to use the bathroom. Two?

Two little human beings were growing inside of her.
Their family wasn't adding one addition but doubling
their children. She didn't know whether to laugh or
cry. One baby was hard enough, but two? That was
terrifying.

After they came home, she called Tia. "We're
having twins."

"Congratulations! That's quite a surprise. Have
you seen Renata singing on the worship team? I'll have
to point her out to you and introduce you although I
don't know her well. She was at another table at our
Mothers of Preschoolers group. She has twins. She had
another child this spring. You should come to MOPS...
You're going to need them once those babies come."

"I'm willing to check it out."

"Good."

~*~

Friday night came, and Johnny watched Katie pull
her top down over her tummy.

"I kind of like the look of it hanging out there."

"No. I am not exposing my belly for all and
sundry."

"Well, aren't those posh words."

"Sorry. I think I sounded like my mother just then,
didn't I?"

Johnny nodded. "Yeah, you did. It scared me."

"I'm a little nervous meeting with our mentors.
We've not been able to connect with everything
happening, and life is still moving ahead at warp
speed."

"Yeah. I need to check out an accountability group
this week too. Dan said one of the members passed

away and they had an opening."

"That's your Wednesday morning group?"

"Yeah."

"How's that going to work when you have studio trips?"

"I can fly out on a Wednesday afternoon, play Thursday, Friday, and even Saturday morning if I need to and be back. Or leave Sunday afternoon and be back Tuesday night. Most of my jobs don't have to take too long. They usually want me for only one or two tracks."

"OK. I'm not sure I'll like it when you travel."

"Hopefully I won't have to do it too much, but it helps pay the bills. Niko's already starting to work on another album, so we'll be laying down tracks here. That might mean a tour next year, though."

"That'll be something to figure out too. Our family has exploded at a rapid pace." Katie rubbed her tummy.

"I'm not complaining."

"Me, neither."

~*~

Katie hustled to make sure everything was perfect before Dale and Terri Walker arrived for their marriage mentoring. It would be the first time meeting face-to-face. Terri had called once in the midst of the chaos and had prayed for Katie. Katie was aware that Dale had also connected with Johnny during his isolation, but she didn't know what they talked about. Now that they had come through the most difficult phase of his treatment, she had hopes that maybe, just maybe, things would start going better for all of them.

Johnny put his hand around her waist as she finished getting the coffee going. "Relax, we are not being tested on how clean our house is or graded on the level of hospitality you provide with the correct beverage and dessert."

"I'm acting like my mom, aren't I?"

"Kinda." He massaged her shoulders, and she took a deep breath to try to relax.

"Everything always had to be perfect."

"Do they need to be perfect for you?"

"No. I mean I like the house clean, but we have kids, right? I don't mind things being slightly messed up."

"Good, since you married me and I'm only slightly messed up." Johnny put his lips on her neck, making her squirm. "I like you messed up too."

"Stop it. We have company coming any moment. This is not the time to be fooling around. And the kids could come out any time."

"They are watching a movie and seem content. Besides, I warned them that if they came out, we'd start kissing."

Katie giggled. "You are trouble."

"But I'm your trouble."

The doorbell rang.

Johnny held her hand, and they strode to the door together to let in the older couple.

"Dale and Terri Walker. How wonderful to finally meet you both face-to-face."

Terri was a heavyset woman with a big smile. She reached forward and wrapped Katie in a hug. "I have been praying so hard for you both over the past few months."

Katie found herself released and watched Dale

wrap Johnny in an embrace too. The man was huge in comparison to her husband, who still hadn't regained all the weight and muscle tone he lost during his illness. She grinned as Johnny staggered back a step. She saw the grin on his face, though, and knew he liked this couple already.

"Why don't we come to the kitchen. I have some fresh brewed coffee and some brownies for us as we sit and talk."

"Brownies? You don't have to ask me twice." Terri hooked her arm through Katie's. "Lead the way, young lady. Now when are you due?"

"Mid to late January. Did I tell you we were having twins?"

"No!" The older lady maneuvered herself into a seat, and Katie poured the coffee. Johnny and Dale joined them, and soon all four were catching up on all that had happened in the past few months and how they were doing right now.

"We've been married forty years now and have five children and sixteen grandchildren. We've been through war, illness, bankruptcy, and church splits along with moves and some other hardships. Our heart now is to help young couples make their way to having a successful marriage. While the mentoring is primarily during the first year, our hope is that we'll become close friends and can help out if things get rough in the future." Dale sipped his coffee and reached for his wife's hand and then Johnny's.

"Let's hold hands and pray," Terri said. They bowed heads and each took turns praying for the concerns of all of them, including Terri's upcoming knee surgery and Dale's plans for retirement.

They rose to leave. "Call and let me know when

you find out more about those precious babies."

Dale shook Katie's hand and then Johnny's. "You're a great couple. I can tell God's got great things in store for you and your family. Shall we meet again next month?"

"Sure," Johnny responded after getting the nod from Katie. "Let's set it up."

Soon they were gone, and Katie and Johnny put the kids to bed.

~*~

Johnny stretched out on the bed. "They are a neat couple. I hope we're a lot like them after forty years of marriage."

"In what way?"

"Happily married with lots of kids and grandkids. Still able to tease each other and minister to others."

"How about we make it through the next year before we plan for thirty-nine more?"

"Worried, Katie?"

"No, just tired and overwhelmed. Sometimes I wonder if I can do all this. Then I feel guilty for my self-pity when I remember all you've suffered."

Johnny drew her into his arms and held her close. "Let's make a pact right now. No more pity parties unless we invite the other spouse."

"As in Dale and Terri?" she teased.

"No. As in me and you. No pity parties alone."

"OK. Only if you seal that with a kiss." She stretched her face up toward his.

"I'm sure I can seal it with more than that."

~*~

Tia called the next morning. "Johnny there?"

"Yeah, let me call for him."

"OK."

Katie yelled down to the studio. "Johnny, Tia's on the line for you."

"Coming." She heard him trudge up the steps. He'd been back to practicing and slowly exercising more but still tired easily. Recovery was going to be long, and it concerned her. He reached for the phone, and she handed it to him. He walked away into the living room and sat. She resumed folding the clothes in spite of her curiosity. She knew Tia was his manager, but since they had been married, Johnny had not taken any jobs. His only focus had been beating the cancer.

But what if now… She gulped. Johnny wanted to provide for their family. She had been surprised at how financially solvent he was, and now that Robbie had won the battle for her trust account and insurance reimbursement, they had even more resources. Johnny didn't need to work for quite some time if he didn't want to.

He was eager for a project. The months of isolation and recovery left him itching to perform, to take on a challenge.

The reality was she envied him getting to travel and play his music and get noticed for it. Being a stay-at-home mom wasn't quite so fulfilling most days. She rubbed her tummy in wonder at the two little lives growing within. She loved being a mom. But she'd been alone for so much of their marriage already, and she was jealous for time with Johnny.

He walked back into the room and handed her the phone.

"Well?"

"I've got a job."

"Where? When?"

He sighed and pulled her into his arms. "Chicago."

"That's it?"

"Yeah, well, from there I go to New York."

"How long will you be gone?" She wrapped her arms wrap around him, as if willing him to stay.

"I'll leave Sunday, tomorrow, after church and be back Saturday evening."

"A whole week?"

"Yeah. You OK with this?"

"I don't know. What about your accountability group?"

"I'll miss a week. I hadn't joined them yet anyway, so it's not like they'll miss me."

"What about me?"

He tilted her head up and kissed her. He still made her toes tingle. "I'll miss you most of all. But the pay is good and the work is nice. I've been itching to get back in the game."

"We don't need the money."

"It isn't about the money."

"What's it about, then?" Katie stepped back.

"It's about me re-establishing my career as a professional musician. With a cancer scare there's always a hesitation to hire someone, like they'll die before the project is complete. But if they see me taking on work, I'll get more and make more."

She nodded, unconvinced. "You tell the kids."

Johnny's face fell. "Yeah. This will be the first time I've left. None of you have experienced my real life before this."

"Yeah."

"That's going to be hard for all of you."

"Probably."

He sighed and walked away, shoulders drooped. Katie longed to call after him and tell him it was OK. He should go and chase his dreams. They would be fine without him here. The hardest part was seeing him through his cancer, so this shouldn't be that painful or difficult. This was, after all, what she signed up for, right?

Now if she could only convince her heart of that.

~*~

Johnny changed and went for a light jog over to Niko's. He hesitated at the front door. He used to live here and never knocked then. But so much had happened. He rang the doorbell.

"Coming!" Tia soon appeared at the door with Apolo at her heels.

"Johnny. Is everything OK?"

"Yes…and no. Niko around?" He walked in.

"In the basement." She nodded for him to go down.

Johnny took the steps slower than usual. He hit the bottom landing and stood watching his friend working on a riff. "Sounds good," he offered.

Niko jerked up and, seeing his friend, set the guitar aside. "Johnny…what's wrong?"

"You know me too well—it's kind of scary."

"The cancer?"

"No. No news on that yet. It will be a while before we know for sure. Listen, I'm not really up for a full-blown run, but a light jog? I need to talk."

"Sure, let me grab my shoes."

They walked up the stairs together, and Niko called out to Tia to tell her where he'd be, and she responded with an, "Enjoy your run, guys."

Johnny's admiration for his friend's wife rose. She always seemed to understand his moods but also respected the relationship the cousins shared, on and off the stage. What they had went far beyond music, and it was a rare and beautiful thing. Niko met him out on the sidewalk, and they took off in the direction of a park at a light lope.

"So what's got you down? Oh, wait." Niko tapped a finger to his forehead and gave an "mmm." He put the hand down. "*You* have a problem with a girl."

"I'm beginning to think I'm cursed."

"Why?"

"Tia got me two great opportunities, but Katie isn't really on board with me going."

"Why? It's what you do."

"Right. But it's never been what she's experienced. Our whole relationship to this point has revolved around my cancer, and our lives adapted to fit that, and it's changing."

"And you have two kids now and two more on the way…"

"Yeah. So, Katie wants me home, but I need to work. Support my family. I can't coast by on what's in my savings accounts and mutual funds forever."

"Is she saying you can't go?"

"No. I don't think she would ever forbid the trip, but she's definitely not happy with me."

"Ah, I think I see the problem."

"And would you care to enlighten me?" Johnny came to a park bench and sat down, the short run taking more out of him than he anticipated. He heard kids playing in the background and the birds singing in the trees. His life had stopped for cancer, but the rest of the world had moved on without him.

"Did you ask her about the trip? You know, like present it as something you want to do and get her opinion?"

"No. I've never had to…"

"My point exactly. Donna thrived on you being gone. You didn't know until later that it was because your absence allowed her the freedom to carry on with her affair."

"Affairs. There was more than one."

"Whatever. The fact is, your absence fit into her plans. But to Katie, she was without you for months. Everything centered on you and those kids, and now she finally has you. Hopefully healthy and for a long time. She's not ready to share you with the world, but you're itching to take off and do what you do best. Here's the rub. I don't think you realize just how hard this will be for you, either. You've never taken a trip like this and left your family behind."

Johnny frowned. "What do I do?"

"I'm not the marriage expert by any means. You can call Dale for that or even Andrew, but really? Do what you always told me to do. Talk to your wife. Duh." Niko nudged Johnny's shoulder with his fist. "Were there ever two dunderheads like us when it came to women?"

Chuckling, Johnny shook his head. "And yet look how God has blessed us. You got a jewel in Tia, and I got a do-over with Katie."

"So let's not screw it up, OK?" Niko rose. "Do I need to carry you to your house?"

"No." Johnny stood. "But I don't think I'm up for more than a walk back."

"I'm cool with that."

~*~

After the kids were in bed, Johnny drew Katie close to him. "Honey, I'm sorry I sprung this trip on you without even discussing it. I guess I'm not used to having a partner to check in with on things like this. We raced into marriage and cancer treatment at full speed, and we didn't even get a honeymoon. Negotiating what life will be like now is something we never talked about. I took you by surprise and hurt you. I'm sorry."

Katie sighed and squeezed him tight. "I forgive you. I guess I only looked as far as getting you home and well from cancer. I want to be with you, get to know you, spend time with you. Then the twins surprised us."

"Have I told you how thrilled I am about that?"

She giggled. "Yes, many times. It never crossed my mind what your work would mean for me and our family. Being left behind."

"You won't always be left behind. For this trip, it doesn't make sense to take the kids. They're in school. When it's time to tour, though, I hope you would all come, and maybe we could explore some of the cities we visit. But the traveling and prep for shows and interviews—it would be a lot of waiting for you and the kids."

"We'll figure something out. You take this trip, and I'll learn to adapt, as will the kids. You still have to wear your mask, right?"

"Yeah. Not my most attractive look, but at least at the airport, on the plane, and in any other crowds."

"OK. I'm going to check out the Mothers of Preschoolers group on the Friday you're gone."

"That will be awesome. Tia, Stephanie, and Renata attend. I'm sure you'll love it and will make some new friends."

"As I head into this new season of parenting with babies again, it will be nice to have a husband and friends to support me this time around."

"One thing is for sure. You'll not be alone." He rolled Katie over and kissed her. He really did enjoy this part of marriage.

25

When I hear music, I fear no danger.
I am invulnerable. I see no foe.
Henry David Thoreau

Johnny played guitar for the jingle in Chicago, even adding some background vocals to the singers. It was a sweet gig. In and out and off to the airport for his flight to New York. Was it devious that he never told Katie why he was going?

He arrived in New York and entered his hotel room late. He was an hour ahead of Wisconsin time, so he called home.

"Hello? Johnny?"

"Hey, sweetheart, just wanted to let you know I arrived safely in New York and I'm at my hotel. It's been a long day, so I'm ready to crash."

"How did your work in Chicago go?"

"It was fun. Kind of a new thing for me to play and sing for a commercial jingle, but the people I worked with were great."

"Commercial for what?"

"A national hotel chain, but *shh*, not the one I'm staying in tonight."

Katie giggled. "I miss you."

"I miss you too. If things go well out here, it is possible I could be home earlier, but it's too early to know yet. I love you, Katie. Sleep well."

"I love you too, Johnny. Sweet dreams."

"Hold my pillow tight and think of me."
"I will. Night."

~*~

The next morning, Katie got the kids off to school. David and Khloe had both settled in well in their classroom. Khloe still had to wear her mask, which was hard for her. The doctor assured her it was only for a few more months.

Katie did her grocery shopping. Then she headed home, unloaded, and followed a recipe to get things in the slow cooker. Her tummy now seemed to get in her way as two babies vied for limited space. *Who are you two? Do you know what a miracle you are to your father and me?*

That evening after dinner, she set up the computer and the kids did a video chat with Johnny. His face was pale, and dark circles were more pronounced under his eyes. His speech lacked its usual energy. Concern flared within her that this trip was too much too soon for her husband.

After the kids shared their news and ran off to their rooms to play, she sat and stared at her husband.

"Katie? You OK?"

She shook her head. "No. You look tired, Johnny. I'm worried about you."

Johnny grinned. "Well, you are beyond beautiful, and I hate that I can't lean forward and kiss those pretty lips. Things went well today, and I'm excited about this project."

"You are a tease."

"Ah, but the best kind because I'm your husband and can follow through when these miles aren't between us."

"For months, it was the barrier of protective clothing and your isolation—all because of cancer...and now, it's music in our way."

"No. Music isn't in our way. Trust me on this, sweetheart. I may not be able to tell you about it for a while, but when I do, I think you're going to be thrilled."

"You're having twins?"

Johnny laughed. "Touché. Nothing could be as wonderful as that, but still...I just wanted you to know that this trip is really for you."

"Mysterious man."

"I'll be home soon."

"I love you."

"Love you too, Katie."

~*~

Katie walked into the huge room at church. Mommies and their preschool children littered the hallways, and she was conspicuous with her lack of a child to escort to the children's program they called MOPPETS. Cute. She found Tia and was soon introduced to so many women she wondered if she would ever remember their names.

"Katie!" Terri Walker approached her. "I'm so glad you came. I made sure they put you at my table. I'll be your mentor mom here. Thought it might make the transition easier for you knowing you had a friend at your table."

"I won't be with Tia?"

"Sorry, her table is full already, but we had a mom move away a few weeks ago, so we have an open spot just for you."

Katie enjoyed the food and conversation. Some moms had older kids like she did, and Renata was at her table with her newest child, only a few months old. She had twins but didn't bring them, as her husband stayed home on those Friday mornings with the girls so she could be here. She figured this mother of twins would be a huge fount of wisdom as she awaited her own. Suddenly, she didn't feel so abandoned by Johnny. She was going to have friends, and even when he traveled, she would be busy. Never too busy to miss him, but she wouldn't be spending her time pining for him and anxious every minute like she was when he was in isolation.

She went to lunch with Terri afterward.

"I'm not sure I really have room to eat anything after all that food at Mothers of Preschoolers this morning."

Terri laughed. "Somehow I always find more room. I'm glad you came. Even though your babies aren't in your arms yet, you'll make friends and have the support you need when you bring those babies home, and that's important."

"I had heard about Renata and have seen her sing on stage with the worship team, but I'm glad I finally got to meet her."

"She'll be a great resource for you. Girl has an amazing story of her own as well. I'm hoping she'll share it one day from the podium. She says she's fine singing in front of others, but speaking? Not so much."

"I don't know how Johnny can do both. Interviews, playing music, singing in front of huge crowds. He says it's because Niko's the front man and he's just support, but I've seen them together on and off stage and know it's a partnership and that Niko doesn't think Johnny's any less important than him."

"I always enjoyed their music. Are they working on a new album?"

"They will begin that process soon. Now that the worship ministry has transitioned back to Pastor Dan, Niko is freed up to focus on songs for Specific Gravity. Johnny's eager to get working on that too as his energy improves."

"How are you doing with Johnny being out of town?"

"It's been easier than I anticipated. I miss him most at night. Reminds me of all those months without him while he was in isolation and the fear that he'd never come home." Katie wiped a tear away. "I never realized just how traumatic all that would be for me as his wife—watching him suffer, worried that I would be a widow and that our time together would be so short."

"No news yet on remission?"

"No. It's too early. Johnny still has to wear the mask in public, which he hates because it's so conspicuous, but now with the Ebola scare, most people think he's just acting paranoid rather than treating him as if he's sick."

"How convenient."

"Yeah, he said he got a little hassle at security, though. They demanded to take his temperature to make sure he wasn't sick as he boarded the plane. He showed them his note from the doctor, but one passenger refused to sit next to him and was able to find another empty chair and move to it. Johnny said if anything, that was a blessing. He wasn't bothered by anyone."

"Anything special planned for when he returns?"

"Well, I'm going to try to make his specialty, spanakopita, for Saturday night. That's when he's due back. He showed me how to do it a few weeks ago, so now I want to try."

"I'm sure that will please him."

~*~

Katie left lunch and returned home eager for a nap. She pulled into the garage and saw Johnny's car parked there. It reminded her that they needed to shop for a larger vehicle to replace at least one of theirs. Then it hit her.

Johnny was home early.

She rushed into the house and found him in the laundry room dumping his dirty clothes in the washing machine. She wrapped her arms around him, and as he turned to return her embrace, she captured his lips with hers.

Johnny responded, and she dragged him off to the bedroom.

"Welcome home, husband."

He grinned. "Well, if this is how I'm received, I'll have to come home more often."

Katie almost forgot to pick up the kids from school.

26

*Keep your face always toward the sunshine
and the shadows will fall behind you.*
Walt Whitman

November 2014

Johnny walked into the clinic with Khloe. She had gotten out of school for this, which didn't make her brother too happy. They both sat down with Dr. Osgood.

"Khloe, congratulations on finding the best possible parents. Oh, and on being cancer-free. I want you back in a year to check up on you, but you're good to go." Khloe jumped up and gave Johnny a high five. "Why don't you sit out in the waiting room while I speak with your father?"

"OK." She skipped out the door.

Johnny's heart filled with dread. If the doctor couldn't say anything in front of her...it was probably bad news.

"First of all, let me relieve your worried mind. You're fine. The transplant was successful. You're looking great, and your blood work is excellent. I wanted to apologize for leading you to believe the infertility was a for-sure thing. At the time of your treatment years ago, it appeared that was the case. Obviously, I've been proven wrong. Congratulations.

Do you know what you're having?"

"Two humans."

The doctor's eyes grew wide. "Well, good thing we checked this out this time, then, before I pronounced with any kind of certainty. Obviously, this recent battle has not compromised your fertility. Our tests show you are perfectly capable of producing children even after this round of treatment."

Johnny laughed. "As happy as that makes me, I'm not sure my wife would be on board with that idea at the moment."

"Give her time. You will both have your hands full, but it will be worth it."

"How many kids do you have, Doctor? If you don't mind me asking."

"Not at all. I have seven children and sixteen grandchildren now. God's been gracious to us, and trust me…it's worth all you have to go through to get there."

"And how did you convince your wife…"

The doctor winked. "I didn't have to do any convincing. Trust me, some women get the urge to have more kids, and you just have to be ready…"

Johnny rose to shake the doctor's hand. "Thank you."

"Come back in a year. Bring the kids or at least pictures, although I'm sure I'll see you in church. Dedicate your next album to me if you think of it."

Johnny reached forward and gave the doctor a hug. "Thank you. You've given me a new life. I had almost given up, but just look at all God has done."

The doctor's eyes watered. "We don't always get that outcome, but when we do, it's a wonderful thing. Praise God for His healing. Ultimately, He is the one who decides who will come through treatment and who won't."

Johnny went out to collect Khloe, who was anxiously waiting. "I'm good, Khloe. God has been gracious to us both."

Khloe wrapped her arms around his waist. "I hate cancer, but I'm glad it brought me to you."

"Me too, Khloe. Me too. I adore my fuzzy-headed little girl."

"Your head is fuzzy too."

"Funny. You look like my daughter. God must have known, huh?"

"Yeah. As David would say, God is 'cool.'"

"David would say that, wouldn't he? How about we go get some frozen custard to celebrate before I take you back to school?"

"David will be jealous."

"Just don't order a root beer float and he'll be fine. We can have that for dessert tonight to celebrate."

"Don't you need to call Mom?"

"Why don't we do that together?"

When they got to the car, he pulled out his phone, pulled up a video chat, and dialed Katie. She answered, and her frown let him know she had been more worried than she would admit to.

"We have news, Mom."

"Yeah?"

"I'm clear. All good. No more cancer."

"Oh, Khloe, that's wonderful!"

"Daddy has news too."

"Same thing, babe."

"Johnny! We'll celebrate tonight."

"We're going out for custard right now," Khloe said.

"Enjoy your date. I'll plan something special for dinner."

"And I'll pick up the root beer for dessert."

"Sounds good. Love you both. Thanks for letting me know."

"Bye!" Johnny and Khloe said together.

~*~

Katie thought she could pass for the Thanksgiving turkey this year. She was huge. The babies seemed to be doing well. In spite of Johnny's desire to know the gender, the two little munchkins were being discreet and modest every time they had an ultrasound. They would have to be surprised at delivery.

The family went over to Johnny's parents' house for Thanksgiving, with all the children and grandchildren running around wild. There was snow on the ground, and Johnny hung the Christmas lights two weeks previously, ready to plug them in the day after the holiday. They would decorate the interior of the house as a family, having already shopped for everything. Starting over from scratch was going to be fun for all of them this year as they created new memories for their first Christmas together and in this house. She had much to be grateful for.

Johnny had taken a few more short trips, but she made coming home special, making it harder for him to want to go. She grinned at how, even as big as a house, she could still make her husband desire her. Today she was especially anxious because Johnny told her he had a special surprise for her. Niko and Apolo would be joining them later for the big reveal.

She couldn't imagine what it was, although she

knew it must be something good because he acted more excited than a child on Christmas morning.

Mr. Marshall led the family in prayer, and as the food was passed, family members shared what they were grateful for.

Khloe was still quiet and shy in the large group, but she spoke up. "I'm thankful for my daddy's cancer because God used that to bring me into this family, and now I know Jesus and that I am loved. This is the best year of my life ever."

Everybody smiled and agreed with Khloe, but Mrs. Marshall shed a tear. "While it was hard to watch my son go through this, it was a huge blessing to know that he had Katie. And we had a grandson in David and now a beautiful granddaughter in Khloe. I have so much to be grateful for…I fear my heart will burst."

David chimed in. "I got a daddy this year, and he saved my life and saved Khloe. He's my hero."

Brothers, sisters, cousins all took turns, but it often came back to Johnny, and Katie watched his struggle to contain his own tears. The year had been eventful, but more painful for him than many realized. He gazed across the table at her and smiled.

"I'm grateful that God didn't hold my past against me when I turned my back on the love of my life. This year, he returned Johnny to me, but then He almost took him away again. I doubt I will ever take the blessing of his presence in my life for granted. He gave me a family, a home, and most of all, love." Katie held up her water glass. "A toast to God for His many blessings."

Johnny had remained silent, but she knew he had much to thank God for as well. When the meal was cleaned up, Katie was shooed from the kitchen and instructed to put her swollen feet up while others cleaned. Soon the Acton family arrived.

"So, Johnny," Niko asked, "you have something for us?"

Johnny rose and held a package in his hand, wrapped in glittery gold paper. He gave it to Katie. "Open it, please?"

Katie gently slid her finger under the tape. David chided her. "Mom, you're supposed to just rip the paper."

Everyone laughed. Katie opened the box and pulled out the tissue paper. She gasped as she pulled out a compact disc titled *Songs for Katie*. She flipped it over and saw a list of titles. She didn't think she knew the songs. *David's Melody, Khloe's Hope, Forever Friends*, and *Eternal Love* were some of the titles.

"This was the reason I went to New York, Katie. Terrance Manchester, Tia's father, loved the raw music Tia had sent him from when I was in treatment. These are the songs with full orchestration and my guitar playing. It releases to the general market next week."

Katie ripped open the plastic covering and removed the disc. "Play it for us?"

Mr. Marshall opened the stereo and put the disc in. Katie looked at the inserts of pictures from the past year and awash with memories, the tears flowed. "Thank you, Johnny."

"It's primarily instrumental, but since you were listening to the raw version all the time, I figured maybe having a more professionally produced one would be nicer for my biggest fan."

She struggled to her feet and went to put her arms around him and gave him a long kiss.

"Get a room!" one of Johnny's brothers shouted as

the rest of the gang laughed. Except for David and Khloe.

"Kissing? Again? Yuck!" They ran off to find the building blocks.

Katie couldn't wait to get her husband home and alone to show her appreciation more fully.

Best. Present. Ever.

~*~

December 2014

The house was decorated, and Katie was huge. Johnny and Niko spent time at each other's homes with some of the other guys from Specific Gravity, working on songs for the next album and tour. They'd lost some members but would be adding to the group soon. Tia anticipated them hitting the road for more local festivals in the summer, well aware that Johnny's quickly multiplying family was a factor in the plans.

"Got news, Johnny."

"Yeah?"

"Tia's expecting."

"Whoa! Congratulations, man. 'Course, you're going to have to work extra hard to catch up to me."

"Didn't know procreating was a race"—Niko grinned—"and I'm not sure how eager Tia would be to catch up to you and Katie."

"Adoption helps."

"You do realize your situation is unusual."

"True. I'm hoping by Christmas, our gift to Khloe will be our last name."

"I'm really happy for you, Johnny."

"Thanks. After a painful year, I'm finally happy

too."

"Year? Johnny, you lost something special when Katie left all those years ago, and I never really recognized it until your wedding day. You've had far more than a painful year, and I'm glad I got to watch you persevere to reach this point in your life."

"I used to think God had it in for me."

"And now?"

"Now, I see how He blessed me all along. Mostly with you as my best friend. I don't know that I would have had the strength to move past any of the struggles I've had if it weren't for you, and then Tia."

"And finally, Katie."

Johnny grinned. "Yeah, Katie has been a wonderful blessing, but even more than that is just how much closer to God I've grown through it all. I'm not the same man I was at eighteen or even twenty-one. I'm not that old, Niko, but I feel like I've lived a lifetime of heartache and joy. It scares me that there is so much more ahead."

"I pray you have some smooth waters for a while."

Eyebrows raised, Johnny shook his head. "You're forgetting my wife is going to give birth to twins? I doubt there will be anything smooth about that."

"You might be surprised. After all you've gone through, I think you and Katie are more than up for the challenges and the joys of these two precious children."

"David thinks they all need to learn instruments and start our own band."

Niko laughed. "You know, with Apolo, our upcoming arrival, David, Khloe, and your next two...we could have a good start at the next generation of musicians."

Susan M. Baganz

Johnny's phone rang. "Katie?"

He turned to look at Niko. "What? It's too early, isn't it?" He set his guitar down and ran up the stairs, Niko at his heels. Katie was sitting in a rocker, and she turned off her phone.

"The doctor wants me to come in."

"To the clinic?"

She shook her head. "To the hospital. They are worried I might be in labor or that there might be something wrong with..."

"Whoa. We don't even have the car seats yet, or the cribs. You can't be having the babies now."

"Calm down. Just get my coat, please. Niko, could you pick up the kids from school?"

"Sure. Keep us informed on what's going on, OK?"

Johnny nodded. "Will do." He helped Katie with her coat.

27

Love is the greatest refreshment in life.
Pablo Picasso

Christmas 2014

Katie had been instructed to stay off her feet, and it drove her nuts. The baby shower scheduled for next weekend was held early in her own home, and they now had a fully functional baby room. Car seats were installed in the newer model minivan that was now parked in the garage. But Katie wasn't so much excited about the babies today as she was about the special gift they had for Khloe.

They had all attended church last night, and Johnny had played on the worship team. He hadn't wanted to, afraid she would go into labor, but Katie had encouraged him to do it, knowing the congregation would be blessed—as blessed as she was as Johnny, Niko, and Pastor Dan played, sang, and worshipped the newborn King, Jesus. David looked spiffy in his suit, and Khloe sparkled in her Christmas dress. Later today, family would descend on their home with food so that she could maintain her more prone position.

If she thought waiting for a baby was hard, she

found waiting for it while not being able to do anything was harder. She was grateful for Johnny's music, although he insisted they listen to Christmas music as well. The band was starting to work up arrangements for a new Christmas album for next year, which excited her. She insisted they keep the door to the studio open so she could hear them as they played. Nothing like having her own personal concert every day.

Soon the kids were awake and Johnny was flipping pancakes and cooking up sausage in the kitchen for a breakfast.

After they ate, the kids joined her in the living room by the tree.

"Kids, we'll open most of the gifts later this afternoon when Grandma and Grandpa come over, but there is one gift we wanted to share first." Katie smiled at her children. She never knew she would love being a mother so much.

Johnny pulled out the box from under the tree and handed it to Khloe. "Open it, sweetheart."

"Me? I'm the only one with a gift?"

"For now," Katie added.

"Come on, silly, open it." David chided as he nudged her.

She ripped the wrapping paper as her brother taught her to do. She opened the box and removed the layer of tissue paper. Her eyes shot up to meet his.

"Really?"

"What is it?" David asked.

"It's her official notice that she is now Khloe Marshall, David. She is officially ours. She cannot escape us now." Katie smiled as she watched Khloe.

"What's this?"

"Your new social security number. We'll file that away in a safe place, but it shows that even to the government, you are a Marshall."

Khloe started to cry and ran to Johnny's arms. "Thank you, Daddy."

"Hey, princess, this was our plan all along."

She pulled back to look at him. "But not everyone keeps their promises." She turned to Katie, who held her close.

"Thank you, Mommy. I'm so glad I'm yours."

"Me too, Khloe."

David yawned. "I suppose I need to get dressed now."

Khloe ran to him and wrapped her arms around him. "I'm glad I'm really your sister now too." She giggled. "Won't that mess up Mrs. Gardner at school?"

David rolled his eyes dramatically. "I'm never going to live this down with the guys."

Johnny grinned. "Just tell them you're twins."

Shock was written all over David's face. "No. I'll have a sister, and she can share my mommy and daddy, but my birthday is mine and mine alone." He rose and stalked off to his room, shutting the door behind him.

Khloe laughed. "I love picking on him." She rose to go to her room to change as well.

Johnny came to sit beside Katie. "I know staying off your feet is a pain, but you are still beautiful. I love you and, well…the kids will be a while, and there is a lock on the bedroom door…"

"And you want to open a present early?"

"I like the way you think, Mrs. Marshall."

~*~

333

One week later
January 2015, New Year's Day

Katie pushed and groaned as Johnny held her close.

"It's a...boy!" The doctor placed the crying infant in a nurse's arms. "One more time. Push for me, Katie."

Katie gave it her all and fell back, exhausted. "It's a...girl!"

"Go ahead, Johnny. Meet your children." Katie smiled at the awe on Johnny's face. It had frustrated him to wait to find out until now. It was worth it to see the look on his face as he met his newborn son and daughter.

"What are we going to name them?" He brought their son over to her, placed him in her arms, and returned for their daughter.

"We've gone round and round on this forever."

"Yes. But we didn't know we'd have one of each."

"It was always a possibility. For some reason, you were convinced you'd have identical twins."

"I'm happy with what we have. We have a David at home. How about a Daniel Nikolos Marshall?"

"I love it. And for a girl?"

"I get to name the girl?"

"I'm willing to consider your suggestion. You did pretty well for Danny."

"My Danny-boy...a bit Irish, huh?"

Katie grinned. Johnny held his little girl in his arms. He gazed into her face as she stared back at him.

"Who are you, sweetheart? If Daniel has an Irish ring to it, shouldn't you get something Greek?" He glanced over at Katie. "What do you think about Calliope but with a 'K'? We have a Khloe, and now we have a Kalli."

"David, Khloe, Daniel, and Kalliope Marshall?" Katie asked.

"Sure, why not?"

"Middle name?"

"I'll let you pick that, Katie."

Katie thought long and hard as she looked at the little girl in her husband's arms. "How about Anne after your mother?"

Johnny nodded. "Kalliope Anne Marshall. Welcome to the world."

Katie gazed down at their son. "Daniel Nikolos Marshall. Welcome to our family."

The nurses came to clean up the children, and soon Katie nursed them both.

"Double duty, huh?" Johnny asked.

"Double blessing. For someone who was supposed to be shooting blanks, you sure had great aim."

Johnny's face grew red. "Six weeks…"

"Maybe longer."

"Wait, what?" Johnny's eyes grew big, and the nurse in the room laughed.

"You're pretty potent. Not sure I want to take a chance again that soon."

"Guess I'll have my work cut out trying to convince you."

"You keep it up and we'll need a bigger house."

"I'm OK with that."

"Kiss me, dear husband. I do love you."

"I love you too, Katie. Happy New Year."

ACKNOWLEDGEMENTS

It would be impossible to thank everyone who has helped me on my journey, so I apologize in advance for those I will miss. It doesn't mean you are any less valuable, and thankfully God keeps better track of those things than I do, and His "well done, good and faithful servant" has more merit than any thanks written here.

So here it goes. Special thanks to:

Johnny Phillippidis – your journey, although entirely unique from the Johnny in my story, is inspiring. Thank you for being an overcomer and continuing to share your musical gifts with the world.

Heather Holland – beta reader for the early version of this manuscript who gave me valuable insights into how to make it better and encouraged me immensely.

Elisabeth Herman – you amaze me. Thanks for all the ways you've invested in me.

Doris Pollard Wichern – another early reader and one of my most faithful cheerleaders in this writing adventure.

Lisa Lickel – thanks for being such a wonderful mentor, friend, and shoulder to cry on when the publishing process throws me those curve balls. I don't think I would have ever taken that first step in this journey to publication without your gentle push.

Andrea Boeshaar – my carpooling buddy, friend, prayer partner, "critter," and encourager. I'm blessed to know you!

Pastors David Mundt and Ken Nabi – for your love and support and believing in me and the calling

God has on my life.

Community Church Fond du Lac – for being an inspiration for Orchard Hill. We're not perfect—but I've seen great things in our church family, and I'm proud to be associated with you all.

Sally Shupe – my faithful editor. Thank you for finding all those silly errors!

BIOGRAPHY

Susan M. Baganz chases after three Hobbits, and is a native of Wisconsin. She is an Editor with Pelican Book Group, specializing in bringing great romance novels and novellas to publication. Susan writes adventurous historical and contemporary romances with a biblical world-view.

Susan speaks, teaches, and encourages others to follow God in being all He has created them to be. With her seminary degree in counseling psychology, a background in the field of mental health, and years serving in church ministry, she understands the complexities and pain of life as well as its craziness. She serves behind-the-scenes in various capacities at her church as well as serving on the board of her local American Christian Fiction Writer's (ACFW) chapter. Her favorite pastimes are lazy...snuggling with her dog while reading a good book, or sitting with a friend chatting over a cup of spiced chai latte.

You can learn more by following her blog at www.susanbaganz.com, her Twitter feed @susanbaganz or her fan page, facebook.com/susanmbaganz

Thank you

We appreciate you reading this Prism title. For other Christian fiction and clean-and-wholesome stories, please visit our on-line bookstore at www.prismbookgroup.com.

For questions or more information, contact us at customer@pelicanbookgroup.com.

Prism is an imprint of
Pelican Book Group
www.PelicanBookGroup.com

Connect with Us
www.facebook.com/Pelicanbookgroup
www.twitter.com/pelicanbookgrp

To receive news and specials, subscribe to our bulletin
http://pelink.us/bulletin

May God's glory shine through
this inspirational work of fiction.

AMDG

You Can Help!

At Pelican Book Group it is our mission to entertain readers with fiction that uplifts the Gospel. It is our privilege to spend time with you awhile as you read our stories.

We believe you can help us to bring Christ into the lives of people across the globe. And you don't have to open your wallet or even leave your house!

Here are 3 simple things you can do to help us bring illuminating fiction™ to people everywhere.

1) If you enjoyed this book, write a positive review. Post it at online retailers and websites where readers gather. And share your review with us at reviews@pelicanbookgroup.com (this does give us permission to reprint your review in whole or in part.)

2) If you enjoyed this book, recommend it to a friend in person, at a book club or on social media.

3) If you have suggestions on how we can improve or expand our selection, let us know. We value your opinion. Use the contact form on our web site or e-mail us at customer@pelicanbookgroup.com

God Can Help!

Are you in need? The Almighty can do great things for you. Holy is His Name! He has mercy in every generation. He can lift up the lowly and accomplish all things. Reach out today.

Do not fear: I am with you; do not be anxious: I am your God. I will strengthen you, I will help you, I will uphold you with my victorious right hand.
~Isaiah 41:10 (NAB)

We pray daily, and we especially pray for everyone connected to Pelican Book Group—that includes you! If you have a specific need, we welcome the opportunity to pray for you. Share your needs or praise reports at http://pelink.us/pray4us

Free Book Offer

We're looking for booklovers like you to partner with us! Join our team of influencers today and periodically receive free eBooks.

For more information
Visit http://pelicanbookgroup.com/booklovers